The Body in

Nick Louth is a best-selling thriller writer, award-winning financial journalist and an investment commentator. He self-published his first novel, *Bite*, which was a No. 1 Kindle best-seller. It has sold a third of a million copies, and been translated into six languages.

Freelance since 1998, he has been a regular contributor to the *Financial Times*, *Investors Chronicle* and *Money Observer*. Nick is married and lives in Lincolnshire.

Also by Nick Louth

Bite
Heartbreaker
Mirror Mirror
Trapped

DCI Craig Gillard Crime Thrillers

The Body in the Marsh
The Body on the Shore
The Body in the Mist
The Body in the Snow
The Body Under the Bridge
The Body on the Island
The Bodies at Westgrave Hall
The Body on the Moor
The Body Beneath the Willows
The Body in the Stairwell

NICK LOUTH
THE BODY IN THE STAIRWELL

First published in the United Kingdom in 2022 by

Canelo
Unit 9, 5th Floor
Cargo Works, 1-2 Hatfields
London, SE1 9PG
United Kingdom

A CIP catalogue record for this book is available from the British Library.

Print ISBN 978 1 80032 930 0
Ebook ISBN 978 1 80032 929 4

Look for more great books at www.canelo.co

Printed and bound in Great Britain by Clays Ltd, Elcograf S.p.A.

1

For Louise, as always

Chapter One

Jonathan Hale awoke with palpitations, covered in sweat, the bed damp. The digits of the clock showed 5.17 a.m. Gradually he eased himself out, trying not to awaken his wife. Fleeting fragments of a nightmare melted away, but his racing heart reminded him. He had been trying to escape. He didn't need to be told what from. All he remembered, as on previous occasions, was the final image before he woke up. He was looking from several floors above down to the bottom of a circular stairwell. A man in a suit was lying face-down, soaked in blood, on a floor of black and white tiles.

He knew the man was him.

And he knew that he was dead.

He padded through to the en suite and carefully clicked the door closed behind him before switching on the light. Above his pyjamas the top of his chest and his neck were mottled red. Taking a face cloth he sponged himself down, chest, armpits, neck. He reached into his own reflection and pulled open the mirrored door of the bathroom cabinet. Dozens of packets of prescription drugs were crammed in there and without his contact lenses in he squinted to read the names.

There was a time, not so very long ago, that he had been fit, healthy and unafraid. His property law business had been prospering, and he had his choice of wealthy clients. Regular referrals from overseas. He'd run a half marathon for charity, played squash twice a week, cycled and swam. Now, everything was different. He stared at his florid face. The sweep of fair hair was still thick, thank goodness, with only the occasional quill of white showing through above his ears. The dark brown eyes were still clear. But on the lower half of his face, the original firm jawline had been replaced by a series of sagging fleshy pouches. Fifty-four years going on seventy. What he had been through had aged him, the fear and worry. Even now, safely home, anxiety gnawed at him. The tiny chance, the what if. Not only for him, but his family. What if? If it happened, what would he do?

Hale tiptoed down the wide, carpeted stairs to the tiled ground floor. He made his way past his home office into the panic room, installed just three months ago at huge cost. He flicked on the security screen, which showed the nine CCTV cameras dotted around the four acres of grounds. In the darkness, nothing appeared to be moving. He clicked the cameras to infrared. A small shape waddled along the back pastures above the brook. Their regular hedgehog, christened Spike by his daughter, was nuzzling the ground, on a hunt for slugs and snails. It made him smile, a moment of blessed relief before the fretting returned. He tapped on the keyboard and ran the analysis program. It searched files recorded for the last twelve hours looking for unexplained movements. Nothing. The system was smart enough to have learned to recognise and ignore members of the family, the au pair, dogs, cats and birds, anything whose profile had already been registered, anything it was told to ignore. It was looking for unknown humans. The only thing it had flagged up in the last week was a new window cleaner, who'd since been added to the profiles, and the distant vision of a contractor on a ladder fitting a burglar alarm to a neighbour's house.

He left the panic room and padded into the kitchen, his bare feet chilled by the quarry tiles, and crouched down by Duffy's bed. The aged spaniel was watching him with milky eyes, his tail wagging rhythmically.

'How are you doing, boy?'

Duffy stretched and gradually stood up on his arthritic legs, yawning extravagantly. Hale tickled the dog's ears, and watched as the animal limped gamely towards the side door. Hale disarmed the alarm and let him out. He then made some coffee and sat sipping it, watching Duffy exploring the side lawns as if he had never visited them before. He envied the dog for its peace of mind, and its determination to greet every new day with equal excitement. He'd lost that ability.

For Hale, each day dawned with foreboding. Money worries were real, of course, but he'd find a way to deal with them. It was the deeper fear, however irrational, that never quite went away. There was in reality nothing to worry about. That's what Xolwa always said, and logically she was right. But since his little trip abroad he was no longer rational. Anxiety seeped into every solitary moment, the knowledge that even with the huge distance between him and his enemies, there was still a chance that they would track him down, even here in the discreet and leafy comfort of the Home Counties, even at this new secluded home. What they would do to him and his family before killing them all didn't bear thinking about. But at least once every hour, he did think about it.

Chapter Two

Five thousand miles away

North Bluff State Correctional Facility occupies a shallow canyon between two reserves of Native American land in the heart of the Arizona desert. Summer temperatures exceed 110 degrees, and the canyon is reached by a single dirt road. The maximum security complex has a dozen low buildings around a giant windowless concrete dome which houses 2,200 violent felons on five circular floors. Each two-person cell has a barred front facing a huge central atrium, as if they were boxes at a theatre. A narrow glass watchtower, bristling with CCTV cameras, stands at the centre of the atrium. Correctional officers within can see directly into each cell. At the base of the atrium are three subterranean punishment pits.

In one of those pits, a felon contemplated his fate.

There was darkness, and there was a total absence of light. Richard Tyler literally couldn't see his hand in front of his face. The only sound was a susurrus coming from the air purifier high above him, a ghostly moaning. It was unnerving, but blocking it out was hard. With nothing to see and little to hear you were already down two senses out of five. In darkness, touch was useful. In the first few hours of confinement he thoroughly explored the pit. He was at the bottom of a deep circular well, made of seamless concrete. He'd seen it briefly when they lowered him in on the harness. The narrow ledge on which he sat was just wide enough to sleep on. His feet rested on the concave bottom of the pit, which sloped gently to a drain at the lowest point. To circumnavigate the ledge was exactly twenty-three heel-to-toe paces, starting from his folded blanket and finishing when he found it again. In the first few hours he had sung to himself a handful of country ballads he could remember, then some nursery rhymes that his British-born mother had sung to him when he was a child: 'London Bridge is Falling Down'; 'Oranges and Lemons'; 'Pop Goes the Weasel' and, most relevant to his current predicament, 'Ding Dong Dell'. He sang all that he knew, varying pitch and volume, listening to the sibilant echo before the darkness swallowed his voice.

He thought about his mother, snatched away from him by fate, and his long, dark, nasty childhood, isolated by his father, kept locked indoors when he wanted to be outside like the other kids. For your own good, that's what he was told. Always, for your own good. Well, now he was incarcerated all over again. Not just for his own good, but for the good of society. A childhood in isolation, no wonder he turned out this way, returning to the solitude. The scene of the crime, the core of his psychopathy.

That's what she had told him. The penitentiary shrink. Tight white blouse, long legs, short skirt, curves. Had given him the itch.

He licked his lips.

It was warm in the pit, the temperature of blood. Like the blood he'd tasted after killing her. She had begged, which had added to the pleasure. The correctionals were on him in seconds, but he'd already snapped her spine and bitten deeply into her carotid artery. When they got to him, his face was covered in her blood. He'd taken many a pleasurable hour reliving those few seconds of power and freedom.

But in the pit those fleeting pleasures of recollection and imagination needed to be rationed. He quickly discovered you could desensitise a fantasy by overuse. Instead, he tried to gather together the wisps of memories of his trip with his mother across the Atlantic to London in the winter of 1979, when he was six. He recalled the changing of the guard at Buckingham Palace, all the soldiers in red with big black hats, and all the tiny little British cars, the narrow streets that always seemed damp, lined by poky-looking rowhouses. There was garbage everywhere, which his mother said was down to the unions. He also recalled the Tower of London and its Crown Jewels, Big Ben and Parliament, and London Zoo and the waxwork place. Even under the perennially cloudy London sky, he'd had to hide from the light, wearing sunglasses and a baseball cap with a fringe of material to protect his skin. It was easier there than back home.

At least that wasn't a problem in the pit.

But boredom was. Grinding and relentless. There were so few stimuli. Trying to find some, he'd explored his clothing: an already-familiar orange prison jumpsuit with his name and prisoner number embroidered in hard thread above the left breast pocket, one set of originally white underwear in artificial fibres, green rubber shower shoes. He also had six sheets of coarse toilet tissue. No book, because there was no light. No pencil, no paper. When he'd finished exploring his clothing, he explored his body in all the ways you might imagine, then a few you might not. First, he had checked all of his skin lesions, feeling for changes in shape, for desiccation, anything that might indicate melanoma. He had tasted his skin in different places, noting the variations in bodily hair, salinity, odour. By stretching, he was able to lick his own knees and armpits with his tongue, and taste how different they were.

The last sense to intensify was smell, the most neglected of humanity's five. He could smell himself of course, and the powerful stink of his own waste where he'd squatted on the grating. There was the smell of his blanket, clearly used by many others, and a slightly perfumed taint on the unused toilet paper. He hunted in his mind, concentrating on analysing every odour. Even the concrete had an aroma, when he put his nose close to it. It was a little like vinegar.

Time stretched endlessly, until he was awakened from a sleep he hadn't realised he was in. A grinding noise high above. A hatch was opened a good fifteen feet above him, and a searing beam of artificial light burst onto the floor, right over the drain hole. A hose was pointed in, and in the high-pressure jet all the bodily waste he had deposited on the grating was washed down into the drain. Echoing voices ordered him to strip off and stand over the grating. Dazzled by the light even through closed eyelids, he groped his way across the floor into the beam. The water was powerful, cool and welcome, a sensory delight, and he was just beginning to wash himself when it stopped. He stood back as instructed and a metal tray was lowered on a cable to him. On it was a pack of chow, and some more sheets of the coarse toilet paper. After he'd received it, the cable was withdrawn and the lid closed.

That daily two-minute ray of was the only clock in his life.

At the start he been able to number the days this way, but after the first month he lost count. There was nothing for him to think about, except to look forward to that two minutes of brightness. Once he had explored every aspect of the realm, his fingers found every shallow depression or scratch in the concrete, counted every stitch on the hem of the blanket, he began to retreat inside himself and to plan for the moment that he was determined *would* come. Escape. All he had to sustain him until then was hatred. In that respect at least he was well nourished. Every moment that passed, every lap of the pit, every crunch or press-up, made him more determined to seek vengeance. He was here in this hell because of one person. A slippery British lawyer who had broken under interrogation, made a plea bargain with the DOJ and ratted out all three of them. Department. Of. Justice. That's no justice. Six months they gave him! And now he's out. Living the high life somewhere. Wherever in the world he was, he'd track him down. If it took him a hundred lifetimes, a thousand, he'd do it. And then, the pleasure of a slow death.

He threw his head back and roared his fury, as he had done so many times.

'Jonathan Hale, you cannot hide from me. I will destroy you.'

Chapter Three

Hale sat in his home office in his dressing gown and looked at the finances. They were depressing. On the face of it he was a wealthy man, with a prestige home in one of the most expensive and exclusive districts in Surrey. In truth, he had been forced to transfer most of his assets into his wife's name. And even then they were mortgaged to the hilt, following the fine he'd had to pay. Now he had to find a five-figure loan repayment for The Cedars each month while earning less than a third of that from his property consultancy business. It couldn't go on. How he missed the income he used to have. Easy money, taken for granted.

A decision became a little more pressing every day. It wouldn't be an easy one to make. It might mean breaking a promise made not only to himself but to his family. But what was the alternative?

He padded back upstairs just after seven, to see his wife wrapped in a towel emerging from the en suite. Her flawless teak-coloured skin was still dappled with droplets of water on her shoulders and thighs, her cornrows still dark with moisture.

'You got up early,' Xolwa said, sitting on the bed and towelling down her thighs.

'I was a bit restless.'

'You had the sweats again, didn't you? The sheets were damp.' Her soft brown eyes held his. It wasn't an accusation, it was expressed in a tone of concern. He said nothing. 'Was it that nightmare again?'

'Yeah, it was.' He looked up to the ceiling. 'But it's also money.'

'That letter from the mortgage people?'

'Partly.'

He could see in her eyes that she knew what he'd been thinking about. 'We can cut back, Jon. We don't have to do anything desperate.'

'We can't cut back enough. I'm disbarred, I'm just not earning what I did before.'

'I've stopped buying artwork, antiques. I stopped the moment you went away on your little trip.'

'I know. Poor you, no new handbags.'

'No golf for you.' She smiled at their little game of pretend poverty.

He had cancelled all the club subscriptions months ago. That had been making a virtue out of a necessity. There was no point being a member of the golf or squash clubs when nobody wanted to be seen with him. He held both of her hands. 'Xolwa, we're in overdraft on five bank accounts. I'm constantly robbing Peter to pay Paul. We've got almost no equity left in the house.' Hale considered the enormous running costs of The Cedars, the twenty-metre indoor pool, the cars, Azalea's extortionate livery for her horse. And the school fees, my God, the school fees.

'It's still nowhere near enough.'

'I can go back to work. I mean work work, not the shop.' Xolwa worked three mornings a week at a very expensive local fashion shop but was hankering to return to modelling. With her tall, lean frame and high cheekbones she had been a fixture on the catwalk for a decade before they met, twenty years ago.

'No, we have to be discreet,' Hale said. 'I don't want your face out there for them to find.'

'Jon, they're in *prison*, a long, long way away.' They had been through this many times.

'These guys always have friends on the outside.'

'But not *here*, not in Britain, not in Surrey.'

He shrugged and sighed.

'You're not being rational,' she said. 'We have an immediate problem, right now, and I could help fix it. I could do catalogue work, colour supplements, there's loads of it out there. I don't have to do TV. I've always used my maiden name.'

'Well, radio would be okay,' Hale said with a smile.

Xolwa grinned back at him, delighted that his mood had improved. 'You can't model on the radio.'

'What about voice-overs?'

'It's not my shtick, you know that. I'd never be considered.'

'It would be a waste of that wonderful face too,' Hale said, and reached across to kiss her.

'Maybe we should sell the house, start again,' she whispered.

'There'd be no proceeds if we've no equity. We'd just give it to the bank. Even with rising prices we would never be able to afford anything around here.'

'We could move away, we would still have us, our little happy family, we could start again, go abroad. Get some quality back into our life.'

Hale sighed. 'We can't take Azalea out of St Cuthbert's. She's just got settled.' Azalea's piano and cello had come on in leaps and bounds in the four years she'd been enrolled, and she'd found some good friends in the orchestra. 'Besides, you love this house, so does she. She is always in the pool with Zoe and little Lucy.'

'I know. But you've got to keep some perspective. We still have so much. My grandparents watched all their cattle die in the drought...'

'I know.' The story of their 800-mile trek in bare feet for better pastures was part of family lore. 'And like you always remind me, we're not queueing for sustenance in a food bank. We are lucky. It's all true, but it doesn't actually help me now.'

'Jon, truly, we must never forget how lucky we have been. Despite everything.' She stood up and let the towel drop. Even now, after all these years, the sight of her naked, the statuesque Somali princess she once was, made his heart skip a beat. She embraced him, opening his dressing gown and feeling for him, caressing. He tried to relax but then pulled away, and she looked a little hurt.

'We can try without, you know. You take enough pills as it is.'

'I'm sorry, Xolly.'

'You want me to bring you off orally?' she whispered.

He shook his head. 'Thank you, but I'm not ready for it, up here.' He tapped his temple.

She sighed as she reached for her underwear. 'French toast okay?' she said brightly. But her smile never got as far as her eyes.

–

Conversation at breakfast was muted, but he knew she was upset. Clearing up, the cutlery sounded a little louder, cupboard doors slammed, the used plates banged into the dishwasher. 'I think you need one of these today, Jon,' she said, her long fingers placing a small pink pill by the remains of his orange juice. It was the anti-depressant, prescribed by a helpful doctor soon after his return. It was the only one he was reluctant to take. Unlike the others, it worked, but too well. He felt like a happy zombie because they fuzzed his brain.

'I'll be all right,' he said morosely, picking up the *Financial Times*, his brow furrowed. 'I just need a few minutes.'

'Whatever you say,' she said. 'Remember we're picking up Simon at three.'

'Haven't forgotten,' Hale said absentmindedly, before changing his mind and swilling down the hated tablet.

His son from his first marriage was twenty-two, and suffered from cerebral palsy. For many years Hale had kept him out of sight at Ashbourne Court, an expensive specialist care home in Sussex. Hale's visits, few and far between, had found him secretly horrified at Simon's jerky walk, the inward folding wrists, and large flapping hands. In the child, he could accept Simon's permanently inclined head with its drooping mouth, exposed curve of upper gums, and hard-to-follow vocalisations. But now his son was a full-grown young man, still unable to feed himself. It wasn't until the last few months, since returning, that Hale had admitted to himself why his son repelled him. Simon reminded him of failure. The failure of his first marriage, his failure as a father, and now his criminal record. These were hidden under his apparent wealth, the all-encompassing cloak of comfort. He remembered one occasion several years ago when he drove away from Ashbourne Court after a short visit feeling drenched in guilt. Simon had stared at him as he got up to leave, and asked, in the strangulated moan impervious to casual understanding: 'Why don't you love me, Dad?'

In the earliest years, soon after his divorce, Hale had bought off his conscience with a generous allowance to Madeleine to look after their only son. The physiotherapy, the personal care, the adapted bedroom and bathroom at her home. He was happy to pay for all that to keep the reality of Simon away. After he remarried, he focused his entire life on the relationship with Xolwa and their daughter Azalea, the light of his life, now seventeen. In all the years since her birth, he had been to see Simon only half a dozen times.

Now he was determined to make amends.

–

While Jonathan Hale was having breakfast, a hundred yards away on Blenheim Drive a van bearing the BT Openreach logo coasted to a stop. The driver, an undistinguished middle-aged man wearing steel-rimmed spectacles, squinted out of the passenger-side window at the telegraph pole he was to work on. He was wearing a hi-vis tabard, bearing the Openreach logo over his BT overalls. He had all the supporting paperwork in the van to identify him as Kevin Fleet, a BT employee, carrying out routine maintenance. There was even an authentic-looking job reference number.

The man was a skilled telecom engineer, but he did not work for BT. His name was not Kevin Fleet. Everything from the overalls through to the vehicle itself were bogus. The preparations had been meticulous, and the only real worry would be the arrival of a genuine BT employee.

Doing the job on a Saturday morning minimised that possibility.

He emerged from the van and slid a metal ladder from the roof, which he leaned against the pole. He then extended it fully, reaching about halfway up. Returning to the vehicle, he took from the rear a standard BT safety harness and climbed into it, tightening the waist and shoulder straps until they were snug. From a toolbox he took a small grey plastic box labelled PCA81. It was about the size of a cigarette packet and had a single wire protruding. He slid it into his overall breast pocket, along with a couple of screwdrivers and a pair of pliers. He shut and locked the van doors, then climbed the ladder. From the top of the ladder he grasped the pole and ascended further using its metal brackets as steps, each time clipping his fall-arrest harness to a higher bracket. Finally at the apex, he looked at the many wires radiating to individual homes and identified the one to the target house. Then he got to work.

It was the matter of a half minute for him to screw the PCA81 to the wood, adjust the tiny lens, and fit the wire to a junction on the large ISDN controller already in place above it. Once finished, he double-checked that the line of sight to the target was not obscured by the foliage of the many trees. Satisfied, he then descended and made his way into the van. Opening a laptop, he powered it on and then clicked on a web link. This opened a video which gave a fisheye-lens view of the street from the top of the pole, right up to the driveway leading to The Cedars. Closing the video, he logged on to an app which allowed him to monitor the Internet and phone traffic passing through the controller. Satisfied that everything was working correctly, he logged off and closed down the laptop, retrieved the ladder and fitted it back on the van roof.

Just as he was settling himself into the driving seat, he spotted in his wing mirror the approach from behind of a police patrol car. His heart missed a beat as the chequered blue and yellow car slid past at low speed. This wasn't supposed to happen. A female officer in the passenger seat scrutinised him briefly, and he gave her a tight smile in reply. His heart rate didn't return to normal until he'd seen the vehicle continue along the road to a bend which took it out of view. He exhaled with relief, then packed up quickly, fired up the engine, did a quick U-turn and made good his escape.

Mission accomplished.

–

Saturday lunchtime. Simon sat in his motorised wheel-chair at the head of the table, while his father leaned over cutting the cottage pie and vegetables, separating it into manageable portions. 'All right, Simon now you try,' Hale said, offering him the plastic spoon. Simon's left arm moved out slowly, wrist turned inwards, splayed fingers still pointing at his own chest. With the greatest effort, he rotated his wrist so his fingers were poised above the fork. His elbow trembled as he clasped the plastic utensil awkwardly, and dug it into a mound of mashed potato and minced beef.

'That's very good,' Hale said. 'Terrific, keep going.'

'MmmUUGH.' The spoon dug into the mash, and he lifted a small amount until his arm was horizontal. Simon was trying his utmost to control his errant limbs, but with all the concentration going into the left arm, Hale noticed that his son's stockinged feet were curling and rotating on the foot rests, his head leaning to the right, a thread of drool hanging from his open mouth.

'That's it, that's it. You're doing brilliantly.'

Simon emitted a triumphant groan, as he gradually folded his left arm inwards towards his chest, the spoon still horizontal. The hardest part was controlling the ascent of his wrist from chest height to mouth.

'Now, Simon, try to move your head horizontally like you do for Wanda.' The Polish physiotherapist had made great strides in getting him to reassert control over his damaged nerves. Simon's head trembled with the effort of keeping it horizontal, and just at the final moment, the spoon jerked and a thumb-sized dollop of mash dropped onto his bib.

'Never mind, there's still some in there,' Hale said. 'Go on, go on, that's fantastic!' The final connection between spoon and reaching lips felt as monumental to mankind as a docking manoeuvre in space. Forty-five minutes so far, and Simon had managed to eat only a dozen spoonfuls. The temptation was to feed him like a baby, but Simon's willpower to improve was indomitable, and he would groan in protest.

Hale's mobile rang, and after checking it, he switched it off and turned back to his son. Simon was watching, his grey-green eyes expressive, and a distorted but unmistakable smile slipping across his face, knowing his father's priorities had never been that way before.

–

Later that afternoon, Hale walked into the lounge, where the horse racing was on the TV. Xolwa and Azalea were sitting side-by-side watching it, their heads almost touching and a newspaper spread out on the coffee table before them. His wife's delicate head, delineated by the cornrows, next to Azalea's luxuriant dark wavy hair. Azalea was scribbling down details as Xolwa read them out from her smartphone.

'What are you to up to?'

Azalea turned to him. 'We're studying form,' she said. 'For the horses.' Xolwa now looked up, the end of a pencil clamped between her perfect white teeth. 'We are going to make some money and get us out of debt.'

Hale laughed and placed an affectionate hand on each of their shoulders. 'Betting on the gee-gees?' He could now see the paper was the *Racing Post*.

'There's another race starting at Sandown Park in a minute,' Azalea said. 'I've been working out the best odds. It's good maths practice, too. If all these horses are placed in the various races in the accumulator, you can turn a hundred pounds into a hundred thousand.' She pointed to various underlined names in the paper.

'But Azalea, the chances are incredibly slim,' Hale said, ruffling his daughter's hair. 'You will almost certainly lose more than you win.'

'We're just trying to help,' she said.

'I know you are.' Hale smiled indulgently at his daughter, who radiated innocence and always seemed young for her age. When she was born he had wanted to call her Grace, but Xolwa was set on Azalea, her favourite shrub. She had her mother's slender figure and upright bearing, and in repose the same extraordinary face, just a shade or two lighter. Not for the first time Hale wondered what genetic contribution he had made to this lovely well-mannered girl. He hoped she had his common sense and toughness as well as her own academic and musical skills, and Xolwa's sweet nature. But if so, they were late emerging. There didn't seem to be too much sign of his self-confidence either. It was a dangerous world out there, and in a year's time she would be heading off to university. He couldn't always be peering over her shoulder to look out for her, to guide her. She had to go her own way. And that made him extraordinarily uncomfortable.

He could look after himself and accept the consequences if he failed. But for Azalea even more than for Xolwa, he couldn't fight the terrible and gathering premonition that his mistakes, his weakness, had put them all in mortal danger.

Chapter Four

'*Name.*'

A harsh voice jolted me. The correctional officer looked at my attorney and then back at me, then down at his clipboard. He was a big guy. The drone of the air conditioning didn't quite hide the background echoes of metal upon metal, keys and lock, the shouts of the confined.

'*Hale,*' I responded.

'Your full name,' the guard bellowed.

'*Jonathan George Hale.*'

'*He's here to self-report,*' my attorney said helpfully.

'*Offence?*' the guard yelled, looking down at his clipboard. A great long list of names. I craned my neck, trying to read it upside down. What kind of crazy people would I be in jail with? The guard jerked the papers away and snarled. '*Don't you even know what goddamn crime you committed?*'

'*Wire fraud.*'

'*Six months,*' the attorney said helpfully.

'*Right, your new life starts here. Follow me.*'

I barely even had chance to say thank you to the attorney before the guard pulled me away, clipped on handcuffs and leg irons. I shuffled after the big guy, through to a windowless room painted in battleship grey where I was passed across to two more officers, a big mean-looking white guy, and a sizeable black woman, who looked equally short on the milk of human kindness.

'*Name?*' the female bellowed, without even looking at me. I gave her my full name, and went through the same rigmarole, as if the first guard had just tossed away the information I had given him. The wall was lined with stained orange jumpsuits, dangling on coat hooks, legs and arms limp as if they had all been executed that morning.

'*You wear eyeglasses?*' She squinted at me through her own steel-rimmed spectacles.

'*No. Contact lenses.*'

'*Take 'em out. No contacts allowed.*'

I hesitated. '*How will I see?*' I had four months' worth of disposables in my toiletry bag, but hadn't thought I wouldn't be able to use them.

'*Let me help you: there's three walls, a gate and a ceiling, all in grey, and an ugly cellmate. What d'you need to see for?*'

'*Reading?*'

'*What d'you think this is, the Library of Congress? Ask to see the ophthalmologist if eyeglasses are medically necessary. Now strip off.*'

'*Here?*' There didn't seem to be anywhere to put my clothes.

'*No, in the Waldorf fucking Astoria. Fuck's sake, do it now.*'

I stripped off to T-shirt and boxers. My clothes were dumped by the male guard into a clear plastic bag.

'*Watch, jewellery, piercings,*' she yelled.

I slid off my wedding ring, and carefully undid my Tissot. '*Can I get a receipt?*' I asked as I put them carefully into the metal tray.

'*No you can't. Address for postage.*'

I started to give my British address.

'*Fuck sake, do you think we're FedEx? We don't ship overseas. US address only.*'

I couldn't offhand remember the address of my attorney. '*I'll get you the address.*'

'*No address,*' she said as she ticked a box on her clipboard. '*Now the cavity search,*' she said with an almost sadistic smile, sliding on a pair of nylon gloves.

—

I spent six days in the Special Housing Unit, solitary confinement. It's designed to break your spirit and it does. The guard wasn't lying. There really was nothing to see. The first twenty-four hours were the worst. I felt completely suicidal. The guards were sadists, impersonating my accent, asking if I was a fag. All I had for company was a half-roll of cheap toilet paper, a thin scratchy towel, two sheets of A4 and a pencil stub. I asked for a book and was thrown a tatty and stained paperback, a 1950s romance. The print was too small to read comfortably without glasses or contacts, and pointless too. A big chunk of pages at the end were missing.

To my shame, I wept on numerous occasions in that first week. It was little comfort to know that this East Coast federal prison was a lot less harsh than the desert state maximum security facilities I had consigned my former business partners to. I couldn't imagine what it was like for them or how intensely they must hate me.

'Jonathan. Phone call.' Xolwe's voice broke through his concentration. He looked away from the PC and closed his notes. Just reliving the experience had given him palpitations.

'Just coming,' he said.

Writing the story of his incarceration was Azalea's suggestion, one wholeheartedly endorsed by the Harley Street shrink Hale had employed on his return. He could pretend it was for publication, but was much less sure than Azalea or Xolwa that anyone else would be interested. Mainly it was catharsis. But so far it hadn't made him feel any better.

Hale took the call. It was from a client for his property consultancy, one of the very few, and he dealt with it quickly and efficiently. Earning a living had been hard since his return. Being struck off from practice made it almost impossible to return to his legitimate area of expertise. The customers happy to use a bent lawyer were often those who were the wrong side of the law themselves. But with the benefit of a few referrals from the handful of faithful old friends still in practice, he had picked up some dribs and drabs. Mostly it was setting up overseas companies in tax havens to own or trade London property. It seemed there was still investors who were sufficiently keen to avoid paying stamp duty and other taxes on prestige homes in central London, for whom his chequered past was not a deterrent. Perhaps the fact he was charging half the price of the big city firms had something to do with it.

He made his way into his home office, looked up the client's file and checked online the progress with the Dutch Antilles brass plate listing. Fortunately, as far as the tax haven was concerned, there were few awkward questions. When he'd finished updating his files, he looked again at the letter he had received yesterday morning, threatening foreclosure on his mortgage if he did not pay up the six months he was in arrears. It was a six-figure sum and he had thirty days to find it.

He really had no choice. Forget gambling on horses, there was only one way to get that kind of money. He'd have to keep it from Xolwa, and from everybody else. He felt guilty already, breaking his promise. Total secrecy was essential. It always had been.

Hale went to a drawer, and pulled a brand-new dumb phone from its plastic blister pack. He checked the number he'd been given for his contact, then pocketed the phone without turning it on and headed to the garage. He chose the grey Renault estate, the least obtrusive of the family's five vehicles, and the one that Azalea had been allowed to drive since she passed her test a month ago. He hit the door button, and the garage roller shutter slid noisily upwards. He settled himself into the car, drove out into Blenheim Drive, then onto Marlborough Avenue.

It was only five minutes to Waitrose, somewhere he would be expected to go. Once there, he sat in the car park in the gathering darkness and made the call, leaving the cryptic message that had been arranged in advance. After he hung up, he watched the families trundling trolleys out of the supermarket, laden with groceries. Normal people, happy people. How he envied them, always on the right side of the law.

'*Well, that's it,*' he muttered to himself. '*The die is well and truly cast.*'

Chapter Five

Monday

Detective Chief Inspector Craig Gillard knew something big was happening when he arrived at eight a.m. and saw that all of Mount Browne's VIP parking spaces were taken. He recognised Chief Constable Alison Rigby's big new Jaguar, almost always there by seven, and the Audi belonging to the newly appointed assistant chief constable, Stella Anderson. Three more cars, black Range Rovers which he guessed were from the National Crime Agency. They had 2018 plates, which he recalled was the year the agency updated its fleet with seventy-five of this marque.

He entered the CID department, a modern building built alongside the historic house, and found it abuzz with rumours about the NCA presence. Nobody in CID had been briefed, which was of course absolutely typical. Paranoia about leaks wasn't entirely unjustified, given some detectives' relationship with crime reporters, but did nothing for morale for the rank and file detectives who classified themselves as mushrooms: kept in the dark and fed shit.

Gillard sat in his glass office with a mug of coffee, and after checking his emails started flicking through the latest reported crimes. The usual Monday morning crop:

a knifing, three burglaries, a good half-dozen domestic incidents, and a scattering of antisocial behaviour.

His landline rang just after nine. It was the chief constable's secretary, Denise.

'Craig, they've already started, but now Alison thinks they need you. The executive conference room, straight-away if you can.'

'What's it about?'

'An NCA case apparently.' She thanked him and hung up.

That made sense. The executive conference room, a grand and historic room on the first floor of the main building, was normally used just for bigwigs. He drained his coffee and headed out, waving cheerily to detective constables Carrie 'Rainy' Macintosh and Carl Hoskins, each of whom was on the phone. Making his way into the main building, he passed under the portrait of Sir Robert Peel, and knocked on the walnut-inlaid door. He heard Rigby call him to enter.

The room inside was dark, with a trio of screens at the centre arranged in a triangle on the oval boardroom table, so that the dozen people arrayed around it could see. In the gloom, Gillard recognised the chief constable, and sitting appropriately enough on her right-hand side, ACC Stella Anderson. Alison Rigby beckoned Gillard over to a vacant chair on her left. 'Surveillance operation,' she whispered enigmatically.

The screens showed a high, static view over a leafy suburban street, from about the height of a telegraph pole. At the edge of the fisheye lens was a street sign. Blenheim Drive. There were only two parked cars in view and a few large houses, most of them screened by trees. No doubt one of Surrey's more expensive suburbs.

Rigby leaned towards him. 'We're expecting something right now,' she whispered. 'Watch carefully.'

Gillard glanced at his watch and pressed the light button. It was 9.14 a.m. A Royal Mail van turned off the main road and into the street. It made its way under two horse chestnut trees and past a half-dozen discreet private roads. It drove almost under the camera and took the laurel-lined driveway signposted for The Cedars. As it passed out of view, the view switched to a different camera, this one with sound. From this angle the front of a palatial home with a pillared portico could be seen. The red van rumbled in from the left and stopped on a gravel drive in front of the house near to a black Mercedes A3 and a grey Renault estate. A man dressed in a red Royal Mail shirt, a baseball cap and wearing surgical gloves emerged. He was carrying a battered red bag, bearing the official logo. He did not go to the front door, but instead crunched his way across the gravel and then on grass made his way around the far end of the house towards the back.

'Is this the guy?' Gillard asked Rigby. 'Not a real postman I take it?'

She shook her head and raised a finger to her lips.

The next camera offered a good telephoto view of the side and rear of the house. The postman walked briskly along the rear deck, past the back door and to a large glass patio door. He produced a small tool from his post office bag, crouched at the lock, made two or three quick and practised movements, then slid the door open.

The next view was a slightly jerky one, showing the inside of the sun lounge. The picture was obviously from some kind of bodycam, and had the benefit of sound. They could hear the laboured, probably nervous, breathing of the wearer. The man held up a camera in front of him and took close-up pictures of a few objects in the room, before carefully opening the door and going deeper into the house. A vast and luxurious kitchen was next, with numerous deep granite countertops and silvery fittings. Several close-ups were taken of electrical plug sockets.

Finally, Gillard figured out what was going on.

The screens continued to relay the passage of the intruder through the luxury house, all the while taking photographs of household objects, from wall clocks to pot plants, from china ornaments to paintings and sculptures. The reflection of the intruder was caught in one bedroom mirror and showed the cam was mounted below the peak of the baseball cap. A particularly long time was spent in what appeared to be a home office, with a couple of laptops, two big screens and a wall-mounted wifi unit. The intruder, who appeared to be in stockinged feet, made his way back to his point of entry, where his shoes could be seen. The man to Gillard's left clicked a remote at the screens, which went dark as the lights in the room came back up.

'Phase one of Operation Whirlpool is complete,' said the man, who Gillard now recognised as Detective Superintendent Joe Kyrios, the NCA's money laundering expert. Kyrios was a sleek Cypriot with a pockmarked face and intelligent brown eyes.

'That's pretty impressive,' said the chief constable. She turned to Gillard and said: 'Sorry for pulling you in on this late, Craig. It's in your patch, so it's important that you are aware of it.'

'Who's the target?' he asked.

'Jonathan Hale, money launderer extraordinaire.'

'Oh, him. I thought he would still be inside.' Gillard was aware of the blanket press coverage three years ago when the British property lawyer was extradited to the US to face charges that he had cleansed $128 million for L3, a drug syndicate based in Phoenix, Arizona. He was found to be turning truckloads of dirty dollar bills into squeaky clean London-based property assets.

Kyrios laughed. 'He would be, but for the plea bargain. They dropped the major charges in exchange for him helping untangle the route the cash took. The conspirators went down for at least sixty years each, but Hale served only six months for wire fraud and returned to the UK back in February.'

'I hope for his sake none of the drug gang ever find him,' Stella Anderson said.

Kyrios chuckled. 'The Feds offered him witness protection in the US, but he preferred to come home. He's in luck. The L3 syndicate is no more. All were imprisoned for long terms. Since then, one of them is already dead after a penitentiary gang fight, a second has terminal brain cancer, and the third is according to my information in a solitary punishment cell after killing a member of prison staff. He'll die in jail.'

'Excuse me for having missed the start, but Hale is presumably up to his old laundry tricks?' Gillard asked.

'We think so,' Kyrios said. 'The Feds were unable to crack the route the cash took without his help, which means that every criminal enterprise will know that he is the go-to guy. So once we wire his place, we will have a heads up on any criminal network approaching him. If Hale's got any sense he'll probably be no more than a consultant. He knows we'll be watching him.'

'I hope he doesn't suspect quite how intensively,' Rigby said.

'We hope not,' Kyrios replied.

A woman at the far end of the table spoke. Gillard recognised her as DCS Helen McCarthy, head of drug crime at the NCA. 'This for us is very important. As you may know, most of our intelligence is about drugs in transit. In these seizures we only get the little guys, mules, the distribution people. We may seize narcotics by the lorry load and get big headlines, but we almost never get Mr Big. However, at the money laundering end, you are almost always dealing with senior guys, the ones with their hands on the cash, trusted to allocate the proceeds. If Hale offers to buy them a property in London, the chances are they will want to come and see it for themselves, and to see him.'

'It's all going to be very light touch,' Kyrios added. 'We're trawling for contact information to begin with.'

'So where do I fit in?' Gillard asked.

'First, we simply need your crew to leave Hale alone. We need to give him enough rope to hang himself. I don't want him being hassled by some ambitious young officer in the economic crime unit, and I don't want to see any more patrol cars in his street unless there is a pressing need.'

Alison Rigby took over. 'Craig, Operation Whirlpool is going to take over the third floor of the CID building. We are seconding a number of electronic technicians from your team, plus DC Townsend.'

'For how long, ma'am?' Gillard asked. Rob Townsend was his research intelligence officer, needed to lead the team which traced mobile phones and examined the contents of seized computers.

'Six weeks, possibly as long as three months. I don't need to tell you that we need your discretion on this.'

Gillard shrugged. 'Speculation about all the new kit being installed is already rife. I expect my team will be pretty upset to discover that none of it is for their use.'

Rigby nodded. 'I understand, and I regret with the current resource issue not being able to offer you what you need.'

Gillard tried to control his outrage. 'So ma'am, it seems a shame to me that our best technical experts will be on an inquiry waiting for a crime to be committed, instead of being able to tackle the huge backlog of cases where crimes, some of them very serious, have already been committed.'

The room went quiet at this insubordination. Rigby turned her bright blue eyes on Gillard, the famed stare of death. 'My job is to make difficult decisions, Craig. Your job is to execute them.' The silence stretched out. 'Anyway, no need to detain you any longer.' She gestured for him to leave. 'I'll speak to you later on.'

'Yes, ma'am.' As Gillard stood to leave, he could see all eyes turned on him. Almost everyone here was ranked above him, and the looks they gave varied between pity and amusement. ACC Stella Anderson seemed to be displaying both at the same time, but then they had history. She would be the last person to be on his side.

–

On his return to the CID office, Gillard was peppered with questions about the briefing he just been to. 'What's the big NCA deal, boss?' DC Carl Hoskins asked him. Hoskins, shaven-headed and overweight, was the workhorse of the unit, always pulling in plenty of over-time, never grumbling about the hours spent on the most boring of CID tasks, which was reviewing CCTV footage.

'All I can tell you is it's a surveillance operation.'

'That could last months,' Hoskins said, gloomily.

'It's for the wee laddie Jonathan Hale,' Rainy Macintosh told Hoskins.

Gillard rolled his eyes. 'What makes you think that?'

'I earwigged a table full of NCA plods when I was queueing for a gingie and a piece in the canteen.'

Rainy was one of Gillard's sharpest team members. A former Glaswegian junior hospital doctor with an enquiring mind, she had fled a terrible marriage and unrelenting hours in a sometimes violent A&E department to come south with her teenage son, and join the police. Frying pans and fires, was the general opinion. Gillard had put her forward for promotion, and her sergeant's exams were due later in the month.

'Well, keep it to yourself,' Gillard said, looking at each of his team, but knowing full well that it would already be all around the department. 'Do not, let me emphasise, tell any of your contacts in the press.'

'Och, but wasn't our wee launderer back in a flash? I mean, six months, that's a peach result for a plea bargain.'

Hoskins shook his head. 'But surely he ain't so stupid as to reach for the Persil straightaway.'

'He might,' Rainy said. 'The million-dollar fine means he's probably skint, and if he's disbarred as a lawyer—'

'—Then it's probably too great a temptation to resist,' Gillard said. 'That's what the NCA are banking on.'

That evening Gillard was in the middle of preparing one of his quick 'ping' dinners, jacket potato with melted cheese and beans on the side. The microwave was buzzing busily when Sam walked in wearing a full-length raincoat, car keys in hand, her hair wet.

'How was the pool?' he asked.

'Almost empty, but it's a pain they've closed the changing rooms. Covid again.'

'So have you just got your cozzer on under that?'

She opened the raincoat, flashing the black one-piece to him briefly. Her pregnancy bulge was now quite noticeable, as were her enlarged breasts. Seeing where his eyes rested, she said: 'I'm just going up to change. Don't get any ideas, my shift starts in ninety minutes.'

'And dinner will be served in five, your ladyship.' He bowed.

'Well done, Jeeves.' She ruffled his hair, then headed upstairs.

A few minutes later she re-emerged with her thick dark wavy hair neatly brushed, eye make-up reapplied. As they sat eating, he asked her: 'Don't you have an old schoolfriend who lives in Esher?'

'Jenny Barnes. We're in contact on Facebook but I've not seen her since before lockdown. Why?'

'Is she still on Blenheim Drive?'

'I think so. My address book is upstairs. Why do you ask?'

'Just curious.'

Sam gave him an odd look, before kissing him goodbye and heading out to work, to dispatch blue lights all over the county. Gillard collected up the dishes, filled the last few available slots in the dishwasher, and set the machine. Once it was rumbling away, he headed upstairs, and picking up Sam's address book, sat down in his home office. He looked up the address, typed Jenny's postcode into Google maps. He homed in on Blenheim Drive. The northern end of the road was dominated by a large home in extensive grounds. Switching to an aerial photograph, he homed in on the magnificent Edwardian building with its multiple roofs and chimneys, indoor swimming pool, tennis court and what looked like formal lawns around three mature cedar trees.

Jonathan Hale's house, The Cedars.

Jenny Barnes was listed by Sam's address book as living at number nineteen, which he found on Street View. It was a couple of hundred yards on foot from The Cedars, but on the satellite map it was clear that Jenny's long narrow garden in Blenheim Drive backed on to the larger property.

He wondered if Sam would be able to get a lunch invitation from her friend.

Chapter Six

North Bluff State Correctional Facility

Tyler lay on his back on his bunk, enjoying the relative softness of a mattress. His two months in the pit had ended yesterday, and for the first few hours back in the cell he had almost gone crazy. He'd been able to shield his eyes from the unaccustomed dazzle, even though the ceiling strip light was hardly bright. But there was little to be done about the racket. The endless metallic noise of the landing, the shouting, the taunting and the clamour for attention of 2,200 inmates arrayed on five floors around that cathedral-sized space. In his head he'd been to places no one should go, into his own soul. So deep, so unmoving had he been in those final few days in the pit, that correctional officers had not been able to rouse him, even by hosing him down. They had looked at him through night-vision goggles, to be sure he was still alive.

His cellie now was a Hispanic called Morales, a lean, heavily tattooed LA gangster half his age. But Morales had clearly got wind of Tyler's reputation. He moved out of the bottom bunk without any fuss and offered him some of the smuggled chow that his friends in the kitchen had given him. It was the respect that anyone on a 260-year stretch is entitled to. News of Tyler's record-breaking stay in the pit had travelled around the landings, and when he emerged for his first outdoor rec session, there was a round of applause and some good-natured catcalling.

There was even an appointment with TJ, the head of the Bloods, the dominant black gang. TJ was a legendary drug smuggler in his own right, serving a life plus forty-five stretch. He had for a while dealt with Tyler's L3 consortium, and they knew each other by reputation. Three days after emerging from the pit, Tyler was escorted to TJ's cell by two of his tough-looking associates. TJ's single cell reflected his status. There was a partial curtain inside the barred cage front that shielded him from the landing, and a three-foot piece of red carpet along the edge of his bed. Tyler had no doubt that TJ had everything he needed to keep control of his guys on the outside.

TJ was neither big nor particularly muscular. He had few tattoos, except for the three starred tears under one eye, for the cops he had killed. As with Tyler, he would have been destined for death row if it hadn't been for Arizona's judicial suspension of lethal injection in 2014.

Tyler fist-bumped TJ.

'You're a legend, bro,' TJ said. 'Two months in the pit, Jesus. Two weeks was enough for me.'

Tyler extruded a slight smile of satisfaction. 'Was hard.'

'What d'you need?'

'A phone.'

'Can getcha a burner, no problem.'

'No, it has to be a smartphone. Internet access.'

TJ sucked his teeth. 'That's a big ask.'

'I know you got one.'

'Says who?'

'I just heard it, that's all.'

TJ nodded. 'Whatcha got for me on the outside?'

'Ten grand?'

TJ shook his head. 'Not enough. I got big overheads.'

Tyler sighed. 'I got a small condo in a complex in Santa Monica. Secluded, in good repair. Three years left on the lease.' He had inherited the property when his twin brother died in a road accident five years ago. He had regretted that in the two years before he was arrested, he'd rarely had the opportunity to use it.

'Now you're talking.' The gangster looked impressed. 'For that I'll give you one free recharge too. First thing you do with the phone is to email the real estate details to my guy on the out. I'll give you the email.'

Tyler knew that getting a phone into a high security penitentiary wasn't easy. Visitors couldn't help because they only saw you through a glass screen. All visiting officials, even lawyers, were thoroughly searched, and had to pass through a body scanner more sensitive than anything at an airport. But TJ had found a way, and Tyler suspected it was through a night-time drone drop into the outdoor rec cage. It wouldn't be prudent to ask. But Tyler had read about silent drones being used to supply inmates with drugs in jails in California. Of course as TJ clearly had his own phone, he must have access to a charger too. Incredible.

'It's a deal,' Tyler said, and giving a little nod of deference, stepped back out of the cell.

Chapter Seven

Tuesday

'Has anyone here got a second-class postage stamp?' DSU Kyrios was making a presentation in Mount Browne's largest CID conference room. A woman in the front row held up her hand.

'Great, let me give you a pound for it,' he said, advancing towards her. The woman gave him a stamp from her purse.

'Sounds like a good deal, doesn't it?' he said to the rest of the audience, mainly NCA officers, plus a smattering of technical staff that Gillard recognised from the Surrey research intelligence area. ACC Stella Anderson was the most senior officer present. He was trying to stay out of her way, but they had already exchanged a quick, wary glance.

Kyrios held up the stamp. 'Now, ladies and gentlemen, I have a second-class postage stamp, and she has my pound coin, agreed?'

There was a murmur of assent.

'Don't worry,' he said, turning to her. 'I shan't ask for it back.' He then paced in front of the audience. 'Now everybody, this transaction has just laundered one pound of illicit drug money.'

There was a ripple of laughter.

'No, it's true.' He held up the stamp. 'If I came to you with a stamp, or several books of stamps, to offer in payment for something, you wouldn't worry about the origin of my stamps, would you? Because everyone knows that stamps are ultimately validated by the post office which issues them. And everyone would assume that is where the stamp originated. And they'd be right. You see, it is this trick of confidence in the provenance of an asset. Belief. Trust. Integrity. That is what the criminal seeks, and the launderer provides.

'Before moving on to what Hale might be doing now, let's see what we can learn from a little history of those he dealt with.' Kyrios dimmed the lights and pressed a remote control in his hand. A mugshot appeared, an image of a glowering thick-necked individual with a shaven head and fleshy face. 'This is Gary Feinman, one of the Three Stooges, so to speak, in the L3 consortium which Hale served. They had the highest level contacts with the Colombians, and had an almost foolproof idea. Feinman owned a power boat yard in Florida, and usually entered three boats in the monthly Miami to Bimini race. Bimini is twenty miles offshore, but these being high-powered boats they could make it there and back in an hour. Inevitably, though, one would break down, or at least appear to. While the race competitors disappeared over the horizon, the mother ship would pull alongside the stricken vessel, and the drugs would be passed on board. Only then would the rescue boat appear, and tow the failed competitor back to shore, packed with pure cocaine. Feinman was murdered a year ago by a fellow inmate shortly after incarceration.'

Kyrios move the presentation on, to another mugshot, a tanned, smooth-looking individual of Mediterranean appearance. 'This is Nico Christadopoulos. He had the contacts with domestic coke distributors and broke down the packages into manageable sizes. When the money flowed in, in cash, much of it in small denominations, it was Nico who counted, checked and bundled it in cooking oil drums in a Little Havana warehouse, guarded by a bunch of Cuban exiles. He's currently serving eighty years, and has brain cancer.'

'Two down, one to go,' someone behind Gillard muttered.

'Last but not least, Richard E. P. Tyler, a.k.a. the Reptile,' Kyrios said.

A collective *eeugh* greeted the slide.

It showed a mugshot of a middle-aged man, almost bald, with just a few tufts of white hair. His skin was dry, cracked and scaly, scabbed and peeling off in places, but the most shocking thing about that face were the bulbous heavily bloodshot eyes. 'Tyler muscled his way in to the syndicate first as an enforcer, and second because of his loyalty and obsessive attention to detail. He'd worked in the freight industry, and was a logistics expert. Feinman and Christadopoulos trusted him to get the bales of cash trucked from Miami to Arizona, from where it was flown by his bent airline contacts to Mexico, then deposited in banks in the Caribbean, from where Hale took care of it. Tyler refused to say a word during months of interrogation, and is currently in North Bluff State Correctional Facility in Arizona. He's a loner, a depraved and violent psychopath, and has now been linked to a series of unsolved sexual offences against women and minors when he was in his twenties and thirties. He killed a prison psychiatrist in the first week of his incarceration, normally a death-row offence, but with Arizona executions suspended since 2014 his original 130-year sentence was doubled to 260 years.'

'Is he called Reptile because of his skin?' one of the audience asked.

'Yeah, that's right. I knew someone would ask, so I looked it up.' Kyrios looked at his notes. 'It's a rare genetic condition called xeroderma pigmentosum, where the skin has extreme sensitivity to ultraviolet light. Of course, excessive daylight isn't going to trouble him much where he is.'

More nervous laughter.

'Fortunately, we don't need to worry about these guys anymore. They're never getting out of jail. They may be history, but the methods they used are not. They were raking in millions from the speedboat scam. Laundering that much cash in the United States is not easy. Forget what you see in the movies. Used notes are bulky. A million bucks in twenties and fifties does not fit in a briefcase, you need a big suitcase. When it's in fives and tens, and you're talking tens of millions of dollars a month, you need space and you need time.'

He clicked up the next slide, a diagram.

'There are four stages in laundering cash. One, concealing the illegal source of funds. Two, the form the money is in must be changed from small denomination cash to something else: artworks, antiques, a foreign currency deposit, or the ownership of land and property. Maybe even postage stamps.' He waited for the laughter to subside. 'Three, there must be no audit trail that anyone can follow to trace the changed form of this money back to the original source. Fourth, and most important, this whole process from beginning to end must remain under the criminals' control. There is, as everybody knows, no honour amongst thieves.

'So how do they do this? The traditional route is to choose some kind of commercial activity in which lots of cash payments by customers are part of the normal run of business: casinos, bookmakers, pizza parlours, burger vans, second-hand car dealers. So legal cash payments and illegal ones look the same. Of course, the bigger the flow of illicit cash, the harder this is to accomplish without drawing attention. How many pizzas, how many cars? The US Internal Revenue Service watches this kind of thing. That's where the gambling industry serves so well. Backing dozens of favourites in horse racing, baseball, the NFL, you turn cash bets into legit prize money with the smallest loss.'

The next slide showed a suntanned fair-haired man, wearing sunglasses and apparently at the wheel of a sizeable yacht.

'Now, over to Jonathan Hale. This is him. The IRS now owns the yacht, by the way. I'm going to show you a simplified version of the laundering route he designed to obscure the source of the L3 cash he laundered.'

The next slide showed a dense diagram of over a hundred colour-coded boxes, each one representing a commercial entity, with arrows between them indicating the flow of funds. The audience gasped at the complexity of it.

'This, ladies and gentlemen was where our Mr Hale worked his magic. And yes, I have simplified it for you. The full charts are in pages one to twenty-two of the appendices of the briefing on your desks. There are tax havens, numbered bank accounts, brass plate shell companies in the Caribbean and Cyprus, plus blind trusts and attorney-client privilege protecting this money flow. Without his help and the plea bargain, this entire edifice would have taken years to unravel. In many of the jurisdictions in which these transactions took place you need very strong evidence of wrongdoing before the secrecy could be legally uncovered. And of course, without breaking open this monstrous Russian doll of company ownerships, you cannot get that evidence. It's a classic Catch-22.

'While we're talking about domiciles, a word about Britain,' Kyrios said. 'The United Kingdom is heaven for laundered cash. The gentlemanly spirit of my word is my bond still prevails despite many new pieces of legislation. If you walk in off the street with £1 million in cash and want to deposit it, you're going to have problems, as you might expect. But if you have more, there's always a way around. Take NatWest, for example, a bank with a long and somewhat chequered history, rescued by the taxpayer in 2008 during the global financial crisis. Between 2013 and 2016 NatWest took no less than £246 million in cash deposits from a single criminal company, at a rate of £2 million a day. Just imagine the size of that. At one branch in Walsall, where £6.6 million in cash was deposited, bin bags of notes were lugged through a shopping centre, and because they were splitting with the weight, branch staff transferred them into stronger hessian sacks. The notes filled two floor-to-ceiling safes, with lots more stashed elsewhere.

'Suspicious, right?'

'Apparently not. That is an impressive piece of money laundering, enabled by the laxity of bank oversight. Yet get this – even though the scheme was shut down in 2016, no individual at the bank is being prosecuted. Not one. Instead, the bank will probably pay a huge fine, and because it's majority owned by the public, a good portion of this will be levied indirectly on the taxpayer.'

Gillard heard two officers whispering behind him. 'So the government's fining itself for raking in the proceeds of crime eh, nice one.'

'Typical.'

Kyrios laughed, seeing heads shaking in amazement across the room. 'Compared with the US, white-collar criminals in the UK are rarely prosecuted and when they are, they're treated leniently at sentence. Tax haven registered companies can still own huge chunks of prime British property and, by being registered as trusts, can hide their real ownership. Criminals can easily trade big London homes without paying stamp duty or capital gains taxes on the sale. Instead of buying or selling a house, they trade in the companies which exist purely to own the asset. The company owned the house before, and still owns it after. Therefore, no change in ownership and no tax. London, particularly, has a fantastic property market: prime space that keeps rising in value, in a jurisdiction dedicated to preserving the legal advantages of property ownership. And it is so expensive that the purchase of a single home in the best areas can launder the proceeds of years of criminality. The non-domicile tax regime is a soft touch too, and as a nice little insurance policy, the political donation to keep ministers on your side is way smaller than that required in Washington. Some MPs even have a second job representing tax havens to help them keep their privileges. All in all, Britain is a launderer's paradise. The rule of law appears to work, but in practice there's always a loophole. For criminals, it's brilliant: it appears to be strict, but it isn't.'

Rob Townsend raised his hand. 'What happened to the properties bought under this L3 scam?'

'I think I can answer that,' Stella Anderson said from the back. 'I was on the team that helped seize sixteen of those UK properties for the Crown. There was a Scottish castle, a minor airport in the West Country, and a flat overlooking St James Park. In all, £120 million worth, more than half of it now sold to new owners for the benefit of the public purse.'

Kyrios held up his hands. 'Okay, take a break for coffee. In the next session I'm gonna tell you how we think Jonathan Hale has gone back to his criminal ways, and see who the client might be this time.'

–

Gillard, seeing it was gone four, ignored the coffee and headed for the door. He descended the stairs to the first floor, aware that the day's backlog of unsolved crimes had barely been touched. An earlier text from Rainy on the subject had been a call for help.

It was all a matter of priorities. Kyrios' presentation would still be going on for another hour, but Gillard had already got the gist: there were a dozen candidate European drug operations, including the 'Ndragheta, the Calabrian mafia, which might need Hale's laundering skills. There were little nuggets of intelligence indicating renewed activity inside some of these organisations. Kyrios showed the mugshots of a dozen individuals, but there were no hard leads. Not surprising. That was the whole reason the NCA wanted to use Hale. A lot now depended on how smart the former launderer was in covering his tracks. Gillard was thankful that he wasn't in charge of the surveillance operation. Kyrios had admitted what everybody knew – that the majority of such endeavours, despite their huge drain on resources, produced no arrests and little tangible intelligence. But just now and then, they would hit the big time and scoop up dozens of senior organised crime figures.

Now to tackle some crimes which had actually happened, not just those that might.

Gillard entered the first-floor CID office He found DCs Michelle Tsu and Carl Hoskins standing over Rainy Macintosh's desk, where she was poring over a series of burglary reports. A series of large houses from Surbiton to Walton-on-Thames had been targeted over the previous couple of weeks. The thief or thieves specialised in gaining access through rear patio windows during the daytime and chose secluded homes which were not overlooked by neighbours.

'What have they been looking for?' Gillard asked.

'A wee bit of everything,' Rainy replied. 'Cash, jewellery, high-end laptops. Nothing bulky.'

'What about this one in Esher?' Gillard said, pointing at one of the printed-out statements. Fortunately, it was not the address where the surveillance was taking place. That would be a disaster. Still, it was only three streets away.

'Och, I'm not sure this is the same laddie. It's a different MO. First off, it was in the evening. He climbed up a drainpipe and gained entry through an unsecured first-floor bathroom window, then tiptoed down the stairs, pinched the car keys and drove off in the brand-new E-class Mercedes from the driveway.'

Gillard scanned the report. 'The victims were watching television.'

'Aye. They're well pissed off. There was no sign of forced entry so they'll have a rare wee fight with the insurers.'

'But it was the same date as the two Walton jobs, which were daytime.'

The Glaswegian detective shook her head. 'I put the stolen Merc through the ANPR. The number plate hasn't turned up anywhere. Maybe has false plates on it by now.'

Gillard sighed and scratched his head. 'Anything from forensics?'

'They're all pretty clean. Some partial latex glove prints in the Walton and Surbiton burglaries. Of course, with Covid there's nothing suspicious about seeing anyone wearing gloves. Even my postie wears surgicals.'

'Have you tried DNA?'

'I got the feeling we dinnae have the budget for it.'

'CCTV?'

'None of the houses had cameras, or a decent burglar alarm. I put out requests for footage from neighbours, but I wouldnae hold my breath.'

'What else have you got?' Gillard asked.

Hoskins answered: 'A woman being stalked by her ex, a long-running domestic dispute where I'll bet my life she won't give evidence, and some criminal damage on cars in the West Byfleet station car park.'

'Given the resource issue, the word from on high was we should mark these burglaries as NFA,' Rainy said.

'Sounds just like DCS Dobbs,' Hoskins said.

'But he's off sick,' Michelle said.

'Well, you all know my attitude,' Gillard said. NFA, or No Further Action, was widely derided by the public as a police cop-out. Gillard was unusual amongst senior detectives in being reticent to use it, even for non-violent

48

burglaries or car thefts. Burglars and car thieves would go on and on until they were caught. 'Let's brainstorm them, see what we come up with.'

They worked hard together for the next three hours, comparing the MO to known criminals, and eliminating those who were still inside. By seven p.m. they had pulled together a shortlist, all of whom had DNA samples on the database. 'All right, so now we have a plan,' Gillard said. 'Rainy, to hell with the budget, I want you to co-ordinate some DNA lifts in each of the burgled premises. I know it's a long shot, but if we do all indoor door handles, window latches, we might get something.'

They all agreed. 'Let's hope we get a result before Dobbs comes back to work,' Michelle said.

'Och, let's hope so, we might all have retired by then,' Rainy replied.

–

The next morning, Gillard was flicking through newly filed crime reports and saw another evening burglary had occurred in Esher. Nothing had been taken, but an entry had been forced in rear patio doors at the property, and the intruder had fled when disturbed by the householder. Then he saw the address: 42 Blenheim Drive. That was almost opposite the entrance to The Cedars and would surely be on the spy camera footage from the telegraph pole.

He tried Kyrios' direct line, but it was engaged, so he pounded up the stairs to the third floor and punched in the entry code only to find it had been changed. He hammered on the glass until he was let in by the NCA's Colin Williams, a DI who he'd known for years.

'Colin, I urgently need to see footage from the Blenheim Drive spycam.'

'I'm sure we can arrange that,' he said. Gillard cast an envious glance at the fully staffed desks, the extra equipment, all the resources the NCA had. He even saw his own research intelligence officer, Rob Townsend, on the phone.

Williams prompted Gillard to take a seat at a computer terminal so new it still had the protective film on the screen and a polythene sleeve on the keyboard. Williams leaned over, punched a few keys, and the aerial view of Blenheim Drive appeared on the screen. 'What time are we talking about?'

'Just before nine o'clock last night.'

Williams adjusted the time slider and the view became dark, lit only by streetlamps. The view towards number forty-two was obscured by branches. Gillard took over the keyboard, and fast-forwarded from 8.40 p.m. until 9. There were a few vehicle movements, but one particularly attracted his attention. A light-coloured Ford transit van with only one working headlamp moved slowly from the top of the screen and passed under the camera. Gillard went back a further ten minutes to 8.30, and sure enough, the same van moved slowly up the picture. No other vehicle came and went in that time. He froze the image at a clear view of the front of the vehicle, then used the mouse wheel to zoom in. It gave a clear view of the registration number, and some indication that there was only one occupant. Glare from the streetlamps made it impossible to get any more detail.

'Right, that's the vehicle I want,' Gillard said, getting up. He gave a cheery wave to Rob Townsend, who was now off the phone, and then thundered down the stairs back to his floor. The man he most wanted to find right now was Carl Hoskins, who was sitting at his desk eating.

An apple.

Gillard still couldn't get used to the fact his most over-weight team member was keeping to his new healthy diet. The shock of a diabetes diagnosis had completely changed Hoskins' eating habits. Early days perhaps, but he even looked a little bit less overweight.

'Carl, I've got a job for you.' He wrote down on Hoskins' desk jotter the registration number of the white van. 'Get a DVLA check on the owner, then I want you to match this on ANPR to every burglary we looked at yesterday. If it's cropping up in the same places, I think we might have our man.'

'Righto, sir,' Hoskins said, dropping the apple core into a bin.

Maybe this surveillance operation might be good for something after all, Gillard thought.

He looked around for Rainy Macintosh. 'Where's Rainy?' he asked Michelle Tsu, who had the desk opposite her.

'She's not on until Monday. This weekend is that big family wedding in Glasgow,' Michelle said. 'She's been dieting for weeks to get into the dress.'

'Her ex will be there, won't he?' he asked. Rainy was terrified of the man, an NHS paediatrician with a volcanic temper, who had assaulted her in the past. Gillard's attempts to get her to press charges against him had always fallen on deaf ears.

'Yes. But this will be the last time she'll ever be in the same room with him. That's what she said.'

'It's hard to be sure of that when you have a son together.' Ewan, nearly sixteen, lived with his mum in

Reading. But very soon he would be able to make up his own mind. Gillard was determined to give Rainy the support she needed. She was the best new detective he'd had on his team in years. With so many of his resources being soaked up by the team upstairs, he needed to ensure that every member of his team was firing on all cylinders.

—

After another meeting, it was mid-afternoon before Gillard managed to catch up with Hoskins, just getting up from his desk. 'Hi Carl, how's it going on the van?'

'We got quite a few links on ANPR cameras, some in the vicinity of other burglaries. Trouble is the van is carrying a plate from a Honda Civic that was scrapped seven years ago.'

'That's annoying,' Gillard said. False plates always complicated the task of tracing a vehicle. It also meant the van was neither insured nor taxed.

Hoskins continued: 'We found the last owner of the Honda, a middle-aged woman from Chelmsford, who said it was written off after an accident. The details she gave me checked out, and she's got no criminal record. So we don't have much of a lead.'

Gillard considered the options. Licence plates from scrapped cars were supposed to be destroyed, but they often found their way into the hands of criminals. Despite stronger controls in recent years, scrapyards remained magnets for criminality. 'Let's have a look at the ANPR map,' he said.

Hoskins sat back down at his computer and called up a screen on which dots denoting ANPR hits for the van were superimposed over a map of Surrey. Each observation was labelled with date and time, with a dense cluster around the town of Hersham, superimposed on each other.

'Zoom in so we can see the times,' Gillard asked.

Hoskins enlarged the map until the timestamps became legible. 'It seems to spend most of its time around Hersham, so it could be where he lives.'

Originally a village, Hersham was one of many sprawling prosperous suburbs that had grown up along with numerous business parks within London's M25 orbital motorway.

'Have you sorted them by day?' Gillard asked.

'Not yet,' he said.

'Here's a shortcut,' Gillard said leaning over and taking control of the computer mouse. 'Click on colour code, assign a date, say this first Esher burglary, and drag the icon into the control box.' He clicked 'return', and the map changed a good fifth of the dots to red. 'Now within that, sort by time.' The red dots appeared with sequential numbers.

'Ah, I see what you mean,' Hoskins said.

'You can see a pattern. First hit of the day was in Hersham, and so was the last.' He then changed the date to the first of the Walton-on-Thames burglaries. The dots came up in blue. 'And on this one, first and last ANPR hits of the day were in Hersham.'

'So it pretty much proves that's where he's based,' Hoskins said.

'Only the vehicle, Carl. He could be switching to another to go home.'

'True,' Hoskins said. 'I'll get on to the neighbourhood policing team at Elmbridge, see if they can do some more street patrols in Hersham, maybe find the van. Do you want a public appeal for dashcam footage?'

'Definitely not. If he knows we're onto him, he'll go to ground. But if Elmbridge can spare an unmarked van or two with dashcams and leave them parked within Hersham, that would help to narrow down the location.'

'I'll get on to it, sir.'

Chapter Eight

Sam Gillard rang the doorbell at the Barnes' home, admiring the neatly kept flowerbeds, and the glorious display of fragrant yellow roses that climbed up a trellis by the front door. The door opened to reveal Jenny Barnes, in a pinny, flour on her fingers and a phone clamped under her chin. 'Yes, Mum. Look, I've got to go now, I have guests at the door.'

She beckoned Sam in, and they exchanged socially distanced air kisses. She put down the phone against her shoulder for a moment, to summon her daughter Zoe, before picking up the phone again. She was clearly having trouble trying to wind up the call. 'Goodbye Mum, yes, speak soon. No, we'll talk about that later. Look after yourself.' She rolled her eyes at Sam, who was still waiting with a bottle of wine in one hand and a box of chocolates in the other.

The youngest daughter Lucy appeared behind her mother. Eight years old, with huge blue eyes and a shock of dark wavy hair. 'You can give me the chocolates,' she said conspiratorially to Sam.

Sam started to pass across the handmade Belgian selection, but Jenny intercepted the box. 'These are not for you, madam, they are for all of us.'

'I know, but you've got floury hands,' Lucy said.

The phone call now complete, Jenny wiped her free hand on her pinny, received Sam's bottle of wine and said: 'Lovely to see you, Sam. It's been too long.'

Friends at school, Jenny and Sam had lost contact for more than a decade, until Sam's kidnapping had made national headlines just over a year ago. During her long recuperation, Sam had delighted in the wave of messages she got from friends old and new, including a heartfelt message and open invitation for lunch from Jenny and husband Oliver.

'It's wonderful to see you, Jenny. You're looking so slim.' It wasn't a white lie. Jenny's nickname at school had been Podge, but now with spectacles replaced by contact lenses, and her previously unruly brown hair in a highlighted bob, she looked every inch the career woman that she was.

'Where's the heroic Craig, I'm dying to meet him!' Jenny said, looking over Sam's shoulder.

'In the car, finishing off a work phone call. It happens constantly.'

'Criminal classes, eh? Why can't they keep nine-to-five hours,' Jenny said.

'Yes, sometimes I think he is the only detective in the county.' As soon as she said it, Sam realised her mistake.

'Is your husband a detective?' Lucy asked, eyes wide.

'Lucy, stop being nosy.' Jenny ushered them through the hallway into the kitchen, and out of the open back door onto the patio, where a slim dark-haired man with a neat beard was setting a large wooden table with cutlery and glassware. A selection of salads was already laid out.

'Ollie, this is my old school friend Sam.'

'Nice to meet you,' he said, offering his elbow. 'I've read about your appalling ordeal.'

Sam smiled. 'I'm not sure I will ever be truly over it.'

Oliver turned away, perhaps unnerved by having strayed into a serious topic too soon. 'It's just about warm enough out here.' No sooner had he said it, a gust of wind blew a pile of paper napkins into the air.

'Our sacrifices to the pandemic,' Sam said, watching Ollie and Lucy chase around to retrieve them. Gillard, still in face mask, had now arrived at her side, and the greetings were completed.

'I've read lots about you,' Oliver said.

'Nothing good I hope,' Gillard said. 'I try to keep my profile low, it doesn't do to be too recognisable in my line of work.'

'Not much you can do about that when you single-handedly rescue your wife from a kidnapper. The press had a field day,' Oliver said.

'Ollie, did you call Zoe?' Jenny asked.

'Twice.' He made his way back into the house, shouting for his eldest daughter. 'Come on Zoe, it's lunchtime. We have guests.'

Sam took in the long rear garden, bordered by high neat hedges to either side, and descending in a series of terraces to a rear fence about fifty yards away. 'This is a lovely place you have here. You're not overlooked at all.' Sam felt a little envious. She and Craig were in a bog-standard semi, with Craig's appalling and interfering Aunt Trish in a bungalow opposite them. She would love to have this much space.

Zoe finally arrived, with eyes only for the phone in her hand. She was a skinny fifteen-year-old with an elfin face and mid-brown hair cut in a bob, wearing meticulously ripped jeans and a sweatshirt. She looked up for a moment and shyly greeted the guests, before returning her gaze to the device. 'Zoe, put it away now, we're eating,' Jenny said, rolling her eyes at Sam, then heading off to the kitchen.

Gillard and Oliver were soon deep in conversation. Oliver modestly described his role as a stay-at-home dad. In fact he was building and maintaining websites for various clients and looking after the kids. Jenny was a sales director for a medical equipment firm, and now frantically busy because of the pandemic. Jenny arrived halfway through her husband's description of her career. She had a tray laden with a selection of cheeses and a large wholemeal quiche.

'That looks lovely,' Sam said. 'Home-made?'

'Yes, but not by me,' Jenny said. 'Ollie's been hard at work this morning.'

Oliver poured the wine, including a half-sized glass for Zoe. Sam put a hand over her own glass. 'Just orange juice for me, please.'

'Oh yes,' Jenny said, serving out slices of quiche. 'This is your big news.'

'Mummy says you're going to have a baby,' Lucy said. 'Does it hurt yet?'

'Lucy, please don't be so direct,' Jenny said.

'It hasn't hurt at all so far,' Sam said. 'I'm only just over three months along. It's only during the birth that it's likely to hurt.'

'Then it will hurt like fuck,' Lucy said, nodding sagely.

'Lucy! How many times have I told you?' Jenny said.

'But that's what Maya Jenkins' mum said.'

'Lucy, you have no sense of decorum,' Zoe muttered, still staring into her lap.

'What's decorum?' Lucy asked.

'What you haven't got,' Zoe answered, then looked at Sam. The teenager had fashionably heavy brows, and the same shrewd gaze Sam remembered Jenny having at the same age. There was a keen intelligence in the girl's hazel eyes.

'Your mother says you're studying music. What's your instrument?' Sam asked Zoe.

'Clarinet.' She returned to staring in her lap, where a phone was clearly in use.

'Zoe, don't be rude,' Jenny said. 'What's wrong with a proper sentence? "Yes, that's right. I'm studying the clarinet."'

'You wasted seven words, and got no more information across,' Zoe said.

'Smart alec,' her father said, snaking out a hand and grabbing the phone from his daughter's lap.

'Don't!' Zoe said, reaching across to get it back. She failed, but tipped over her glass of wine.

'Stupid fuckwit,' Lucy said mildly, as she chewed a mouthful of quiche.

'Lucy!' her mother admonished, as she mopped up the spillage with a handful of napkins.

'That's what Daddy calls people on the phone,' Lucy whined. 'Every time he ends a call he then says—' she opened her mouth as if to say it again.

'—Lucy, don't you dare.'

Oliver laughed nervously as his wife's basilisk gaze turned to him. 'I might have said it with technical support. After the line went down for the fourth time this week.'

'Do you work in technical support?' Lucy asked Gillard, blue eyes wide in beguiling innocence.

Gillard laughed. 'I'm glad to say I don't.'

'Mum, can I get down?' Zoe asked.

59

'You haven't eaten anything,' Jenny said.

'I don't eat eggs.' Zoe pushed her plate of quiche away.

'Since when?' Oliver asked.

Lucy put a hand to her mouth a leaned conspiratorially towards Sam. 'Eggs are actually murdered chicken babies,' she whispered.

Sam stopped mid-chew, realising that this word of advice was meant for her, the mother-to-be.

'Okay, Zoe,' Oliver said. 'There's some bread and butter in the kitchen. Help yourself.'

Zoe stood up, then held her hand out to her father. Oliver rolled his eyes at Gillard, then pulled Zoe's phone from out of his shirt pocket and gave it to her. She took it and strode away towards the house.

'What do you say?' Oliver called out to her.

'Thank you,' Zoe called out mechanically, then vanished into the kitchen.

'Tch, kids today,' Lucy said, shaking her head. Everyone laughed.

'You've got all this to come,' Jenny said to Sam, with a smile.

'I won't mind a bit,' Sam said.

'This is a fantastic garden,' Gillard said. 'That's the benefit of an older home.'

'Developers tried to buy some of it,' Oliver said.

'They had agreements from three of the neighbours, but we held out,' Jenny added.

'This neighbour too?' Gillard asked, pointing towards the rear of an enormous home a hundred yards or more beyond the back fence.

'Not them, they don't need the money,' Oliver said.

'That's where Azalea lives,' Lucy announced. 'She's got a pony, her own car, a heated indoor swimming pool, a pinball machine and a home cinema. Her boyfriend's just dumped her.'

'Sounds like a very rash decision,' Sam said, exchanging a wry smile with Jenny.

'Azalea is Zoe's closest friend,' Jenny said. 'They're in the school orchestra together. Zoe plays clarinet and Azalea the cello and the piano.'

'I play the violin,' Lucy announced. 'I'm absolutely crap.'

'Lucy, you're only learning, and Zoe was horrible to say that to you,' Jenny said. 'No one is good when they first start.'

'Azalea was. She's a prodigy,' Lucy said.

'No, it's about hard work. Azalea practises twenty hours a week,' Jenny said. 'Zoe doesn't do half that.'

'Her parents are very strict,' Oliver said to Sam. 'No smartphone, no sleepovers at friends' homes.'

'No sex,' Lucy added casually. 'Zoe said that's why Josh dumped her.'

Jenny and Oliver exchanged a glance. 'I know a little girl,' Oliver said, 'whose ears were too big, and didn't know how to control her mouth.'

Lucy giggled.

'You probably know her father,' Oliver said to Gillard. 'He's been in the paper even more than you. Jonathan Hale.'

'He washes money,' Lucy whispered to Sam, who laughed.

'Extradited to the US as I recall,' Gillard said. 'Took about a year for him to lose the case to stay here.'

'I suppose he had the money to fight it,' Jenny said.

'And with a plea bargain, back already,' Gillard said.

'Money brings power, even in the legal system,' Sam said.

'Are you going to arrest Azalea's daddy?' Lucy asked.

'No.' Gillard laughed, more than a little unnerved by the directness of the child. He had assumed that, given the disparity in wealth, there would be no contact between the Barnes and the Hale households. But if the kids were such good friends with Azalea Hale, it would only take a brief mention of a detective visiting next door to blow his cover and ruin the surveillance.

'Jonathan Hale, he's from jail!' Lucy sang, getting down from the table. She continued to sing the rhyme to herself as she scampered into the house.

'Lucy is so adorable,' Sam said, taking a sip of her orange juice. Gillard noticed his wife's wistful expression. Hopefully this time, he thought, now we're past the worst time for miscarriages. Third time lucky.

'They both seem very bright,' Gillard said.

'Too bright, sometimes,' Oliver said. 'Apart from her musical side, Zoe is also bit of a computer whizz.'

'Years ago, Ollie used to sit Zoe in her highchair in his office while he worked,' Jenny said.

'I think she absorbed everything she saw,' Oliver added.

'Do you know,' Jenny said, 'when Zoe was five, she changed all the fonts on Ollie's computer.' She eyed her husband. This was clearly a much-retold anecdote.

'Lime green on a yellow background,' Oliver said. 'Utterly illegible.'

'Very enterprising,' Gillard said. 'And she's friends with Jonathan Hale's daughter?'

'Yes, it's quite an age difference,' Jenny said. 'But Azalea is a young seventeen. Despite being so pretty, she hates being tall. But then that's not surprising as her mother used to be a fashion model.'

'Do you have much to do with them?' Gillard asked.

'Socially, no, they're a bit out of our league, even now,' Jenny said. 'But they're very nice, considering.'

Gillard smiled, then checked to make sure that the girls were not within hearing. 'I understand one of our men came to fit a burglar alarm a few weeks ago,' Gillard said quietly to Oliver.

'Don't worry, we didn't say anything to the girls. They think it's just a normal alarm,' he replied.

'Perhaps you be good enough to tell them that I'm a traffic warden, not a detective,' Gillard said.

'That might fool Lucy, but knowing Zoe, she's probably already googled you,' Jenny said.

'Can she keep a secret?' Gillard asked.

'Yes, unlike her sister,' Oliver said.

'It's really important that they're not tipped off next door.'

'I'll speak to Zoe about that,' Jenny said.

Gillard nodded. 'Look, I don't know if they've told you, but when this comes to a head,' he nodded towards the Hale home, 'a raid could come at any time of day, and be pretty alarming. Lots of vehicles, maybe armed cops. Just keep the kids close to you and stay away from the windows.'

'When will that be?' Jenny asked.

'I have no idea.'

Chapter Nine

The same day

North Bluff State Correctional Facility

It was two a.m. when Tyler stirred, awaking with a sense of excitement. He was lying on the bunk, and under the blanket in his hand was a brand new Samsung smartphone. One of TJ's associates had delivered it to him in a sock that afternoon when Morales was out. His cellie was now snoring above him. Tyler eased himself to a cross-legged position and pulled the blanket over him to suppress the glow from the phone. He'd already set the brightness to minimum, and checked the signal, which had been one of the things that most worried him. Two bars. Not great, but adequate. The display showed it had plenty of juice.

He pulled up Google and searched for the property details of his brother's condo. It had briefly been on the listings of a few real estate agents, so it wasn't hard to find and save them. He looked at a bookmark in his prison copy of *A Tale of Two Cities*. It had TJ's outside contact details. Tyler set himself up a Gmail account, typed out a brief email, attached the property details, and sent it to the address he'd been given. Then he started on the real search, the first step on the road to vengeance.

He typed in the name Jonathan Hale and hit return. There were hundreds of them. He added the word lawyer and found dozens of British press articles about the extra-dition fight years previously. He scanned through half a dozen, but none mentioned a home address, only the office from which he worked. As Hale was now disbarred that wasn't any help.

There were plenty of photographs of the man, however, and he saved them in a folder. When he heard the sound of the night-time landing patrol, he turned off the phone and pretended to be asleep. He'd made a start, but there was more to be done.

—

Simon's arrival in the Hale household had upended normal routines. If he fed himself the messy process would take at least an hour, so Jonathan, Azalea and Xolwa took turns to sit next to him after they had finished their own food. Tonight was Azalea's turn. Hale could see his son was being particularly difficult, shouting a lot and gestic-ulating. She seemed to understand about a third of what he was saying, but then she had much less experience than he did. Xolwa understood little but there was something about her empathy and caring that allowed Simon to relax more when she fed him. Perhaps it was the traditional Somali songs she crooned to him, that calmed him. The love and affection that both women willingly bestowed on Simon was a source of pride.

'Dad, I've got a piano lesson in half an hour, can you finish him off for me?' Azalea said.

'Yes. Do drive carefully.' He looked meaningfully at her.

'Dad,' she said, rolling her eyes. 'It's only five minutes away.' She enjoyed her private lessons. The tutor, a rather fierce lady, had been at the Royal College of Music and in under a year had brought her from grade eight, where she had got a distinction, up to higher diplomas.

'You only passed your test a few weeks ago,' her father reminded her. 'There are some mad drivers out there. Drive defensively, anticipate what other road users might do.'

Azalea glanced mischievously at her mother before answering. 'Um, can I remind you who it was who reversed the Maserati into a bollard last week?'

Simon squawked with laughter, his arm jerking upwards, his clawed fingers twisting towards his father. He never missed a trick.

Hale smiled sheepishly at his daughter. 'Yes, I know, I failed to anticipate that it was going to jump out behind me. You can do better!'

Xolwa chuckled. 'A £1,400 bill for just a dent. That's more than Azalea's Renault is worth.'

'What will you be playing on Wednesday at orchestra practice?' Hale asked his daughter, clearly anxious to change the subject.

'I don't know. Zoe messaged everybody on Facebook, but forgot that I'm not on…'

'Not this again,' Hale said with a sigh.

Xolwa turned to her husband. 'Jonathan, come on, she's old enough to drive, so she's obviously old enough for a smartphone.'

'It's not about her age, as you well know. Social media can be used to trace people, from anywhere in the world. She's vulnerable.'

'But they're in *prison*,' Xolwa said. 'An ocean away. They're not getting out for decades. And they're not allowed to go online when they're in there.'

'Dad, I'm missing out on everything,' Azalea said. 'Everyone at school exchanges messages, and I never get to see them. I'm a social leper.'

'You're being ridiculous. Your friends can email you. You've got a powerful top of the range laptop. If those so-called friends can't be bothered to do that, then they're not...'

Azalea's face dissolved into frustration. 'Kids today don't *use* email. It's WhatsApp, Telegram, TikTok. I'm always behind. I never know what's going on. That's why I've hardly got *any* friends.'

'Oh come on, you've got loads of friends,' Hale said. 'Zoe and Lucy are always around here, in the pool.'

'Lucy is not my friend, she's eight! Even Zoe is two years younger than me. That's how desperate I am.'

'Come on, you've got your friends from the orchestra, and more friends at the stables...'

Azalea suddenly jumped up from the table and fled from the room, slamming the door behind her.

Xolwa grasped Hale's hand, and said: 'Go easy, Jon. She is a little volatile at the moment.'

'I know, I know.' Azalea's boyfriend Josh had recently inexplicably dumped her. She had been distraught, and cried for days, especially after Josh was seen with another girl. Hale couldn't help thinking it was all his fault. His daughter was a pariah because of his criminality, his stigma.

'Come on, Jon,' Xolwa said. 'She'll be off to university in a year, and she'll definitely need to be on social media by then. You can't stand in the way of progress, and you can't sacrifice her freedom for your own paranoia.'

'I am not bloody paranoid,' Hale said, a wave of anxiety pulsing through him. 'My enemies are real. They do exist.'

He looked at her again, at the caring concern in her face, and sighed. 'All right, all right, I'll think about it.'

–

'We've just had a detective come to lunch.' It was the first thing Zoe told Azalea when she opened the front door to her friend, who had popped in after driving back from her lesson.

'Really?' Azalea said, slipping off her shoes and following Zoe upstairs to her room. 'I'd better not tell Dad, he's paranoid enough as it is.'

Zoe waved a dismissive hand. 'Nothing to be excited about anyway. It was just a tedious social call.' The two girls kicked off their shoes and sprawled on Zoe's bed. Azalea propped herself up on one elbow, while Zoe adopted her usual position: lying on her front, her chin on one hand and phone in the other. 'His wife knows Mum from years back.' She laughed. 'I mean you can't imagine him chasing bank robbers or anything. He must be at least fifty.'

Azalea laughed. 'Fifty's not that ancient. Dad's fifty-four, though he's behaving like an old woman.'

'Time to divorce your parents,' Zoe said. 'Was it about social media?'

'Yeah.'

Zoe looked at her friend and could see that there was something else bothering her. She thought she knew what it was.

'Have you heard from Josh?' she asked.

Azalea rolled her eyes. 'He's been badmouthing me on Facebook. He said I was uptight and boring. Georgia showed me.' Zoe too was friends with Georgia and had seen the comments, which had been widely reposted with approval by Azalea's enemies and condemned by her few friends. It was a rolling argument that looked to go on for weeks and weeks.

'Well, I've got some good news,' Zoe said, reaching into her bedside cabinet and bringing out a mobile phone. 'Dad's upgraded to a new iPhone, and offered me his old one. It's got less memory than my existing one, but I thought you could use it. I've set it all up for you.' She passed the device across.

'Oh, Zoe, that's so kind,' Azalea replied. Zoe knew it was a year or two since Azalea had been allowed to use a smartphone, and she gave her a quick revision course.

'I'll have to find somewhere to hide it from my dad.'

'Good idea. I already set you up a new email address, all random letters, and you can use that to set up Facebook, if you want to keep tabs on Josh,' Zoe said.

'I can't have anything with my name on it. Dad would go ape.'

'Whatever. Hey, your screen name could be Cello Babe.' The two girls laughed out loud.

'What about Princess Piano?' Azalea said with a chuckle.

Zoe stuck her head over the edge of the bed and made energetic vomiting noises. 'That is so stuck up!'

Over the next forty-five minutes, Zoe assisted as Azalea set up accounts on Facebook, Instagram, TikTok, WhatsApp and Snapchat. The screen name they settled on was DarkRider49, and where she needed to give a registration name, she used Emily Rider. Zoe reminded her how to set up her privacy controls to limit who could see her personal details.

'That at least will make your dad happy,' Zoe said. 'Put in a false birthday, and don't mention your address.'

'I'll have to email the details to Georgia and Merrilyn, they'll never find me.'

'Yeah, it's a bit laborious, but once you're on the WhatsApp group for the orchestra you won't miss out on anything.'

'That's great.'

'So who *are* the bad guys who want to hunt your dad down?' Zoe asked.

Azalea groaned and rolled onto her back with her hands cupped behind her head, staring at Zoe's boy band posters pinned to the ceiling and said. 'They're all in prison, with really long jail terms.'

'So he's worrying over nothing?'

'That's what Mum says, but then he told me some really scary stories about being in jail. How frightening some of the other prisoners were, even though he was in with only non-violent ones.' Azalea yawned and added, 'The scariest one is called Richard Tyler.'

'What jail?' Zoe asked, tapping in the details on her phone.

'I can't remember. Some high security place in Arizona.'

It took Zoe only a few seconds to find the website of the Arizona Department of Corrections Rehabilitation and Re-entry. 'Cool, you can search by prisoner name.' She typed the surname in, and it produced a list of seventeen felons with mugshots. Adding the initial cut it down to four.

'Wow, they have a lot of people in jail in America,' Azalea said, looking over Zoe's shoulder. 'All those Tylers, just in Arizona.'

'We could narrow it down,' Zoe said. 'There's a lot of detail here. It's got height, weight, date of admission, eye and hair colour, and the expected date of release.'

'Well, it won't be that one,' Azalea said, looking at the first mugshot thumbnail Zoe had pulled up, a young scowling black guy. Zoe tapped on the prisoner number to expand the record.

Azalea shook her head. 'This one is due out in five years. Tyler's not out for a couple of centuries or something.'

Zoe emitted a peal of laughter and looked up at her friend. 'What's the point of that? He'll be dead.'

'I think that's kind of the idea,' Azalea said.

The second mugshot showed another black man with a fairly long sentence.

'Tyler is white, I think,' Azalea said.

Zoe went down the list. The third thumbnail showed a white man with just a swirl of fine silvery hair, and what looked like red-eye from flash. Only when she tapped on the prisoner number and got the full-size mugshot did she see the full horror of Tyler's appearance.

'Eurgh,' Azalea said. 'Dad never told me about that.'

'Well, there's an address here if you want to write to him,' Zoe said, with a laugh.

Azalea looked suddenly serious. 'Just the idea makes my blood run cold.'

They jumped when the door opened. Standing there was Lucy, stroking the cat, Socks, in her arms, Bond villain style.

'Go away, trouble,' Zoe said. 'Why can't you ever knock?'

'Who's Tyler?' Lucy said, ignoring her sister's comments and making her way towards the bed.

'Never you mind,' Zoe said, hiding the phone under a pillow.

'That's Daddy's old iPhone,' Lucy said. 'I should have that.'

'You're not old enough,' Zoe said.

'You can't have two, it's not fair.'

'I'm lending it to Azalea, because she hasn't got one,' Zoe said.

'I haven't got one, and I'm family.'

'You're not family, you were adopted,' Zoe said.

'I wasn't!' Lucy wailed, close to tears. Socks bailed out onto the bed, with his ears backwards.

'No need to be cruel, Zoe,' Azalea said, punching her lightly in the arm. 'You know that's not true.'

'She's just so annoying, every *bloody* day,' Zoe said, rolling on her back with her hands over her eyes. 'She listens at doors, looks through keyholes. Sometimes I think she works for the Stasi.'

'What's a Stasi?' Lucy asked, a well-formed pout on her face.

'Just *go away*,' Zoe said.

'Is he Azalea's new boyfriend? Is that why you're checking up on him? Is that why you might write him a letter?'

Zoe collapsed with laughter, but Azalea was stern-faced. 'Lucy, this man is dangerous. I would rather die than write to him.'

Chapter Ten

North Bluff State Correctional Facility

Tyler had hit a brick wall and needed help. He had some familiarity with the web before being imprisoned, but generally stayed off it, fearing the Feds would trace him. Besides, he wasn't of a technology mindset. L3 had been a strictly last-century crime syndicate, set up using burner phones, codewords and physical drops of merchandise. Anything else had been contracted out, just like laundering the dough. For a long time it had worked. But now he needed someone to help him.

Someone young, who grew up with the Internet.

'Morales, wake up,' Tyler hissed, easing himself out of his bunk.

'What's up?' he asked, propping himself up on one elbow.

'Sshh. Did you use the web much?'

'Sure. Before I came inside.'

'I need to find somebody. In England. And I got a smartphone,' he whispered.

'Holy shit!' Morales gasped, now seeing the device in Tyler's hand.

'Lower your goddamn volume,' Tyler hissed. 'Help me now, you get to use it for an hour when I finish. Squeak a word, and I will cut out your liver. Understand?'

'I ain't no rat,' Morales whispered. 'So who got you the phone?'

'Never mind that. Help me find the rat who put me in here, and I'll see your family is all right on the outside.' Tyler knew that Morales' mother was suffering from cancer.

'Sure thing. You got an address?'

'I got an office address, in London. But he's been busted. I need to know where he lives now.' Tyler passed him the phone.

'What's the name?'

'Jonathan Hale.' Tyler spelled it out, while Morales typed it into Google.

'There's quite a few. A professor of architecture, some famous dead Canadian, and an actor. Then all the other guys.'

'He's a lawyer. Put that in too.' Tyler leaned over Morales' shoulder.

'Jonathan Hale, property lawyer. Is that him?'

'Sure.'

Morales saw dozens of British newspaper articles about Hale's fight against extradition.

'Money laundering, was he on your team?'

'Mind your own fucking business. I have a score to settle with this guy.'

Morales started scanning through the newspaper articles.

'Look, I already did that,' Tyler said. 'They all give his home address as Kings Parade, Fulham. But that's not his home address, it's his office address. And I reckon he's not practising anymore.'

'Maybe you can try LinkedIn. Set up your own profile, false picture, that kind of thing and reach out to him.'

'I thought of that. But he ain't on LinkedIn. If he's got any sense, he's not on any social media accounts. Just like I wasn't. You got to be hard to find.'

'Maybe he had a secretary, an associate, someone else who worked with him.'

'I thought of that. There was someone called Robinson, Amy Robinson. I spoke to her a couple times. But there's a billion Robinsons in England. No, I need something better.'

'Well, he ain't gonna be in the phone book, that's for sure.'

'What about the voters' register?' Tyler asked.

Morales typed in *voters register England*. 'They call it the electoral roll.' He found a website called 192.com and tapped out Hale's name. 'Fuck, there's more than a hundred. Where's he live?'

'That's what I'm trying to find out, asshole,' Tyler growled.

'I mean the city or the town, then you've got a chance.'

'Somewhere near London, that's all I remember. Jesus, I wish I had access to my documents. There was all sorts of stuff there. The Feds have got it now.'

Morales started reading out the towns on the electoral roll listing. Tyler shook his head. 'I'd know if you said it, I'm sure he told me.'

'But if he's smart, he would have moved, right?'

'He's smart all right. Let me think,' Tyler said.

A high-pitched howl of agony from the landing made them look up. Tyler grabbed the phone and turned it off, stuffing it under his pillow. The screaming came in long breathless bursts, followed by sobs, echoing through the atrium. Morales got up and pressed his face to the bars, sniffing the air like a dog, his ears attuned.

'Pazzo Salvatore again,' Morales said. Salvatore would often scream all night, convinced he was being attacked by demons. Everyone knew that the highly disturbed prisoner should be in a hospital wing, or a proper mental institution. But in Arizona there weren't often spaces. A lawsuit was pending against the prisons department accusing it of 'cruel and unusual punishment' in failing to provide adequate mental health care for the incarcerated. The trouble with Salvatore's outbursts was that they kept everyone else awake, stirring up the other schizophrenics, the psychos, and the violent. Which between them was just about everybody. His keening wail somehow seemed to encapsulate the hopelessness of incarceration.

Tyler turned over and pressed the pillow into both ears. He had to get out of this place. He had to find Jonathan Hale. Otherwise he'd end up just like Pazzo Salvatore.

–

It was nine p.m. and Lucy should have been in bed, asleep. Instead, she was under the bed with the cat. This was her favourite hiding place, one that she used for illicit spying activities. Chief of these was the misuse of Zoe's phone. It was pretty hard to find a moment when the precious mobile was not in her sister's possession, which made it all the more of a prize. Lucy had only ever succeeded in the evening when Zoe was in the shower and their parents would be watching TV downstairs. From the moment the whirr of the shower pump began Lucy knew she had about ten minutes. To be caught would earn Zoe's unrelenting enmity. It was a thirty-second dash from her room across the carpet to Zoe's, to grab the phone from the bedside table and rush back.

Lucy had long ago observed and memorised her sister's unlock code. First priority, as always, was to check Zoe's messages, to see who she been talking to. She was very keen to discover if Zoe was secretly seeing a boy, because that could give her useful leverage against her sister. There had always been a kind of war between them. Zoe excluded Lucy from as many activities as possible, cut her dead in front of friends, and derided her as a child. In response, Lucy had learned to use tears to manipulate her father. She had also learned very quickly that information was power. With practised fingers she scrolled back through Zoe's texts and emails. Most of it was boring, but there were a couple of male names, Zach and Ben, who she seemed to be in regular contact with. She was particularly excited to see if any naughty pictures had been sent between them. She had overheard her parents talking about 'sexting' and looked it up online. Pictures would give her tremendous blackmail power. But scrolling through the images on Zoe's phone, there was no sign of anything incriminating.

How boring.

Lucy finally turned to Zoe's recent search history and scrolled through pages and pages until she came upon the name Richard Tyler. She clicked on the prisoner record, and gasped at the horrible face. She wondered if it would be possible to email him. A love letter to him in Zoe's name would be brilliantly wicked! But reading the prisoner record only gave a correspondence address for the jail, not an email. She started to write it down in biro on the palm of her hand, but the shower pump had just gone off, which she calculated gave her about two minutes grace while Zoe dried herself in the bathroom. Lucy wriggled out from under the bed, opened the bedroom door quietly, and scampered across to her sister's bedroom. She turned the handle and eased it open, darting across to the bedside table to return the phone. She could hear the buzz of Zoe's electric toothbrush now, which usually meant there were only thirty seconds left before she'd emerge. Lucy sprinted back into her own room and jumped into bed. Socks, who had been waiting for her, started purring.

Lucy transcribed the prison address onto her notepad. She would have to think about this. But she was excited to have a go.

–

At two a.m. the landing was quiet. Pazzo Salvatore seemed to be taking a night off from screaming. Hopefully, the nurse had sedated him. Tyler had been working on an idea for tracing Hale. He had waited and waited, anxious to use the phone, but knowing that it was only in the dead of night that he could rely on not being disturbed.

Tyler began working the phone under the covers, but there was enough movement to disturb Morales on the top bunk.

'Whatcha working on?' Morales whispered.

'Trying to find his family. He had a Somalian wife, I think.'

'What was her name?' Morales slipped out of bed to crouch next to Tyler.

'I heard him say it, starting with a zee, zol something. I don't how it's spelled. She was a catwalk model in London.'

'You can ace it then,' Morales said. Tyler passed him the phone and he typed a search into Google. 'I reckon Somali, models, Hale and London will show her.'

'I tried that, but it's just pictures, and I ain't ever seen her.' The image search Morales made seemed to confirm it, a parade of beautiful dark-skinned women, labelled only with the names of designers whose clothes they were wearing.

'Okay, I'll switch to text results,' Morales said, bringing up a whole series of trade journals from ten years ago. 'Is this her?' he said, showing an interview with a woman called Xolwa Sebusi. The accompanying picture showed a tall and slender beauty, with huge eyes and sharp cheekbones, wearing an absurd magenta hat.

'Xolwa, I ain't sure,' Tyler said. 'Type Xolwa and Hale without the rest.'

Morales did so, and on an image search found a London society portrait on a red carpet, of the same woman with a man in a tuxedo with fair, swept back hair.

'Fuck, that's Hale!' Tyler hissed.

'Right, so she is Xolwa Sebusi. And damn hot too.'

'How old is that picture?' Tyler asked, squinting at the phone.

'More than a dozen years,' Morales said. 'But it don't matter, you got her modelling name.'

Further searches found nothing recent. 'Maybe she's retired,' Morales said.

'Yeah, not surprising. She might even have changed it now. But anyway try it in the electoral roll website. As Sebusi and as Hale.'

Morales did so. 'Nothing.'

'Just try it with the initial.'

'No dice,' Morales said. 'Did they have kids?'

'Yeah, but I can't remember the names. He had a crippled boy, from his first marriage. Lived in a special residential centre.'

Morales looked up at him. 'If you know the type of disability, we might be able to find the specialist places that look after someone like that.'

'Sure,' Tyler said. 'The younger kid, he mentioned she played great piano, and cello.'

'Maybe she's been in some competitions? Do you remember her name?'

'Hell, no. I was up to my balls trying to understand the laundering structures the bastard created.' He grabbed the phone from Morales and turned it off. There was some movement across the landing. After sliding the phone under the pillow, Tyler made his way to the bars and peered out into the aura of light created by the flashlight of the correctionals. Some guy had been coughing his lungs out from that cell earlier in the day, and was now being hauled out. The correctionals didn't sound like they were addressing him, only each other. It was too low-key. The cougher didn't make a sound, not even a wheeze. Maybe he was heading out to the sickbay, or just maybe he was just another poor bastard for the Covid cemetery.

Tyler closed his eyes and gripped the bars. *I just got to get out of this place.*

Chapter Eleven

Sunday breakfast time in the Barnes family. Oliver had got his laptop at the table and was eating a piece of toast. Zoe had her own phone well-hidden on her lap.

'No phones or computers at the table,' Lucy announced. She was still wearing her pyjamas, and had Socks on her lap. She has been trying to feed a satsuma to the feline, but despite it being peeled very carefully, the animal showed no signs of interest, and simply thrust his head under Lucy's hand, purring loudly.

Oliver looks up at his youngest daughter. 'Okay, Lucy, I'm finished now.' He closed the lid and moved the device onto the kitchen worktop behind him.

'Why has Mummy got to work today?' Lucy asked, feeding herself a segment of satsuma. 'I'm bored with your cooking.'

Oliver laughed. 'I told you before, she has an important meeting in London. The Covid virus won't wait you know, and she's hoping to make a sale to the government.'

'Why can't she do it on Zoom?' Zoe asked.

'You'll have to ask her,' Oliver said. 'Now who's for some scrambled eggs?'

'Can we have it with smoked salmon?' Zoe asked.

'Yay, posh breakfast!' Lucy shouted.

'We haven't got any smoked salmon,' Oliver said.

The two girls looked at each other and in unison chanted '…Because Daddy messed up the shopping again.' Both girls dissolved in laughter.

'Azalea probably has smoked salmon whenever she wants,' Zoe said.

'Because her daddy's rich,' Lucy said. 'He's got money coming out of his ears!' She giggled and waved her fingers to either side of her head. 'And a trophy wife.'

'Lucy, listen,' Oliver said, suddenly serious. 'For God's sake, don't ever say that when you go over there.'

'Why not?'

'Because it's rude. Xalwo would be very upset.'

'But you said it, Daddy. And so did Mummy. She said Xalwo was so skinny she might break into bits.'

'Well, we didn't know you were listening,' Oliver said.

'Jonathan Hale, he's still from jail,' Zoe said.

Lucy started giggling.

Oliver pointed a warning finger at her. 'And never, ever say that in front of him.'

'So is Sam's husband really a detective?' Lucy asked her father.

'No. He's a traffic warden.'

'Haha, he stops people parking,' Lucy said.

'What?' Zoe looked up at her father, her brows knitted. He raised a finger to his lips. *Don't let on.* She shrugged and returned to her phone.

'Can a traffic warden arrest Azalea's daddy?' Lucy asked.

'No. He can only issue tickets.'

'For washing cash?' Lucy asked.

'No, not for money laundering,' Oliver said, standing up and reaching for eggs from the fridge.

'Why is that naughty?' Lucy said. 'It's good to make things clean, that's what Mummy says when she sells her hand sanitisers.'

Oliver cracked four eggs into a bowl and reached for a whisk. 'Ah, money laundering is different. It's when you get cash stolen from somebody, and pretend it's come from normal business.'

'So it doesn't have to get wet?' Lucy asked.

'No, not at all.' Oliver prepared the scrambled eggs, and served them on slices of toast which he distributed on plates round the table.

'Daddy, you didn't warm the plates.'

Oliver groaned at being skewered again on one of his wife's many domestic standards by the ever-observant Lucy. He picked up Lucy's breakfast and put it into the microwave.

'Daddy! You'll make the toast soggy,' Lucy said.

'You better make up your mind: cold plates or soggy toast?'

Lucy gave way at this blackmail and accepted a cold plate. Zoe had already eaten half of hers.

After they had both finished Oliver said: 'All right girls. Music practice!'

Their synchronised groan was almost musical. 'We're going swimming at Azalea's,' Zoe wailed. 'It's already arranged.'

'What time?'

'Eleven o'clock,' Zoe said. 'And Margarethe is making us lunch. This afternoon she's taking me to ride Billy.'

Oliver and Jenny had quietly agreed after the Gillard visit that they were going to try to discourage their kids from visiting the Hales. For a long time they had been uncomfortable with the amount of time they spent at the neighbours' house, and the expectations it was giving them. Nevertheless, the lure of a heated indoor swimming pool, the pinball machine in the basement, and Hale's home cinema were hard to beat. Above all was Billy, Azalea's chestnut gelding that Zoe was learning to ride. His eldest daughter might be a boffin at school, hard-headed and shrewd, but when it came to the horse she was just a besotted kid. She had begged him for a pony for years.

'Okay, but that's the last time this week.'

'She offered us a sleepover on Friday!' Lucy wailed.

'You'll have to cancel it,' Oliver said. The plaintive cries of the girls only made him more determined. The idea of his two young daughters being caught up in a police raid was terrifying.

They needed to sever the link to Jonathan Hale and his family.

–

The September sun was warm when Zoe led her younger sister out into the garden. Already in their swimming costumes, they ambled beyond the end of the formal lawn, down the stone steps, past the sundial, beyond the shed and the overgrown raspberry and blackberry bushes to the ivy-covered fence at the bottom. Here they finally reached the wooden gate and slid the bolt back. Lifting the latch, they emerged onto a grassy bank, then crossed the stream on the little wooden footbridge. A path led across the public right of way which ran along the far edge of the stream, then through a few yards of rough pasture to the high brick wall which marked the boundary of The Cedars. The girls reached the big metal gate. Zoe went to the keypad and punched in the six-digit code that Azalea had given her, and heard the buzz of the door release. She pushed open the gate, and took in the magnificent house and its four acres of sweeping gardens. From this aspect, at the back of The Cedars, the modern extensions dominated. To the left, under the stand of cedars, were the glass panels of the indoor swimming pool, steam baths and the sun lounge. To the right was the extensive mahogany deck on two levels with its white metal pergola, large circular tables, space heaters, barbecue set and colourful table umbrellas. Beyond the deck was a Victorian green-house, filled with exotic ferns, and then above that the complex mullioned windows and intricate roof and chimneys of the house proper, its decorative brickwork in tones of marmalade and cream.

The two girls paid no attention to the various CCTV cameras, one above the gate they had just entered, and another half-dozen at the rear of the house. They ignored the fact that two of these swivelled slightly to track their progress over the lawns, and to the back door of the house. Zoe had just texted Azalea's dumb phone that she was on her way, and the older girl was there to open the door.

Azalea led the two girls through the kitchen where the Austrian au pair Margarethe was preparing a meal, a collection of salads laid out on the huge marble slab that was their kitchen table.

'We're just going to the pool,' Azalea said.

'Okay, but don't forget that lunch is at one,' Margarethe said.

'Are we having smoked salmon, Margarethe?' Lucy asked.

'Not today,' the au pair replied. 'Avocado, cheese, walnuts and lots of apples.'

As they talked, Jonathan walked into the room wearing jeans and an open-necked pink shirt, a mobile phone clamped to his ear, his plume of hair combed backwards and daringly long at the nape of his neck. He was talking rapidly to whoever was on the other end and gesticulating with his hand as he did so.

'Well, it's got to be ready by next week. I'm meeting a client and he will need to see the contract.' Jonathan laughed. The person on the other end was talking. 'No, you can drop the final two clauses. I don't think we'll need them.'

Lucy nudged her sister, and pointed to Jonathan's bare ankles, above his dock shoes.

He stopped only long enough to pick up a glass of orange juice from the counter, and then with a smile and a wink at the three girls, returned the way he had come, his patrician voice still carrying to them words that seemed confident and in control of whatever situation it was.

'Your dad is so cool,' Zoe said to Azalea. 'He's like someone off the telly.'

'But why doesn't he wear socks?' Lucy whispered to her sister.

'There are some shoes you don't wear socks with,' Azalea said. 'I mean, you wouldn't wear them with high heels.'

Lucy laughed. 'But men always wear socks, and we wear them to school. Even Socks wears socks. Made of fur!'

'Only three of them,' Zoe said, chuckling. 'His fourth foot is as black as his back.'

The girls made their way to the swimming pool, pushing open the fogged glass doors to be greeted by a steamy heat and the aroma of chlorine. While Azalea went to arrange the loungers, Lucy turned to her sister and asked, 'Was the money for this house dry cleaned?'

Zoe smiled 'Probably, Lucy. Who could get this much dosh any other way?'

She threw herself backwards into the pool, and after a huge splash came up to the surface. 'It would be great if Dad had this much money, wouldn't it?'

Chapter Twelve

Monday

The entire third floor of the CID building at Mount Browne had been turned over to the NCA. The combination codes on the entry door had been changed, new equipment had been installed and most of the rest of Surrey's detectives were persona non grata. However, Gillard reckoned he had a reason to visit, to update Kyrios on his meeting with Jonathan Hale's neighbours.

He found the money laundering expert making himself at home in DCS Brian 'Radar' Dobbs' old glass-walled office, with the door open. Kyrios was leaning back in Dobbs' leather chair, with his hands cupped behind his head and feet up on the desk, as he took a phone call on speakerphone, loudly and with extravagant hand gestures.

Gillard walked in, until Kyrios stopped him with a raised palm. 'I'll just be just a moment, Craig,' he said, gesturing for him to wait outside.

He could well understand why the NCA had got under the skin of most of his colleagues. But there were other problems too, because of the cull of senior officers. ACC Stella Anderson had already got half a dozen desk jockeys to go early, along with a couple of pretty good detectives who just hadn't shaped up in the current political climate. Stella's blitzkrieg tactic was to put the dinosaurs down for a compulsory five-day LGBTQ+ policing course, usually one where every other officer was under thirty-five. By day three, most of the diehards were happy to grab the pension, seeing the imminent extinction of the policing world they knew. Not so Dobbs. He had gone off on sick leave on day two, with a recurrent bout of depression. Gillard wondered how long it would be before Stella came for him. He'd had a disastrous one-night stand with her decades ago after a training course in Basildon. It had ruined their friendship and still cast a shadow over their working relationship.

It took ten minutes for Kyrios to finish up, but he seemed enthusiastic to hear Gillard's tale. 'That's very good intel, Craig. We tend not to favour in-person surveillance from neighbouring homes these days, knowing that kids always spill the beans. Besides, the technology allows us to do so much more.'

'Oliver Barnes told me about the bogus burglar alarm.'

'Yeah,' said Kyrios expansively. 'It's got a good tele-photo lens and reaches to the back of Hale's place. We are already building up a pattern of the family's movements. The camera on the telegraph pole, and the other burglar alarm camera on a neighbour's home near the front of Hale's home, give us full exterior coverage. That was stage one. The next stage is much more interesting.' He eased himself out of the chair and beckoned for Gillard to follow him. He led them to a room that had been used for storage and photocopying in the past. Kyrios tapped out the combination quickly, and pushed the handle. Once Gillard was inside, he closed the door behind him, unlocked a metal storage cabinet and brought out a fat silver briefcase. From it, Kyrios laid out three electrical wall socket faceplates, a wifi router and a half-dozen rear-view driving mirrors of different types.

'Special Branch has done a fantastic job,' Kyrios said.

'I recognise these,' Gillard said, pointing at the sockets.

'Yes, fitted with the standard voice-activated mic, with a range of fifteen feet. They're set into faceplates that exactly match the ones photographed inside Hale's home office, kitchen and master bedroom.'

'And are these the bugs for the cars?' Gillard said, pointing at the mirrors.

'Yes, exactly matching the rear-view mirrors in each of Hale's five vehicles. They have a microphone as well as a GPS tracker so we can listen and keep tabs on them in real time.'

'I take it the router will just capture his Internet searches?'

'Yes, belt and braces really. We're filtering out all his calls at the telegraph pole, where we also installed a new micro cell site. Any mobile calls within a hundred yards of that virtual tower get tagged before being handed off to the main cell site, then recorded and downloaded automatically at the switch.'

'That must have been quite a warrant application you wrote for such an intrusive data trawl,' Gillard said.

'Yeah, tell me about it.'

'When we will you substitute them in?'

'Thursday morning. It's the best day. The daughter's at school and has a cello lesson, the wife works at a shop in the town, it's the au pair's day off, and Hale himself has just been notified of an appointment with a trio of senior probation officers in central London. He'll be away most of the day.'

'Convenient, that.'

'It just seemed too good an opportunity to miss,' Kyrios said with a grin. 'We knew everybody else would be out bar the man himself, so the probation service were very happy to co-operate.'

'What about Hale's own CCTV system?'

'Ah, that. It's developed a rather annoying fault. It copies old records over the newly recorded footage, every half hour. Hale probably won't notice, but if he does call in to get a service, it will be one of our undercover technicians who goes. We'll then engineer something more subtle.'

'So you've got it all covered by the sounds of it.'

Kyrios extruded a smug grin. 'We're ready for Thursday. Once the full surveillance kit is installed, we will know everything that happens in that house.'

Gillard smiled. It was an elaborate operation, which always meant a lot could go wrong.

–

Lucy looked down at the letter she had been working on. 'Dear Mr Tyler,' she had begun before changing it to 'Darling Richard'. She had never written a love letter before except the Christmas cards she sent to the cat. It was hard to phrase. He would probably be lonely in prison, so even a kindly word or two would be welcome. She went down to her mother's books and looked through them for inspiration. There must be some ideas. She found a whole row of books, quite old paperbacks. Some of them had pictures on the cover of men with bare tummies ridged like car radiators embracing half-dressed women. She started to flick through. After five minutes she had only got one useful phrase, and she wrote it down. 'I've got a burning for you in my soul, it consumes me like a fire.' She liked the ring of it, the urgency. But she needed more ideas for what to write in the rest of the letter. 'Is it hot there?' That seemed like a good idea and she wrote it down, before hiding the pad in the drawer of her bedside table.

—

North Bluff State Correctional Facility was under siege from Covid. Every night now, coughing and gasping came from a dozen cells. Pazzo Salvatore had been one of the first to die. His absence didn't mean a better night's sleep, just a different kind of being kept awake. The prison staff were going down with the virus too. There weren't enough correctionals to allow the full rec time each day, and the atmosphere was going from edgy to angry. Tyler had stuck toilet paper into his ears, and searched his memory for the name of Hale's cello-and piano-playing daughter. He wished he'd paid more attention to the Brit's small talk on those few days they'd met in Phoenix. It was an unusual name. He roped in Morales during the day to help him.

'Kind of flower name, maybe.' Tyler squinted at the wall.

'Daisy? Rose? Tulip?'

'No, something more exotic. I keep thinking something that grows here in the state.'

'Desert rose? Saguaro is the state flower.'

'Nah.'

The guessing game kept them going all evening until lights out.

Why did he think it was associated with Arizona? Finally, at midnight, he realised the postal service abbreviation AZ was what he was thinking of.

'Hey, Morales. It's Azalea.'

'That's not a desert flower, man.'

'Yeah, but I reckon it's the girl's name.'

'Whatever,' Morales said. He was clearly sore that for all his help, Tyler had refused to let him borrow the phone yet. Well, tough. He had things to do, and the cellphone's charge had already begun to drop. Credit used was a worry, too. Thirty bucks remaining. At one a.m., unable to sleep from the coughing echoing throughout the atrium, Tyler retrieved his phone, and began to use it under the blankets. He started with Azalea Hale, which turned up a couple of dozen hits on Facebook, Instagram and other social media posts. It took ages for Tyler to comb through them for hints of location. There was one Facebook member with that name in Hertfordshire, England which he thought might be the one. It wasn't too far from London, but there was no mention of playing music. That was the one thing he did remember, Hale was so proud of his daughter's musical ability. So he searched within Facebook for Azalea Hale plus piano. It got him nowhere. So, having wasted an hour of precious phone juice already, Tyler went back to Google and added the word 'cello' to the search on her name.

He wished he'd done that first, because it produced a clear result. A news story with a photograph from a local paper, the *Surrey Comet*. A dozen uniformed schoolgirls, posing with musical instruments inside a large concert hall, looking very pleased with themselves. The caption identified them as members of the prize-winning school orchestra of St Cuthbert's Independent School in Surrey, but their surnames were identified only by initial. Azalea H. was fourth from the right, in the back row, a tall young woman with masses of dark hair. And cute. Very cute.

'Bullseye,' breathed Tyler.

Metallic noise on the landing indicated a patrol. Tyler turned off the phone, slipped it back into his pillow, and lay down, covering himself with a blanket.

'What's goin' on here?' A flashlight shone in Tyler's face. He recognised his voice. Sergeant Elliott, a Mississippi hard-ass.

'Nothing.'

'If there's moonshine in there, Tyler, you'll go straight back to the pit.'

'Ain't no moonshine here, sergeant,' Morales said sleepily.

Elliott took a deep sniff. 'If I smell it out, boys, I'm gonna bust your asses.' He ran his nightstick noisily across the bars for emphasis. 'Now y'all go back to sleep.'

Tyler waited twenty minutes before daring to resume his use of the phone. He pulled the blanket over his head and looked again at the school photo of Azalea and her friends.

'I'm coming for your sweet ass, honey.' He chuckled to himself.

–

Mondays were always a drag. Azalea Hale was sitting in the physics class, chin in her hands, listening to Mr Potts droning on. It was last period, 3.52 p.m. She was willing the clock to wind down to four p.m. It had been an awful day. In the morning, while she was doing cello practice, someone had broken into her locker and filled her lunchbox with soap powder. As she had opened the Tupperware container in the dining room, it spilled all over the floor. The sandwich was ruined. It was no great surprise that Andrea Cornwell and Imogen Foulkes-Brierley, her two tormentors-in-chief, were there to laugh, along with half a dozen of their hockey cronies.

'As your dad's a money launderer, that makes you a scrubber,' Andrea had hissed before turning away. The elderly Mrs Bird was on dinner duty and had missed the whole thing, only berating the girls for their unladylike cackling. Azalea was certainly not going to tell. It had been made very clear to her that grassing up her tormentors would incur even worse treatment. Today's humiliation was only the latest in a long line of slights, teasing, and the worst of all: social exclusion. Not being invited to parties. Being snubbed in the corridors. Being whispered about.

It wasn't universal. Azalea had good friends too, Georgia and even Merrilyn, the viola player whose father was a crossbench peer in the House of Lords. But their friendship was clandestine. They would never stick up for her in public or online, although Georgia had shown Azalea some of the abusive Facebook messages exchanged about her. Perhaps there was something to be said for not being online. In truth, most of the school week wasn't too bad. There were only three periods in which Andrea and Imogen were in her class, but anxiety hung over her for the whole week, getting worse as they approached.

The only relief was music, two periods of tuition with Mrs Smedley and two hours' orchestra practice each week. That was where her friendships prospered, and where her dedication was recognised. And that was why she valued Zoe so much. Younger, but never judgemental. They had talked about setting up a quartet together, with

Merrilyn and Georgia, and playing in grand houses for money and applause. Because of her age Zoe was in a lower form, and completely unaware of the bullying. Azalea didn't want to mention it because it would make her appear to be a loser.

Azalea had never dared tell her father either, because he had so much else to worry about at the moment. She had given slight hints to her mother about bullying, but she had reacted so angrily that Azalea backpedalled immediately. The last thing she needed was to have Xolwa march into the school casting accusations of racism here and there. Her mother was finely attuned to discrimination, which had defined her early years, and saw everything through that lens. Azalea had tried to explain. It wasn't race, it was *class* prejudice. Inherited money versus supposedly dodgy money, that's what it boiled down to.

Besides, she didn't want to complain. Bad as it was, she had no enemies like her father's. Nobody was going to torture or kill her.

–

Lucy was in the garden shed with Socks, working on a new hat for the cat made out of an old tennis ball. It was only faintly green and lacking in fluff, but the rubber was still much tougher to puncture than she'd imagined. Having done so, she was working to cut out a segment with a Stanley knife from her father's toolkit, something that had been specifically banned from using after earlier accidents. The cat looked down from the top of the toolbox, purring as Lucy muttered away to herself.

'Now Socks, what colour should this be? Red, yes red. I'll put a brim on it, so you'll be an elegant tomcat for your Instagram followers.'

Lucy then pressed too hard and cut right across the ball, just missing her hand. 'Whoops.' She looked at Socks, who lazily returned her gaze. 'Yes, it's messed up.' She dropped the ball, then pulled out from her pocket and unfolded the letter from Zoe to the prisoner she'd been working on. She'd not go much further despite several attempts, and lots of it was covered now in scribblings out.

'Yes, that's messed up too, isn't it Socks?'

The cat stretched out a paw and tapped the paper. 'Do you want it?' Lucy asked. The cat batted the paper onto the worktop, then jumped down on it, as if it was alive. A couple of half-hearted taps, and a bite, and the paper was torn.

'Okay, so you think it wasn't a good idea,' Lucy said, picking up the scraps and scrunching them into a ball.

Chapter Thirteen

It was eleven a.m. on Monday morning and Gillard was on the phone when DC Rainy Macintosh walked into the first-floor CID room and hung her damp raincoat on the coat rack.

'How was your weekend?' Michelle Tsu asked, though Gillard thought one look at her colleague's face made it obvious.

'Shite, frankly.'

'I'm so sorry to hear that. Did your ex misbehave?'

'Aye, you could say that. We had a blazing row from almost the first minute. I tried to reach an agreement with him on the terms of the divorce, but now we will have to go to court.'

'How awful for you,' Michelle said.

'And he's publicly accused me of mental cruelty, when it was the other way round. He is also doing all he can to stop me getting any money from him.'

'How was the wedding itself?' Michelle asked, clearly anxious to return to lighter topics.

'It rained, but otherwise it was okay. Except I popped a button on my dress, just as they were giving their oaths. It pinged right across the stone floor of the church.'

'Oh dear.'

'Sometimes I think I'm just a fat failure.'

Hoskins looked up from his terminal a few feet away. 'Oi, you can't snatch my title. There's only one of us in CID.'

Rainy grinned, the first smile Michelle had seen on her colleague since she came in. 'Aye, Carl maybe we should both go up and sit on the bastard, eh?'

'Just say the word, Rainy, just say the word.' He winked warmly at her.

—

That afternoon Gillard joined a meeting at Mount Browne where DSU Kyrios was presenting the next phase of Operation Whirlpool. Most of those present were senior officers, including ACC Stella Anderson and the NCA's head of drug crime DCS Helen McCarthy, who both needed to sign off on it.

'The first phase was the remote monitoring of Jonathan Hale's home,' Kyrios said. 'The second phase will be Thursday's planting of listening devices within his home and inside most of his vehicles, together with the electronic tapping of his communications. I am eager for that to be ready, because we urgently need to get phase three up and running.'

He clicked on the next slide. 'Our information is that several major European drug syndicates are switching money laundering systems following the Operation Dark Sky takedown last March. Just to remind you, this was when Dutch, Belgian and French police hacked a criminal phone network allowing them to look over the shoulders of suspects who communicated with customised encrypted hardware. They were sharing not only details of drug plots but also tantalising hints of the money laundering routes used.'

Gillard remembered the news. Immediate raids netted eighty people, and hundreds more were caught in the police dragnet as they decrypted months' worth of data.

'As a result of this, there are billions of euros worth of drug money seeking new routes to legitimacy. Europol's intelligence is that one man, an elusive individual known as Pegasus, has broken cover to act as go-between for the Calabrian Mafia. We don't know who Pegasus is, but we expect him to make contact with Hale pretty soon. A physical meeting isn't guaranteed, but however it does materialise it will give us the end of a trail which we can follow to find this guy.'

Anderson asked a question from the back. 'Hale must guess he is being watched, so how can he do it?'

'That's a good point. Our best guess is that he will not undertake the transactions himself, but act as a consultant, advising on exactly how to set up a similar banking network to that which he used to obscure the flow of laundered money from the L3 consortium.'

Kyrios was in full flow when the vibration of a couple of phones in the audience could be heard.

'Joe, the monitoring team are trying to get hold of you,' said McCarthy, inspecting her phone. 'There's something happening at Hale's home.'

–

Two minutes later, Kyrios, Gillard and a handful of the senior NCA officers were crowded into the Operation Whirlpool control room, watching a wall-mounted TV which showed a view of the rear of Jonathan Hale's palatial home. A slim man in orange hi-vis over a hooded top was walking across the back patio. His face was hidden by the hood, but he moved with the casual ease of youth. He was wearing gloves and carrying what looked like a tool bag.

'Is he one of ours?' McCarthy asked Kyrios.

'Shouldn't be,' he said. 'There's no one going in for three days.'

'It might be legit,' said DI Colin Williams. 'Some kind of tradesman Hale called in. His wife is in the house.'

'Are you certain?' Gillard asked.

'Her Merc hasn't left,' Williams said. 'Hale is out and the daughter is at school.'

The intruder made his way across to the back door of the house.

'There's an au pair,' Gillard said. 'What about her movements?'

'Not sure, to be honest,' Williams replied. 'We've only got external cameras right now.'

'For fuck's sake,' Kyrios said, punching out a number on his mobile. 'It had better not be one of ours. He's going to blow our cover.' He held the handset to his ears. 'Hi Dave, there's an intruder at Hale's house, I need to know he isn't one of yours. No, that's right. Just now.'

Kyrios held his head back with his eyes closed and seemed to be swearing under his breath as he waited for the subordinate to check for him.

The intruder was now crouching down, briefly inspecting the lock of the rear door which led to the kitchen, before moving on.

'He'll be on Hale's CCTV,' McCarthy said.

'Actually, he won't, ma'am,' Williams said. 'It was sabotaged in phase one.'

'Of course, wiped every half hour,' she replied.

Kyrios now seemed to be listening. 'So it's not one of your guys, okay good.' He cut the call and turned to the rest of the officers. 'Not one of ours.'

'Can you switch to the telegraph pole camera for a moment?' Gillard asked. 'I have a hunch about who this may be.'

Kyrios leaned into the monitoring room and asked them to switch the feed. A few seconds later the screen was displaying the view over Blenheim Drive. There were a few vehicles parked in view, but no Ford Transit.

'Okay, maybe I'm wrong. We're tracking an active burglar, but the suspect's van isn't there,' Gillard said, indicating that the screen could be switched back.

'There's nothing we can do,' Kyrios said.

'He still doesn't look legit to me,' Gillard said. 'Far too cautious and stealthy.'

'I agree,' Williams said. 'Look, he's trying the exact same sliding door that we used.'

'I see someone at an upper window,' Gillard said. 'White, female. Presumably the au pair. But I don't think she can see him from there.'

The man slid the door open and disappeared inside. 'Right, it's officially a burglary,' Williams said.

'I'll call Elmbridge Police Station,' Gillard said, starting to punch out a number on his phone. 'They can have a patrol car there in five minutes.'

'No way,' Kyrios said, resting a hand on Gillard's phone. 'If they go in, we blow our cover.'

'There is at least one woman in the house, possibly two,' Gillard said. 'Our duty is clearly to protect them.'

DCS McCarthy weighed in. 'Is our suspect violent?'

'We don't yet know who he is,' Gillard said.

'Was violence used in any of the burglaries you're investigating?'

'No, but—'

'Then we leave it,' McCarthy said. 'This is two years' work involving more than a hundred officers, to try to break open drug gangs which have killed dozens of people. I am not going to jeopardise it for a non-violent burglary. I'm the senior ranking officer here and that is my decision.'

'Yes, ma'am,' Gillard said. He wasn't going to stick his neck out any further. If the burglar did end up attacking either of the women in there, heads would roll. But not his. He'd publicly made his position clear and been over-ruled.

Kyrios was still furious. 'This idiot is still jeopardising the operation. If Hale discovers they've been burgled, or even checks the CCTV and find it isn't working, he might skip his meeting with the probation team.'

The intruder had disappeared from view for a minute. As they watched, the view switched back to the telegraph pole camera. From the bottom of the picture, Jonathan Hale's Maserati came into view, and turned into the drive of The Cedars.

'Shit!' Kyrios said. 'They're going to run into each other.'

They switched to the camera that covered the front of the house. Hale parked the car on the drive and emerged from the vehicle. He was wearing a light grey suit and sunglasses. He stopped for a few moments to inspect the back of the car, knelt down and scrutinised the rear bumper. Satisfied, he straightened up, picked up a briefcase from the passenger seat and walked into the house.

Switching back to the rear camera, they could see the intruder re-emerging through the sliding door, with his tool bag. He carefully closed it and made his way diagonally at a brisk walk across the lawn towards the left of the screen and disappeared from view.

'Is that the way he came in?' Gillard asked.

'Yes,' said Williams.

Gillard knew that the footpath behind the Hale property ran a couple of hundred yards between Blenheim Drive to the right of the picture and Neville Crescent to the left. If this was their burglar, and he was using the Ford Transit, it would probably be parked in Neville Crescent.

There were still ways to catch him so long as he moved fast.

–

Gillard was on the phone to Elmbridge Police even as he ran downstairs. He wanted a patrol car to Neville Crescent ASAP, and gave him the number plate of the Ford, as well as a description of the guy. Trouble was, almost anyone out and about with a tool bag would be wearing hi-vis these days.

He put his head in at the first floor where he spotted DC Michelle Tsu, yawning and stretching at her desk. 'Michelle, drop what you're doing. I need you for an hour. Meet me in the car park in one minute.' He raced downstairs and hurried across the car park to his unmarked Vauxhall. He started up the vehicle and swung it round in front of the CID building just as Michelle was emerging. Two minutes later they were on the road, heading out of Guildford towards Esher. Placing his phone in the cradle, he called into the NCA operations room as he raced down the A3 with blues flashing. Kyrios was soon on the line.

'Joe, we are going to try and pick up this intruder. Eldridge already has a patrol car one minute away, and I'll be there in twenty.'

'It had better be well away from our surveillance operation,' Kyrios said.

'It is. By my reckoning, the suspect will have left his vehicle in Neville Crescent. We'll be lucky to get him in that street, but we still have a good chance of intercepting the van on its way back to Hersham. We know which route he normally uses.'

'Okay, keep me in the loop. We're going to have enough of a shitstorm if Hale notices he has been burgled.'

–

Jonathan Hale heard the barking before he had opened his front door. Once he was inside, Duffy came limping up to him, whimpering and whining, then hobbled away. After a few feet the arthritic dog stopped and looked back over his shoulder.

'I'm back,' he called to his wife. 'What's up with Duffy?'

'He's probably seen Socks in the garden,' Xolwa called from upstairs. The Barnes' family cat enjoyed parading up and down in front of the sliding doors when Duffy couldn't get at her. It drove the dog crazy, which was presumably the idea.

'He seems very agitated,' Hale said as the dog once again came to fetch him, barking and whimpering. Hale crouched and ruffled Duffy's ears. 'What is it, boy? Is Socks tormenting you again?' He followed the dog, which led him into the kitchen, into the dining room and on into the sun lounge, with its full-length glass sliding doors. Nothing looked out of place.

Xolwa joined him. She was wearing a long white sheath dress, stiletto heels and the large diamond earrings that he had bought her for their tenth wedding anniversary. He feasted his eyes on her, before wondering why she was so dressed up.

'Are you off somewhere?' Hale asked.

'I'm seeing Jane, don't you remember? She thinks she has some modelling assignments that would suit me. The *Financial Times* 'How To Spend It' colour supplement.'

'Ah, yes I remember.' He spent all of his time thinking about how to earn it.

'They won't use my name, and I get to keep some of the clothes.'

'Great,' Hale said absentmindedly, picking up a sheaf of post.

Xolwa looked at the dining table and her expression turned to a puzzled frown. 'Where's my Birkin bag?' she asked.

'Hmm?' He saw there was another letter from his mortgage provider.

'The white Birkin bag. I could have sworn I left it on the kitchen countertop.' Xolwa looked at her wristwatch, and gasped at the time. 'I've got to go in a minute.'

Hale looked around. 'I don't see it. Why don't you take one of the others?'

'It's the only white one, and more importantly it's got my purse in it.'

They were joined downstairs by the au pair. 'Margarethe, have you seen my white Birkin bag?'

'You had it upstairs,' she replied.

'Yes, but I'm pretty sure I brought it down.'

'I'll go and look upstairs,' Margarethe said.

'Never mind,' Xolwa said, picking up her mobile. 'I've got to go now. Jon, could you lend me a hundred or so? Just in case.'

'There's some in the drawer in my office, I'm not sure how much.'

Xolwa headed off to his office, and called back. 'There's only a tenner here, Jon.'

Hale frowned. There should have been £200 there. Azalea had been known to help herself to the cash drawer, but not usually without telling him first.

'Well, you can take that. Plus this.' He took out his own wallet and passed her five crisp twenties.

'Thank you, love. Bye,' Xolwa said as she left the room.

-

Gillard was five minutes from Esher when the control room relayed a message from a patrol car now in Neville Crescent. No sign of the Transit van. This was no surprise. The pattern revealed by ANPR showed that when the burglar finished a job, he'd head straight back to Hersham, a fifteen-minute journey.

'Are we too late?' Michelle asked.

'Not if we take a shortcut just here.' Gillard blue-lighted it off the A3 onto the A245 heading north, then took a right turn into Seven Hills Road, the B365. It was a long straight road, and with the aid of the twos and blues they were able to do ninety, with traffic ahead of them pulling over to let them past. At the junction with Burwood Road, Gillard took a screeching right-hand turn towards Hersham. As they approached the built-up area, he flicked off the siren and blues, and slowed to the speed limit. Two minutes later they went under the main London railway line.

'That's the camera our burglar keeps tripping,' he said, pointing to a discreet bridge-mounted ANPR device. He pulled over just after the bridge and rang DC Hoskins' direct line.

'Carl, has our suspect tripped the Hersham railway bridge camera in the last ten minutes?'

There was a few seconds' delay before he replied. 'Yes, two minutes ago, heading north.'

Gillard thanked him, cut the call and indicated to turn out into traffic. In the past five minutes they had seen half a dozen white vans, two of them Ford Transits, but neither matching the suspect's registration number. 'Any ideas, Michelle?'

'Try this next right,' she said. 'It's a light industrial and retail park.'

He made the turning, past a Tesco Express, and saw a promising-looking Transit next door in the front pull-in next to Screwfix. The registration plate was obscured by shrubs. Gillard eased the Vauxhall into the hardware store's pull-in and coasted past the van.

'It's our van,' Michelle said. Gillard reversed into a space two cars over, ready for a quick getaway, and called in their location to the control room for a patrol car to assist. As he was doing so, the door of the Screwfix shop opened, and a slim dark-haired man wearing orange hi-vis emerged, carrying a small cardboard box, and heading towards the Transit. Gillard emerged from the car, while Michelle took a photograph of the suspect on her phone. It was the first time they had seen his face. The man opened the van's driver-side door and Gillard approached him from the rear. In his peripheral vision he could see Michelle behind him.

'Excuse me,' Gillard said, holding up his warrant card. 'I'd like to have a word—'

The man swore, and smacked his right elbow straight into Gillard's face. Momentarily unbalanced, Gillard caught a hefty follow-up punch to the jaw which knocked him over, spilling mobile phone and car keys from his pockets. Michelle, lightly built but fast, grabbed the suspect by the right arm as he was trying to get back into the van. He turned and punched her hard in the stomach, sending her sprawling. Gillard was up again, head spinning, and seized the van door, to stop him closing it. The suspect was fiddling with the van keys, trying to get them in the ignition with his left hand while trying to pull the door closed with his right. He gave up, wriggled across to the passenger side and opened that door, just as Gillard was heaving open the driver-side door. The suspect jumped out the opposite side and fled the van, with Michelle in hot pursuit. Gillard ran after her, as they sprinted up a narrow driveway between Screwfix and an adjacent warehouse.

If the punches hadn't already done it, the speed of the man demonstrated a high level of fitness. While Gillard soon overtook Michelle, he wasn't making any progress overhauling the burglar in the next sixty yards. But it was when the suspect jumped at an eight-foot-high brick wall at the back and somehow scrambled over that Gillard realised that there was little chance of catching him. Only then, when he and Michelle were bent over catching their breath, did he hear the sound of sirens.

'Are you all right, Michelle?' he asked.

She was winded by the punch and was in no state to answer apart from lifting a hand in acknowledgement. Gillard jogged back to meet the patrol car as it drove in, and realised there was blood dripping from his nose and onto his shirt.

Gillard directed the two male officers in the patrol car around the other side of the industrial estate and retraced his steps, picking up the various objects that had fallen from his pockets.

It was fifteen minutes and two more patrol car arrivals later when it became clear that the suspect had escaped. With a throbbing jaw and a tender face, Gillard reflected that this was the supposedly non-violent burglar that Kyrios and company were happy to leave roaming around the Hale household. Thankfully, the intruder had got what he wanted without encountering either Mrs Hale or the au pair. And what he had wanted was found in the van – a large white designer handbag, containing a matching purse. The purse contained cash and credit cards in the name of Xolwa Hale.

Chapter Fourteen

Monday afternoon, three o'clock

Back at Mount Browne, Gillard attended to his bruised face in the CID second floor gents' toilet. While he was dabbing at the bloodstains at the mirror, DC Carl Hoskins wandered in. 'Ouch, that looks painful,' he said, making his way to the urinal.

'Elbow in the face from our bloody burglar. But Michelle got it worse. She's gone home with stomach cramps.'

'After all that, I hear he got away.'

'Yes, but we've uncovered a lot of evidence in the van. His mobile phone in the glove compartment, plenty of fingerprints, and a surprisingly large number of unfenced stolen items. There's plenty there to link him to the burglaries.'

'He'll probably lie low,' Hoskins said, finishing up then washing his hands at the next basin.

'I've asked Rob to triangulate the phone,' Gillard said, dabbing with a paper towel at his bloodstained shirt. 'It was never turned on during the burglary jobs, but if he has used it at home, we'll find out where that is.'

'Sounds like a plan.' Hoskins waved his hands at the dryer, which groaned weakly. After five seconds, he wiped his still-wet hands on his trousers. Gillard rinsed his hands, rubbed them under the dryer a couple of times, then followed Hoskins out.

DC Rainy Macintosh was sitting at her desk checking the latest crime reports as Gillard approached.

'Has anyone in the Hale household reported a break-in?' he asked. 'The theft of a white designer handbag and matching purse?'

'No, sir,' she said. 'I heard about the recovered loot. Och, to my mind, Xolwa Hale probably hasn't even missed it, and if she does she'll probably blame the au pair.'

'She's bound to have loads of handbags,' Hoskins said.

'All right for some,' Rainy said. 'I carry my valuables in an Asda plaggy bag. If she doesn't claim the Birkin bag, I'm first in line at the auction.'

Hoskins turned to wave a finger at her. 'Now, now, we're supposed to return identifiable stolen property.'

'He's right,' Gillard said. 'And, actually, that has given me an idea.'

–

It was a filthy Tuesday morning, cold, wet and dark. Gillard was sitting in his unmarked car in one of the least desirable areas of Hersham with the heater on maximum. With him were DC Michelle Tsu and family liaison officer Gabby Underwood. A van full of uniforms all togged up for a raid were parked on the other side of the road. They were watching a third-floor flat where Kieran Michael Coughlan, a man with a long criminal record, was thought to be staying with friends. Coughlan's finger-prints had been found all over the Transit, and this location matched the burglar's triangulated phone, as Gillard had predicted. The expected presence of children explained why Gabby was there.

He checked his watch: 4.59 a.m. One minute to go. The rear doors on the unmarked police van opened, and half a dozen of Surrey's finest clambered out, their breath pluming into the sky. The door ram was carefully manoeuvred out, in the hands of the giant of the force, PC Tony Tunnicliffe.

Gillard stepped out into the rain with Gabby in tow, leaving Michelle behind.

No lights in the flat. Thirty seconds to go. The uniforms made their way quietly up the path to the door of the block, where the locksmith, having already disarmed the lock, was waiting.

On the signal, Gillard followed the six male officers up the stairs. Tunnicliffe's booming voice demanded the door was opened, but he waited only ten seconds before using the ram. The door crashed open immediately, and in the uproar of voices and the thundering of constabulary boots the crying of children soon followed. By the time Gillard went in, Coughlan was in handcuffs on the same sofa that he had apparently been surfing on for the last few months.

Five minutes later, once Coughlan was securely in the car, Gillard called the control room with the news. 'I'm returning with Kieran Michael Coughlan. I've already cautioned him and intend to charge him with at least six burglaries in this area. Can you make sure there's a nice cold cell for him in Staines?'

As Gillard ended the call, he smiled to himself. Rainy Macintosh would be pleased to get this news. These were the crimes that she had mentioned DCS Dobbs wanted tossed aside and marked NFA. Thanks to the spy camera, the surveillance of Jonathan Hale had marked up its first arrest. He just hoped there would be plenty more of them.

Chapter Fifteen

Wednesday night, 10.15 p.m. and the London streets were slick after recent rain. A black unmarked NCA Range Rover was waiting to turn right at traffic lights in Streatham from the eastbound South Circular into the southbound A23. DSU Joe Kyrios was in the front passenger seat. Behind him were DCS Helen McCarthy, NCA head of Narcotics Interdiction, DCS John Stevenson, head of Organised Crime Command, and in the driving seat Detective Constable Simon Parish. They were returning after an evening meeting at the Home Office. Parish was planning to drop Stevenson home near Streatham Common before returning to Guildford with the other two.

The lights changed, and on the green filter Parish followed the car in front, a blue Mini. He had noticed a white long-wheelbase van, waiting at red to come in the opposite direction. It was because of the size of that vehicle that he didn't see behind it the black Audi, lit only by sidelights, travelling at almost three times the speed limit. Just as Parish was turning, the speeding car shot through the right filter lane opposite. Had he noticed it, as Kyrios just had, he would have known that there was no way the Audi could avoid hitting them.

The impact was colossal. The Audi, already airborne after hitting a kerb, smashing into the Range Rover's front passenger side at window height with a combined speed of 96 mph. The roof section of the range Rover was peeled back like the top of a sardine can. Kyrios died instantly before his airbag could detonate, McCarthy suffered severe head injuries and Stevenson suffered life-changing spinal injuries. Parish's life was saved by the one-thousandth of a second delay between the Audi's radiator hitting Kyrios and heading for him. In that moment his airbag inflated, protecting him from all but a dislocated shoulder and cuts.

–

Gillard was awoken by the call in his Surrey home less than half an hour later. ACC Stella Anderson broke the news of the elimination of the entire senior NCA team who were running Operation Whirlpool. With only sketchy details so far, Gillard expressed his shock. He then had one question.

'Was it a hit, ma'am?'

'Unlikely. All we know so far is that the Audi was stolen, and being driven by a fifteen-year-old with a history of joyriding. If and when the youth comes out of intensive care the Met is going to put him through the wringer.'

'Sounds like they were in the wrong place at the wrong time.'

'Definitely. Kyrios was irreplaceable. I'm going to do my best on the money laundering side, liaising with the NCA's own experts. But I need somebody to take charge of the surveillance operation. That person is you. You're being loaned to the NCA, just until this operation plays out. You've got some relevant experience, and Alison has great faith in you being able to learn the rest quickly.'

'Thank you, ma'am.' It didn't escape Gillard's notice that Anderson was pally enough with the chief constable to refer to her by her Christian name.

'Don't thank me, Craig, it wasn't my decision. I'm temporarily SIO, and you will report to me. I'm pulling together the team for a briefing at Mount Browne at one a.m. Be there.' She cut the call.

Gillard rubbed his eyes. So much for the early night.

'What was all that about?' Sam asked, leaning up on one shoulder.

He was already out of bed and pulling on his underwear. 'I've got to go in. The proverbial has just hit the fan. Half the National Crime Agency NCA bigwigs have been wiped out in a road accident in Streatham. So muggins here has to take charge.'

'Of what?'

'The surveillance of Hale, to start with, but a pound to a penny there's more.'

'There are two clean shirts in your emergency wardrobe,' she said, getting up. 'Shall I make you a bite to eat before you go?'

'Thanks, but no. I'll grab a handful of cereal bars in case get I get hungry later.'

Thursday

Suppressing a yawn, Gillard arrived at Mount Browne fifteen minutes before the meeting to find it like a disturbed ants' nest. He popped his head into the first floor where he normally worked, and said a quick hello to the night duty officers before heading up to the third. His first problem was that even now, no one had told him the new combination for the third-floor security door, so he had to tap on the glass to be let in. He was let in by the NCA's Colin Williams and Detective Sergeant Lewis Lytton, a tall young officer from the NCA's Special Capabilities unit. He was best known as deputy chair of the National Black Policing Association, and for winning the right to wear dreadlocks on duty.

'All right,' Gillard said, looking around. 'Is Anderson here yet?'

'She will be on Zoom from home,' Williams said, with a slight inflection to his eyebrow.

Of course she will, Gillard thought. *Stupid of me to think she would have to get out of bed at silly o'clock for the meeting that she convened.*

'The undercover postman is going in this morning, am I right?' Gillard said.

'Yes. 10.45 a.m. DC Ian Harris from Special Branch, as before.'

'What time does the real postie get there?' Gillard asked. 'We don't want Harris to run into him, do we?'

'It's generally an afternoon delivery,' Lytton said. 'On foot. Harris will be in one of our reconditioned post office vans, used for tracked items, which get higher priority than the normal round. Even if they meet, the only issue will be that Harris is an unknown face.'

'Okay, good. Look, there's one other thing I want Harris to do when he's in there.'

'What's that, sir?'

'I want him to subtly put back the designer handbag and purse that Coughlan stole. Ideally somewhere it might have been overlooked by the owner. I'll have DC Hoskins bring you the evidence bag.'

'That's brilliant,' Lytton said.

'Just to keep them nice and relaxed, you understand.'

Gillard sat at a terminal, and after being given the access code by Lytton pulled up Kyrios' plan of campaign. It looked meticulous. Lytton and Williams then took him through to the operations room, a windowless office with three workstations and plenty of high-tech kit.

'Our voice technician John Horncastle sits here,' Lytton said, of a workstation in the corner. 'The filtering unit is underneath, and we can get an audio feed with only a few seconds delay.'

The display looked similar to a music production desk, with six horizontal panes, each visually displaying an audio feed that gradually snaked from left to right.

'Hold on,' said Gillard. 'You have, what, nine or ten bugs planted, including the cars, and only one technician to monitor it all? How does that work?'

Lytton smiled. 'The filtering unit uses artificial intelligence. As soon as we get some test voice prints from the house, we can identify Hale himself, separate his print from the rest of the family, and prioritise that feed. Hale can only be in one place at a time, and the system will switch to prioritise whichever device he can be heard on. Whoever is on monitoring duty can either listen on headphones, patch it through to another terminal or feed it out on loudspeaker. There's also a keyword detector, which was developed by the Americans for filtering phone calls by terrorists, and a contextual analyser.'

'What on earth is that?'

'Contextual analysis looks for arguments, disagreements, changes in voice tone – whispering for example – anything that may alert us to conflict or secrecy.'

'Sounds pretty impressive. Round-the-clock surveillance the old way needed dozens of technicians.'

'True. Same thing with the cameras. They've already got recognition patterns for the family, and their vehicles. The analysis software simply looks for anything unusual occurring, and when it finds it, opens a live feed on the master screen.'

'And all in real time?'

'Give or take a couple of seconds.'

A few minutes later, bleary-eyed officers assembled round their desks, and the face of the assistant chief constable popped into view on a large suspended screen.

'Good morning everyone, sorry to have to pry you from your beds so early, but as you are aware this is an emergency.'

Gillard noted that she had at least changed into formal uniform. Gillard had briefly wondered whether Anderson would be wearing pyjamas. She hadn't worn anything the only time he spent a night with her all those years ago.

He heard her call his name and blinked to clear the image.

'DCI Gillard, I want you to quickly familiarise yourself with Operation Whirlpool rules of engagement, plus the operational background.'

'Yes, ma'am.' He had in fact already read a summary copy on Wednesday, courtesy of Kyrios, and was already halfway through the briefing background document.

'We are to proceed as planned,' she said. 'Surveillance and a small operational unit remain based in Guildford, but most of the NCA drug intelligence team will deploy at Citadel Place.'

Gillard could see that was reasonable. The NCA's south-east London headquarters had all the capabilities and back-up needed. He wasn't worried about that. He was more concerned about why he had been chosen for this role, when there were more experienced NCA officers of equal rank who lived, ate and breathed the fight against organised crime.

Was Stella Anderson setting him up to fail? By parachuting him into a different organisation it certainly made it likely that any screw-ups, big or small, would be pinned on him as the rest of the NCA closed ranks. There was only one answer. He had to succeed. He had to make sure they caught Jonathan Hale red-handed with his crime gang contact.

—

Less than ten miles away, and ten hours later, Jonathan Hale was stuck in a mid-morning probation meeting, drinking awful machine coffee as three middle-aged grey-haired women in face masks sat around a table asking intrusive questions about how he planned to provide for himself and his family now that he was struck off as a lawyer. As he'd never been charged with a crime in the UK, he resented the kind of oversight they were imposing, and even more the assumption that he should welcome their well-meaning attempts to ensure he didn't fall back into a life of crime. Could this *really* not have been done on Zoom? He barely glanced through the many leaflets they handed across to him, knowing that even in his diminished career, three mornings a week, he was probably earning more than all three of them put together.

But it wasn't enough. He knew that.

The household's financial situation was getting ever more dire, while all Xolwa could do was to fret about a mislaid handbag. She had even suggested to him at breakfast that morning that Margarethe might be responsible. It was nonsense, and Hale had told her so. It had started to deteriorate into a full-scale row, the last thing he needed when he had so much more on his mind. Thank God it was the au pair's day off and she wasn't there to witness it.

He realised he'd stopped listening.

'So is that clear?' repeated one of the probation officers, looking over her spectacles at him. 'There are support services available if you get into difficulties.' She pointed at the leaflets in front of him. 'We'll bring you in again in a few months' time. Hopefully you'll get yourself back on your feet by then.'

'Yes, let's hope so,' he said, with a deliberately false smile. How patronising these people were.

As they all stood, he thanked them for their interest, gathered up the leaflets they had handed him, and after exiting the building, dropped them in a litter bin outside. He walked briskly to the car park, climbed into his pale blue Maserati, and exited onto the road outside the probation office. One of the women who had interviewed him was standing on the pavement talking to a colleague and looked up when he pipped the horn. He waved cheerily to her, laughed at her unsmiling response and then roared off, heading back towards Surrey. Heaving a huge sigh of relief, he turned on the radio and readjusted the rear-view mirror.

He wasn't aware that the mirror assembly had been switched while he was in the meeting. This identical one contained a tiny voice-activated mic.

Jonathan Hale was thinking about money. About the long planned secret rendezvous that would get him out of debt in one fell swoop. In an hour's time he would meet for the first time the man who he hoped would be his saviour.

Which is why he also missed the dirty white Hyundai Tucson, one hubcap missing, that had followed him out of the car park, and settled in to tail him, two vehicles behind.

–

Forty minutes later, the pale blue Maserati turned into the station car park in the Surrey town of Sunbury-on-Thames. Hale emerged, wearing a smart grey single-breasted suit and pink tie, briefcase in hand, and made his way on foot to the railway station entrance. The white Hyundai parked on double yellows within sight of the station. From the driver's seat Detective Constable Binita Patel watched Hale entering the station, then called in her observations to the Operation Whirlpool control room, adding: 'Permission to follow on foot?'

'Please hold,' said the operator. 'We're getting you the train times.' Seconds ticked by, and Binita tapped the steering wheel impatiently. Finally, permission was given, and she was told that the next train was due in four minutes, for London, and in twenty-two minutes for Shepperton. She scrambled out of the car, grabbed her bag and after locking the car headed off briskly. She entered the station, checked the ticket office and the refreshment kiosk, then emerged onto the nearest platform. There were a dozen commuters on each of the two platforms, which were at least 200 yards long and connected by a pedestrian bridge. Jonathan Hale had vanished. The gents' toilet was on her platform side, the only place that he could be hiding. She walked the full length of the platform, and by the time the first train arrived was certain that Hale was not there.

Only then did she notice that there was a second exit from the station, on the other side. She walked over the footbridge, down onto the second platform and out into a quiet cul-de-sac dotted with modern office buildings. Having now wasted three or four minutes she realised that she had lost her quarry. Hale had escaped. By now he could be anywhere.

With a sense of impending doom hanging over her, she called in her position to the control room, and relayed what had happened. The operator passed her to DS Lewis Lytton.

'I'm really sorry, sarge,' she blurted out. 'I thought I was doing the right thing.'

'Don't worry about it. Hale is clearly taking sensible precautions, and it just shows we shouldn't underestimate him. The double exit railway station is a textbook evasion manoeuvre, so don't beat yourself up about it.'

'Thank you, sarge.'

'Besides, things get better from now on. Since this morning, we now have listening devices in twelve places across Hale's home, we've got a copy feed of his own domestic CCTV, we've tapped into his wifi, we're able to hear any phone calls made or received within a hundred yards of his house and there are microphones and GPS trackers in two of his other cars.'

'Three, including this one, sir.'

Lytton laughed. 'Yes, but that one appears not to be working.'

'Oh, I watched the technician put it in.'

'It might need adjusting. You say he's left his Maserati in the station car park?'

'Yes.'

'Look, this presents a second opportunity. I'm sending the technician back over. He should be there within fifteen minutes, and once he's in it will take only ninety seconds to refit the bug. Stay exactly where you are and call me immediately if you see Hale coming back.' He hung up.

DC Binita Patel pocketed her phone, looked up at the bright sky with its fluffy white clouds and smiled. Maybe she hadn't screwed up after all.

–

St Stephen's was a small and undistinguished Roman Catholic church less than five minutes' walk south from Sunbury railway station. The door, usually locked on a Thursday afternoon, had been left ajar, and Jonathan Hale slid through into the semi-darkness of the nave, and closed the door behind him as instructed. The boom of the heavy wood echoed into the quietness. The stained-glass windows had been boarded up from the outside, and there was a smell of incense. As his eyes adjusted to the gloom, he noticed a collection of life-sized plaster saints, mostly in poor condition, standing along one side of the apse. Building work had clearly been taking place in the chancel, and there was a scaffolding platform reaching up under the tower.

He sat in the third pew on the left, as he had been told. And he heard behind him the soft approach of feet. A large man sat behind him, making the pew squeak with his weight.

'Are you Pegasus?' Hale asked.

'I am. Have you got it?' he whispered, his breath carrying the taint of tobacco, and what Hale thought was the wisp of a Belfast accent.

'Yes.' Hale dipped a hand into his pocket and pulled out a data stick, which he held up as if it was a votive candle. 'There's everything you need, including instructions on how to contact me securely in future.'

A large hand in a dark sleeve reached forward and took the device. 'The banking chart?'

'Yes. The companies are all set up, ready, in the names you supplied to me. There is also my own Cayman-registered company, for the commission we agreed.'

'That's grand,' the big man whispered.

'When is the first transaction?' Hale asked. 'I'll need to check its progress online.'

'You will be told. Are you being careful now, Jonathan?'

'Very. I wouldn't be surprised if the boys in blue were keeping an eye on me. So I don't want to be hands-on. Just a consultant, you understand.'

'Oh, that's understood.' The big man got up, and his soft footfall and breathing receded. Jonathan Hale now risked turning to glance at the back of his contact. He was shocked to see he was wearing a priest's soutane.

Chapter Sixteen

North Bluff State Correctional Facility

Tyler was sure Azalea was the weak link in Jonathan Hale's defence. Hale had removed himself from every professional database, and like his wife Xolwa, did not appear on social media. Every reference to them was way out of date. The last news story on Hale, mentioned his return to the UK after serving his joke of a sentence. *Just six months!* It showed a picture of him arriving at Heathrow with Xolwa, and behind them – though he couldn't be sure – was Azalea, with her distinctive mass of dark curls.

It was a while before he could safely follow it up. Night-time patrols were intensified for the next few days. A couple of cells were raided after a fight on the landing below his. Elliott and his goons enjoyed making cell raids, especially at night. Tyler couldn't allow them to find the precious phone. He had a hiding place for it in a recess behind the strip light housing. He could only just reach it standing on tiptoe on the top bunk.

A week later, at three a.m., he had his next chance. Morales had gone down with Covid, taken it bad, and had been moved to the new wing, where all infected felons were grouped. Tyler took out the phone, switched it on, and reappraised himself of the bare facts.

Azalea's daughter attended St Cuthbert's, which according to its website was an independent girls-only school between the towns of Esher and Cobham. There was even an aerial view of the school and its extensive grounds and woodland, which was pretty helpful. It was obvious this was a place for rich kids. What the Brits called 'posh'. He laughed when he saw the publicity pictures of young girls wearing straw hats with the school's magenta ribbon around it, running happily together towards the camera, all gappy smiles and privileged futures. He found the school's address and fed it into Google, first with a satellite picture to get a feel for the surroundings, and then on Street View, marching Google's little yellow stick man along the nearest country lane until he could view the school entrance.

Apart from a few staged publicity shots, there were no pictures of the kids, and no way of searching by name for the students in school. He found a lot of confusing British-isms: boarders and day girls, scholarships, terms instead of semesters. It was all pretty cute but didn't get him very far. He tried to break into the students' portal with the name Azalea Hale. No dice. After three failed attempts with various passwords, he was locked out.

This was frustrating. He had guessed that Jonathan Hale would live within easy reach of the school if the girl went there every day. But what if she was a boarder? He hadn't known that schools incarcerated kids as if they were felons. He'd assumed that all ended in the days of Dickens.

He fell back on his last great hope. Azalea was a teenager. She was bound to have a page on Facebook, Instagram or one of those social media sites. He'd already set up a Facebook account in a bogus name, with the minimum info. Yet after a full hour of searching he'd found not a single British-based Azalea Hale. He tried pairing Azalea's name with her mother's surname, then with the county of Surrey, and finally and laboriously went through a couple of hundred global entries for the name Azalea on its own. There were two that looked promising, until he pulled up the portrait picture. Neither matched the photograph he'd seen in the *Surrey Comet*.

Tyler swore softly to himself in frustration. After all the use, the phone was now halfway out of juice. Getting it recharged once was in the deal with TJ, but a second time would not be cheap. He had to get this completed quickly, but so far he had been blocked at every turn. The Hale family had taken serious precautions, which was smart. He went back to the school photograph and stared at all the young girls on it.

He was suddenly inspired. He knew exactly what he was going to do. He should have thought of it before.

–

The breakthrough came the next night at three a.m. Tyler was sitting cross-legged on his bunk, the blanket over his head to mask the screen. He'd been on Facebook working through the names of some of the other girls captioned in the newspaper. The pupil standing next to Azalea was a self-confident looking blonde with a hell of a body, identified only as Merrilyn K-S. Maybe she was Azalea's friend. He hoped so, just looking at her gave him the itch. According to the caption Merrilyn was, like Azalea, a sixth former. Tyler could see that this was not equivalent to the US sixth grade but more like eleventh or twelfth. That would make them both seventeen or eighteen years old.

He soon found other references to the girl by pairing the school, her musical instrument and her forename in the search. She turned out to be Merrilyn Kidley-Swinton, a mouthful that was easy to find on Facebook. She had 800 friends, and seem to be very active, even though he could only see a few of her posts. It was only after he had sent her a friend request that he paused to consider what she would see about him: no portrait photograph, no details, just the pseudonym John Fletcher. She might even be able to see his age, which Tyler had put at thirty-five.

He wanted to watch to see what Merrilyn's reaction would be. Would she accept? It was breakfast time in the UK, but he didn't want to waste too much juice on the phone by waiting. Most of the other girls in the orchestra had less distinctive names than her, and it would take ages to work through all the Facebook possibilities. Then, in a final act of inspiration, he searched for the name of the school orchestra.

Much to his surprise, St Cuthbert's Chamber Ensemble had its own Facebook account.

It turned out to be a goldmine.

–

By the time Morales was transferred back from the Covid wing, Tyler had made huge progress. He was excited enough to wake his cellie in the small hours to show him.

'Look at this,' Tyler whispered. He played him a muted video on the phone.

'What the fuck is this?' Morales said, squinting at the tiny screen. It showed a small orchestra of schoolgirls.

'Azalea is on the piano,' Tyler said. 'That's Merrilyn on viola, and the girl with the clarinet is called Zoe Barnes.'

'Some fine young pussy,' Morales said, approvingly.

'Yeah, but I think Merrilyn has deleted my friend request.'

'I ain't surprised.' Morales struggled to contain his laughter. 'Even if she didn't already know you're a psychopathic murderer, sex criminal and drug dealer.'

Tyler stared stonily at him for the insubordination.

Morales held up his hands in apology. 'Okay. I'm sorry.'

'Damn right you are. I've killed people for less. Much less.'

'I didn't mean nothing by it.'

Tyler gave him the unblinking reptile stare for a good half minute, then said: 'I was thinking I need a better Facebook profile. Like a young Greek god, with pictures of fast cars and jet fighters. That's how to lure them. A Romeo trap.'

Morales nodded and asked to use the phone. He swiped and tapped and then said, 'Nah, these might be innocent kids. Maybe something more subtle. How about another musician who wants to join their band?'

'I can't play the fucking piano.'

'And you ain't eighteen with killer abs, neither. Point is, you don't need to be.' He tapped away, and then showed Tyler the phone screen. On it was a teenage girl playing the piano in front of a tuxedoed orchestra. 'That's the kind of friendship they're gonna want, Tyler, guaranteed.'

'So how do we do that?' Tyler.

'Step one, set up a Facebook account in a false female name with a new email address, and a date of birth to match. Then find the right music video, copy it and add your own labels and stuff with your assumed name, and send her the link.'

'Sounds good.'

'Which girl you gonna target? You can't choose Azalea if she ain't on Facebook.'

'I wanna target that cute Merrilyn.'

Morales looked at Merrilyn's Facebook page. 'This babe's hyperactive, look at all the friends and pics. Jeez, don't seem no restriction on what she's made public. She's travelled the world already, and look at the picture of the fancy cars. No, you want someone more easily impressed. What about this Zoe Barnes?'

'Sure, why not.' Tyler grinned. 'She's a bit younger. More innocent.' His grin widened even further.

'Okay, Zoe Barnes it is,' Morales said.

–

At the same moment in a quiet residential road in Surrey, Zoe Barnes was cycling to school, one-handed, with her phone in the other and a cycling helmet on her head. She was wearing a magenta blazer with the school coat of arms of a rampant golden lion and a salient dragon on the left breast, over a white shirt – top button undone – with a black pleated skirt and dark woollen tights. The regulation striped red and yellow tie, loosened to a casual noose the moment she left the house, fluttered over her shoulder, matching the daringly pulled out rear shirt tail. Although Zoe was a cavalier cyclist, who texted with one thumb, rode on the pavement when it suited her, and who spurned cycle lights because they were boring, she was in reality cocooned in safety. There was only one busy road to cross, and there was a dedicated cycleway for most of the last half mile. At this time of day, in the 20 mph limit, the parents' Range Rovers, Lexuses and Jaguars eased slowly past each other, disgorging pupils to the various schools, the mums and occasional dads inside waving to their friends. Her mother and father constantly worried about her and Lucy's safety, and on many occasions in the dark winter mornings one or other would insist on driving them to school.

But for all the parental worries, this particularly wealthy part of Surrey was low crime. Little vandalism or anti-social behaviour, no fear stalked the area at night. Young children could safely play in the streets, though they rarely did. Stranger murders and abductions? None, at least since the horrifying killing of schoolgirl Milly Dowler a few miles away in 2002.

It isn't written in estate agent windows, but that is what money is actually for. To buy safety and security for family and children, to insulate against the unknown and the threatening world that the TV and the newspapers warn about. The real dangers to Zoe Barnes were invisible, but growing by the day in a place far away, a world she would scarcely be able to imagine.

Chapter Seventeen

In the dead of that same night, Tyler and Morales were hunched over the phone on the bottom bunk. A screening blanket tucked in on the bunk above masked the light from the phone. They were looking at YouTube videos of young female clarinetists.

'You don't want anyone famous,' Morales whispered. 'You don't want anyone who might be recognised. So it's gotta be someone who is good but not *that* good. No one in front of a full orchestra.'

'I get it,' Tyler replied. 'What about this one?' He'd selected one where a girl with a Russian name who looked about fifteen was playing some piece of music he had never heard of. She had long dirty blonde hair and was wearing jeans and a T-shirt.

'I don't know shit about this kinda music, but there's lots of notes and it's played fast,' Morales conceded. He looked at the name of the piece, the 'Flight of the Bumblebee', and saw the comments beneath. 'Says here it's a tough piece.'

'All these hotshots playing it with orchestras too,' Tyler said, having looked at the YouTube playlist.

'What about the girl?' Morales said. 'Would Zoe Barnes wanna be her friend?'

'Maybe. She could pass for English or American, I guess. So are we ready to go?'

'No way. You're gonna have to get some friends to fill your profile with,' Morales said. 'If you message this girl, and she sees you have zero friends, it makes you look like a loser. She will turn you down flat.'

'So how d'you get other friends? I ain't never been a fifteen-year-old girl.'

'If she's like my stepdaughter, it's easy. All you need to do is post a bunch of popular online jokes, trawl some pictures of other girls playing instruments, some dumb pictures of cute animals, set your Facebook privacy level to minimum, then make a heap of friend requests to other clarinet players. Once you get to fifty friends, make a friend request to your target bitch. Then, my friend, you're ready to rock and roll.'

Chapter Eighteen

A week later

Zoe was on her bed, lying propped up on her elbows, looking at her phone with her calves crossed behind her. She had just posted Lucy's latest cat portrait on Instagram. This one was Socks wearing a black beret, with a background of a cubist Picasso print. Lucy was extremely good at getting the cat to co-operate, wearing silly hats, joke spectacles, and on one occasion a false moustache. As always the cat looked singularly unimpressed. His expression remained haughty, dignity intact, which was exactly why the pictures were so good. She flipped across to Facebook, which showed she had twenty-eight notifications, and three friend requests. With 650 friends, Zoe had the third largest network in her class. Many of them were musicians, who had posted videos of their own playing. Zoe's own clarinet rendition was a rather faltering version of Philip Sparke's 'Party Piece'. She needed to master it for Grade 5, but felt it wasn't good enough to upload yet. More practice required.

Amongst her direct message, she noticed one from someone called Tiffany Dolan, based in Arizona, USA, which had come in a day ago, together with a friend request.

> Hi to u from USA. RU in the band at St
> Cuthbert's? It's real cool. ☺

Zoe looked up her profile. Tiffany aka the Clarinet Queen had just thirty-two friends and hadn't posted very much for full public view. She was fifteen, in a relationship, and liked cats and dogs. The photographs of her were all very similar, showing a slender blonde holding a clarinet. However, there was one video, a three-minute long piece showing her on the clarinet rendering an absolutely faultless performance of the 'Flight of the Bumblebee'. Zoe gasped with amazement, and immediately reposted the video on the timeline of her friends. She then emailed Azalea, and messaged a couple of her closest friends in the school orchestra. 'You have got to see this!!'

Zoe messaged Tiffany back, saying how impressed she was with her playing and asking how she had heard about St Cuthbert's. Then she waited. Zoe was used to getting immediate replies, and when she hadn't got one in fifteen minutes decided it was probably because of the time difference. She accepted Tiffany's friend request. At this rate she should soon have 800, which would be pretty cool, though still a long way behind Sophie Coulter, who was a skateboarding chick and an influencer with thousands of followers on her Facebook and Instagram sites.

Zoe whiled away the next half an hour liking her friends' replies, posting answers to those who commented beneath the video, and generally absorbing the kudos that comes with being the centre of attention.

–

Next day, Zoe was having a bowl of breakfast cereal in her room when she got a message from Tiffany.

> Yo Zoe where do u live? Have u got any pets?

Zoe immediately replied:

> Hi Tiffany. Gr8 to hear from u! 😊😊 We're in Esher, in Surrey. We have a cat 🐈 called Socks, and I sometimes borrow Billy, Azalea's horse 🐴. What's Arizona like? Is it hot? How long have u been playing the clarinet?

After sending it, Zoe looked up and saw Lucy watching the screen. 'Who is Tiffany?' Lucy asked.

Zoe held the phone away from her sister and said: 'Never you mind. She's my new friend in America.'

'Would she be friends with me?'

'You can only be friends when you have a phone. You're not old enough.' She gave Lucy a wicked smile.

'Azalea hasn't got a phone, and she's your friend,' Lucy said plaintively.

'Yeah, well Azalea is really cool. You're not.'

'You're horrible.' Lucy ran away, to their father who was sitting in his home office. Right on cue, Zoe could hear Lucy's crying begin. Zoe knew their father was a sucker for Lucy's tears. She could hear her sobs, and breathless complaints. It didn't take long for Oliver to come in and berate her.

'Do you have to do tease your sister so much?' he said. 'And why aren't you ready for school?'

'I wasn't teasing her.'

The return message took half an hour to arrive, just as Zoe was clearing away her breakfast bowl:

> It's hotter than hell. Not like England with its cool rain 🌴 Who's Azalea?

Zoe sent an immediate reply.

> Azalea is my best friend in the chamber orchestra, and lives in a big house just over the back from us. She's a brilliant pianist, and her dad allows us to use their swimming pool and home cinema. Do you have a big house? The ones I see on TV in America are all huge. I'd love to visit the USA, one day. 😊

–

Tyler couldn't believe his luck. He read and reread the message then turned the phone off and hid it in his pillow. He needed to think about what he'd just discovered. Azalea lived 'over the back'. He was within a hair's breadth of getting Jonathan Hale's home address. All he needed to do was to persuade this girl to give him her own address. He lay back on his bunk to think about it. What kind of excuse could he have to ask that? In this day and age no one of her age needed the postal system, everything was transmitted online. He'd also have to play it cool, especially now she had accepted his friend request. From what Morales had told him, the British teenager would now be able to see almost everything on his account and the lack of activity would seem really weird. To avoid that, his cellmate had advised him to set up a couple of different email addresses, and then build Facebook accounts on each of them for other imaginary teenage girls. Conversations between them, however brief, would make Tyler's Tiffany Dolan character seem real and sociable. But what Morales had described would require logging in and out of numerous accounts, and just a description of it made Tyler's head spin. So he tried a different tack, trying to quickly get the information he needed.

> Tell me about your family? What's your pop's name? 😄 Mine is called Joe, and he works in insurance

The message that came back was useful.

> My dad is Oliver, he builds websites. Mum is Jenny and she works for a medical supplies company. I've got a younger sister called Lucy, 8. 😠😤 she is such a pain.

Tyler chuckled with delight. Searching *Oliver Barnes websites Surrey* found the man's business website, and that in turn produced an address: 19 Blenheim Drive, Esher. He then fed that address into Google Street View, and saw both on the map and on the aerial photo that an enormous home backed on to Zoe Barnes' address. He took screenshots of the maps and saved them. The street view itself gave very little extra information except the name of the home, The Cedars, which was written on a sign at the entry to its private drive. He searched on the house name and the same postcode as Zoe Barnes, and got a listing on a property website. This showed that the house had been bought two years ago, just before the extradition, for £5.6 million.

'My money paid for that, you bastard,' Tyler muttered.

Further searches brought up real estate agent listings, and with them an unexpected bonus: a floor plan of The Cedars in its entirety, and thirty-five professional photographs showing every room. Tyler began to laugh. *I know everything about you. You thought you could get away from me.*

He lingered on all he might do to the wife and daughter, while Hale was forced to watch. Then on to Hale himself.

All he had to do now was escape from jail and get over to the UK.

Not easy. Not by a longshot, but something he'd been mulling for more than a year. Plotting away in all the empty hours in the pit. The schemes and the ideas. It was like that saying. If you had a bunch of monkeys banging away on typewriters, eventually they would produce the complete works of Shakespeare. You just needed time. And time was one thing that he had in abundance. Time and determination.

Chapter Nineteen

The following Saturday, Oliver Barnes and family went out to breakfast at a new American-style cafe in the town, where a friend of Jenny's was the manager. They had waffles and maple syrup, fruit smoothies, and plenty of coffee. Oliver noticed that his eldest daughter seemed to be in a particularly good mood, far more outgoing than usual. However, her smartphone habit was as bad as ever, and she was tapping away through much of the meal.

'Zoe, can you join the human race for a change?' Oliver said.

'I'm in it more than you are. I'm busy talking to my friend in Arizona.'

'What friend?' Jenny asked.

'Tiffany. She is an awesome clarinetist.' A few more swipes and she showed her parents the video of Tiffany Dolan playing the 'Flight of the Bumblebee'.

'That's amazingly good,' said Jenny. 'Where do you know her from?'

'We just hooked up online,' Zoe said with a casual air. 'She was impressed by some of our stuff from the school orchestra site.'

'How old is she?' Oliver asked. The idea of his daughter randomly hooking up online with people anywhere around the world quite unnerved him.

'She's just had her sixteenth birthday, and she is really cool.'

'You're not meeting boys like this, are you?' Jenny asked.

Zoe rolled her eyes and sighed with utter impatience. 'Duh. No. What would be the point?'

'There is such a thing as online grooming, you know,' Jenny said. 'Has anyone ever asked you to, you know, take a picture of yourself?'

'Of your pussy,' Lucy explained, as she casually speared a piece of waffle loaded with maple syrup and cream.

'Lucy! Do not speak like that,' Jenny hissed. Zoe was convulsed with silent giggles.

'But I take pictures of Socks for the Internet,' Lucy said with wide-eyed innocence. 'What's wrong with that?'

Oliver sometimes thought Lucy was a genius – either that or an ingénue. Maybe both. She was certainly playing on the sensibilities of both of her parents with extraordinary sophistication. It made him proud in a way, but also terrified him. What she would be like when she was Zoe's age he had no idea. But he was pretty sure she would be an even bigger handful than her older sister.

'I would strongly advise you not to give out any personal information,' Oliver said to Zoe. 'Not your birthday, mother's maiden name, names of pets, stuff like that. Hackers can build up a picture of you, and use it to create false bank accounts, things like that.'

'For God's sake, Dad,' Zoe said. 'I wasn't born yesterday.'

Oliver and Jenny shared a glance. It was the soft kind they used when looking at pictures of her when she was a baby. Jenny spoke, reaching out her hand, which Zoe ignored. 'Darling, it's for your own good. We just couldn't bear anything to happen to you.'

–

When she got home, Zoe went up to her room and messaged a few of her friends telling them about her boring parents and how they treated her like a child. Then she shared on her Facebook page a picture of Socks wearing a small colander on his head, one that she had recently put on the cat's Instagram page. She sent it with the message, 'The difficulties of maintaining one's dignity in the modern world.'

She then sent a long message to Tiffany on the subject of boring parents and lack of trust, adding: *I know it's unlikely, but it would be great if you could come over here and stay with us, and be a guest player in our orchestra. If you come to Heathrow, Azalea and I can pick you up in her car. Then we can show you Billy.*

Satisfied with what she had written, she plastered it with emoticons, then hit send. Excitedly, she emailed Azalea to tell her the latest.

North Bluff State Correctional Facility

Tyler sat in the crowded chow hall, eating the gruel of rice and beans that was the regular Saturday meal. The Tex-Mex infused menu was supposedly a nod to the preponderance of Hispanics in this particular jail. From all he'd heard they hated the bland spiceless slop and the cardboard-like tortillas even more than he did. He hardly noticed the taste, however, because of his rising sense of excitement. The Facebook friendship with Zoe Barnes was going well, though he could hardly keep up with the blizzard of messages she sent him. He'd found some more YouTube videos from the Russian girl and, having been taught by Morales how to pirate and edit them, had posted those on Tiffany Dolan's Facebook page. He'd built up the personality of the mythical Tiffany: a girl who was always grounded by her strict parents, who'd had a cruel upbringing because she was forced to play music from the age of five. So he went a little further, and played up how much Tiffany would like to come to Britain one day, to see the sights in London. He had invented a British-born mother for Tiffany, based on his own mother's background, and added some family in Scotland. For a few days the messages had gone back-and-forth.

And then Zoe had invited him to Britain.

Unbelievable.

He'd been thinking about getting to Hale for months and now had a tenable plan to get there. His twin brother's personal effects were in storage in Dallas. Amongst these he knew was his passport. When they were younger, he and his brother had looked very much alike, and he was pretty sure he could pass for him even now, when his scurf wasn't flaring up. Not in the States of course, with its biometric checks and registry of passports of the dead. But overseas was just fine. The Mexican border was a day's drive south, a bit over 400 miles. If he could get over the land border, he could take a flight from Mexico City to London with minimal ID checks.

And those cute girls Zoe and Azalea would come and pick him up. Sweet.

–

Zoe Barnes awoke early the next day. It was just after seven, first light visible behind the curtains. She yawned and surveyed her bedroom. Posters of horses dominated, along with a framed enlargement of her astride Billy, a picture that had been taken last year. All of her childhood dolls and teddy bears were either on the windowsill or on top of the wardrobe. She was too old for them now; there were far more exciting things to do. She reached for her phone on the bedside table. It was always the first thing she did, to see if any Facebook messages had come in overnight. But waiting for messages from America made it even more essential.

She was thrilled to see she had half a dozen new notifications, including two direct messages from Tiffany. She had commented on or liked almost all of Zoe's posts, usually just using a single word like awesome or cool. But it all made her more popular. In fact there was a lot of traffic now, lots of the girls in the orchestra had made friend requests to Tiffany, and been accepted. Her discovery of this American musical prodigy might mean she'd get invites from some of the coolest girls at St Cuthbert's. Zoe hurriedly swiped through to Tiffany's direct messages, and gasped.

> Yay! I persuaded my parents to take us to England on vacation. ☺☺☺☺ YOLO! Maybe soon, if I can swing it. We could play some music together. 😺

Hey Zoe, btw, your pa just sent me a friend request! 😾 Uncool!

Her excitement at the first message was almost wiped out by her irritation at the second. How dare Dad try to spy on her friends? This was outrageous. She knew some of her school friends had left Facebook because elderly relatives were on it and kept asking questions and making stupid comments. She sent an immediate message back to Tiffany, expressing her excitement at the visit and suggesting that she delete her dad's request.

That was something she'd be taking up with him over breakfast.

–

'Don't you take that attitude with me, Zoe,' Oliver said, after his daughter had launched her own furious first salvo. He was preparing cereal for the two girls and himself. Jenny was already on her way to work.

'You cannot elbow your way into my circle of friends, it's gross,' Zoe said. 'Tiffany will think I'm just a child.'

'You *are* just a child,' her father said with a smile.

'I'm fifteen. If I was born in Afghanistan, I'd have children by now.'

'Well, thank goodness you weren't born in Afghanistan.'

'I wish you were born there,' Lucy said. 'Then I'd get your big bedroom.'

Oliver pointed a spoon. 'You are fortunate enough, Zoe, to be born in one of the most privileged generations in human history, in one of the most stable and safest

146

countries, to parents who love and cherish you. You have no idea how lucky you are.'

'I'm being suffocated. I can't be myself. I'm creatively repressed.'

Oliver set down the two bowls in front of his daughters, then brought his own bowl over and sat opposite them. 'Well, you will no doubt be pleased to know that she hasn't accepted my offer of friendship.'

'Obviously she wouldn't, duh! The Internet is full of creeps and perverts and for all she knows *you* could be one of them.'

'What's a creep?' Lucy asked her sister.

'I notice you didn't ask what a pervert is,' Zoe said, then grinned at her father.

Oliver sighed and said: 'All I want you to do is to be careful, Zoe. Your mother and I get no credit for giving you all the freedoms that Azalea doesn't have.'

'All the freedoms?' Lucy asked.

'Yes. Absolutely.'

'Can Zoe have sex then?' Lucy asked. 'Azalea can't. That's why Josh dumped her.'

Oliver rolled his eyes. 'Lucy, I wasn't talking about that particular freedom.'

'You said *all*,' Lucy said.

Oliver turned to his youngest. 'I tell you what, young lady, I think I'm going to put you down to study law. Because you would make one hell of a lawyer.'

Zoe waved her cereal spoon at her father. 'Anyway, Tiffany's coming to England. I said she could stay here before she heads off to see family in Scotland.'

'For God's sake, Zoe!' Oliver said with a note of alarm. 'You could have asked us first.'

'She only told me this morning. I suppose I was just being spontaneous,' Zoe responded, waving her arms theatrically.

'When exactly is this royal visit to take place?'

'Dunno. She said she'd let me know.'

'Maybe it's easier if she stays with Azalea,' Oliver said. 'They'd hardly notice her in that huge place.'

'No! She's *my* friend,' Zoe shouted, suddenly feeling anxious.

'Possessive, eh?' Oliver chewed a spoonful of cereal.

'My sister's got a new American doll and wants her all to herself,' Lucy said.

Zoe scowled at her sister and father and took a huge spoonful of cereal.

'All right, Zoe, just keep me in the loop, okay?'

'Dad, you worry too much. It's going to be fine.'

Chapter Twenty

North Bluff State Correctional Facility

The girl's invitation had tickled Tyler. She had no idea. It was like taking candy from a baby. All that young, pale, untouched English flesh.

There would be time for that later. He'd been working hard to write like a fifteen-year-old, downloading a website of teenage jargon, and looking at how the other teen girls he had lured to become Tiffany's Facebook friends talked to each other. There was a whole language of emoticons and abbreviations to master. Writing was never his skill, and fortunately, he never had to write very much. That allowed him to keep his phone use below half an hour a night. He'd already used up his free recharge, and the phone's juice was again down to just over a third. TJ had said an extra recharge would cost ten grand, which would make a big dent in the dough he needed for his own escape.

Those plans were in place. Tyler had aced all the easy parts. Emailing a couple of trusted contacts on the out had gotten him his late brother's passport and other ID, ready in Phoenix to be picked up. He had a volunteer to get him out over the Mexico border, a former drug mule who'd evaded identification when L3 folded. He'd even located a former IRA operative and fundraiser, protected from prosecution under the Good Friday Agreement, who promised to borrow a Glock 17 from the guerrilla group in Belfast and get it to London in time for his arrival. That would be the gun that would dispatch Hale, once he'd finished some play time.

Neither of these guys would he describe as friends, but they had kept their mouths shut at the right time, and for some years. Tyler had kept his side of that bargain too, knowing he'd need allies on the out. He promised them that the remains of the L3 syndicate cash, which he had hidden in a lock-up in Dallas, would be provided to them.

The trickiest part of all was the first step. It was so big and so overwhelming that it gave him a headache. How to escape from North Bluff Correctional. From the facility itself it had never been done, not even in the riot of 1995. Two had made it in 1984 while in transit to a hospital, but were recaptured in a couple days in Winslow.

North Bluff was twenty miles off Route 17, halfway between Phoenix and Flagstaff in the desert between reserves of Native American land. The nearest settlement was thirty miles away, Black Canyon City, population 2,837. Between the jail and town there was no cover, just rocky sun-baked wasteland. The Feds would have a chopper out in no time to hunt him down. But the medical escape route was a clue. Tyler's big idea was that with Covid cutting a swathe through the prison population, he would pretend to be infected and be transferred like many others to the low security South Bluff prison, which was more modern and had an on-site hospital, not just a sickbay. South Bluff was close to Scottsdale, and the getaway route would be less exposed. Trouble was, despite being vaccinated, he could actually catch Covid from those he was transported with. And they would test him, for sure.

Then something happened which made getting out immediately even more important.

Hard ass Sergeant Elliot and his crew had come to the cell late afternoon one day. 'It's your lucky day, Tyler. Nurse Kruger wants to see you, get yourself ready. You know the positions.'

Tyler stood up so that the cuffs and leg irons could be fitted. Elliott made a habit of always using the smaller sizes, which chafed at wrists and ankles. Once ready, he jangled along between a pair of Elliott's goons. Down three flights of stairs, and two long corridors. Just before opening the sickbay door, Elliott whispered to him. 'It's cancer, boy, you're gonna be dead by the end of the month.'

Tyler was unimpressed. He'd been called in to the North Bluff nurse on many occasions. Earlier that week she had removed a scab from the back of his neck, not the first time she'd done it. With his skin condition, he was covered in these kind of ugly lesions, which could easily be cancerous, and had had dozens of 'em cut out over his life. Never been a bad one yet.

Nurse Kruger, inevitably known as Freddy, was a bony woman of indeterminate age, with her grey hair cropped flat like she was a marine or something. The narrow-hipped masculine physique reinforced the impression. Rumour was she was unmarried, and preferred girls. Whatever. She discharged her duties efficiently and without humour.

Tyler was shown into the room where Kruger was looking at a file. Then she looked up, and told the guards to stand outside, something she'd never done with him before. He suddenly realised Elliott was right. This was the death notice. Once the correctionals had gone and closed the door, she looked down at her notes and said: 'I have to tell you that the latest lesion has come back positive for melanoma.'

'Okay, so I got the big C. How long have I got? Must be less than 260 years.' He smiled at her. The tough guy who didn't care.

This time she looked up at him. 'Not so fast. This ain't the dark ages. I've recommended that you get treatment. Surprisingly, you'll be seeing a big-shot dermatologist down in Phoenix. If she works fast, they may get it nailed before it takes over the lymphatic system.' She was making a big effort to pretend she didn't want him to die. She'd seen his record. On balance, she probably didn't care either way. But getting him treatment was a professional duty, and she carried it out.

'When do I go?' This was crucial information.

'Probably this week. You'll be told the day before, because you have to stop applying the lotion for twenty-four hours before.'

'Right.'

'I don't know if the government should be spending taxpayers' money on garbage like you. This woman is outta reach of my own insurance plan, but I guess you make for an interesting case given the rarity of your condition.'

That was the first time he could remember that suffering the scurf, as he called xeroderma pigmentosum, had ever done him any favours. It might be his last chance. Dying inside, or breaking out and dying of skin cancer weren't great options. But if he had just enough time to kill Hale, he'd be satisfied. If he got to sample some cute English rose too, so much the better.

Azalea was sitting at the school grand piano practising arpeggios when Zoe walked into the music room, with a satchel over her shoulder and her clarinet case in the other hand. Orchestra practice started in five minutes, and it was Azalea's best chance to see Zoe in school. Being two years apart, they were in different classes for everything, and there were limited opportunities to catch up in the corridor.

'Hi there,' Azalea said. 'Brilliant news about Tiffany coming over.'

'Yeah, it's pretty wicked that she has won her parents over,' Zoe said, with as much insouciance as she could manage. 'But Dad is already cross with me for saying she could stay at ours. Have you told your mum and dad?'

'I told Mum, and she reckons we should keep it to ourselves for now,' Azalea said. 'Dad would go crazy I think. I get the impression she thinks Tiffany is just boasting, and wouldn't be able to come at short notice, so there's no point winding Dad up unnecessarily.'

'No, no, she's definitely going to come, she's really excited,' Zoe said.

'Okay, let's see. We have to take her to see Billy!'

'I'll ask whether she likes horses. Living out in the wild west of America she is bound to!'

Mrs Smedley, the music teacher, walked in and clapped her hands sharply. 'All right girls, cut out the chatter, let's get some work done.'

—

First thing next morning, Zoe sat up in bed and grabbed her phone to check Facebook. Yesterday evening she had messaged Tiffany to ask if there was a date for the flight yet. She had helpfully enclosed a link giving the various American carriers who flew from Phoenix to London. Most of the flights were indirect, and Zoe linked pages of details. She had also asked Tiffany whether she rode horses as she lived in cowboy country, and if she had any dietary requirements.

The replies this morning were a little odd. No emoticons, no niceties. Just a little angry.

> Geez Louise gimme a break! Things to arrange this end.

Who the hell was Louise? Zoe was still wondering, when a short time later a second message came.

> Hi Zoe, I'll let you know when it's all fixed.😂😂😂😂 Here's a pic of my brother on his horse.

The attached photo was a proper cowboy image, a piebald horse, expertly ridden by a hunky young guy in a checked shirt and western chaps amongst dusty rocks. Was that really her brother? Wow. Another plus. She reposted the picture to her friends.

—

Tyler lay on his bunk silently cursing himself. He knew he'd screwed up when he sent the first message without thinking. It was stupid and risked the whole enterprise. He'd been in a hurry, and impatient because even as he tapped it out the guards were busting some cells on the floor above. Rumour had it they'd already seized a phone, and Elliott's goons needed no excuse to widen the search. The second message was an attempt to straighten things up with the girl, but he hadn't taken the trouble to write it like Tiffany Dolan would have. The cowboy picture was a last-minute piece of inspiration, but he now realised that using a stock image might uncover his deceit. Morales had warned him about reverse searches, where you could find the origin of a picture, checking where else it had been used online. In this picture, boy, when he did the search it showed it had been used all over. He prayed that the girl wasn't suspicious, or some kind of geek. She was only fifteen, so chances were he would get away with it. He'd have to have a story ready.

There was a lot of thinking to be done now. There was only 15 per cent charge left on the phone, and a couple of days' worth of data use in credit. He might still have a lot to do. His arrangements were still up in the air. He'd have very little notice about the transfer and wouldn't know the exact time even if he knew the day. Big Sal, a guy who really was a friend from way back, had been amenable to helping Tyler escape jail, for a five-figure sum. Asking him to hang around for a day wouldn't be too onerous, except he wouldn't know what to look out for. Tyler wouldn't know whether he was being taken in a corrections department van, an ambulance or a minibus. He thought about approaching a few cons who'd ridden the sick train to South Bluff before, but quickly realised they would guess he was planning to escape.

He couldn't afford to deal with any more rats. One big rat was more than enough.

Chapter Twenty-one

It was four a.m. when they came to fetch him. Four goons, who roughly fitted him into handcuffs and leg irons. It had been a close-run thing. He'd only just finished using the phone, which had now died, out of charge. He had concealed the fingernail-sized sim card in a scrap of polythene under his dressing just ten minutes before, but the phone casing was still in the cell, under the strip light housing.

To process him through took a good hour. A cavity search, the radar chair for anything he might have swallowed, and a basic medical check to show he was healthy enough to be moved. They looked at the dressing, but didn't dare unstick it and incur the wrath of Nurse Kruger. It was just before dawn when he walked the long corridor to the out. Fourteen sets of security gates, a few good-natured catcalls from the felons he was leaving behind. Those who knew he was due for the sick train had made requests for contraband. He agreed to them all, not wanting anyone to suspect he was breaking out. Finally, he was under open sky, a correctional on each side of him. The cool breeze of a desert morning filled his nostrils with the taste of freedom. A grey seven-seater minivan reversed into the vehicle cage. It was the worst kind of vehicle for Sal to identify. Too generic for him to be sure that it was a prison vehicle. Sure, he'd be in an orange jumpsuit, and the goons would be wearing the uniform, but there was little chance Sal would spot any of this through the tinted windows.

Tyler's last message to Sal was that he would try to get a stop for a comfort break just before reaching the highway. But there was no guarantee he'd accomplish that. If not he would try to wave an arm out of a window or something. That now looked unlikely. He was pushed into the middle seat of the vehicle, with an officer each side of him, handcuffed arm to arm with the guy on the right. It all suddenly looked a long shot, a stupid fantasy.

The first long fingers of dawn were creeping over the horizon as the exit gate was withdrawn. The civilian driver took them down the ramp, and onto the single-lane exit road, which after winding out of the canyon ran straight as a die for twenty miles before reaching Route 17. Once the first slab of desert heat hit them, the AC was maxed, drowning out the country music on the radio. The guards closed the curtains, giving Tyler little idea where he was. After fifteen minutes Tyler started to impersonate stomach convulsions. He let saliva drip from his mouth.

'What in hell is up with you?' asked the guard on his left, who had a southern accent. What in Hale, it sounded like. How right that was.

'I need a bathroom break.' He heaved, and spattered saliva onto his jumpsuit.

'We ain't stopping,' said the other, a big bullet-headed guy with just a fuzz of white hair.

'Gonna throw up,' Tyler gasped. His heaving was sufficiently powerful that he thought he might manage it.

'No, you ain't,' said bullet head, whose own left wrist was cuffed to Tyler's right.

Tyler really gave it his best attempt and managed a fair amount more drool. He was genuinely starting to feel sick now.

'Hey guys,' said the driver, looking in the mirror at them. 'If he chucks in here, you gotta clean it up. I've got a deductible to worry about.'

There were heavy sighs from the two officers, and they gestured for him to pull over. The minivan lurched to a stop, and they let him out, still cuffed and shackled. Bullet head undid the cuffs, and stepped aside as Tyler bent over, heaving. They were in the middle of nowhere, rough sun-baked ground and just a few black blackened fragments of creosote bush. Tyler leaned further and heaved again. He could feel the burning of the sun against the back of his neck. UV scorching him. He'd pay for that in the coming days.

'Now you hurry up, boy,' said the southern guard.

Tyler straightened up and squinted at the horizon, where he could see the glare of a vehicle approaching in the opposite direction, from the highway. 'Gimme some water,' he demanded.

'When you're back in the van,' said bullet head.

The approaching vehicle shot past. It was a small truck, a U-Haul. *Sal! He must have seen me.* Tyler let himself be dragged back and put in his seat, the safety belt fixed. Before getting in he saw the U-Haul had stopped a few hundred yards past them. They set off again, with the driver repeating his warning about not messing the uphol-stery. Tyler glanced over his shoulder. He could hear another vehicle behind but couldn't turn far enough to see it through the gap in the curtains. He lowered himself, his head almost to his knees.

'What the heck?' the driver said, as the U-Haul start to overtake. There really wasn't the space.

'I'm calling this in,' said bullet head, reaching for his radio.

He never got the chance. The first sideswipe tipped the minivan off the blacktop onto the rough, stony margin. The next turned the world over, again and again. His last memory was being squashed, the meat in a correctional sandwich.

–

Tyler was still dizzy when they reached Black Canyon City limits, the town shimmering in the heat haze. Sal pulled the U-Haul into a parking lot, behind a derelict gas station, and brought it to a stop out of view of the road behind the roofless brick shell of a former burger joint. Right there in the shadow was an off-white GM sedan. Sal used a fob to unlock the GM, then got out of the U-Haul and helped Tyler get into the car.

Once they were back on the road in this clean car, borrowed from Sal's sister, Tyler let himself relive the last half hour: coming to, upside down, suspended from the seatbelt, largely unhurt due to the cushioning effect of two large human airbags, one each side. Next thing he recalled was the deafening sound of shots, Sal dispatching each of the two guards and the driver with a single bullet to the head. Unshackled thanks to the keys Sal found on the bodies, he recalled being tugged out of the bullet-shattered side window, dragged to the U-Haul, and then watching Sal slosh gasoline over the minivan before setting it ablaze. Sal had brought him some fresh clothing, so the prison jumpsuit went on the blaze too.

Only now did Tyler start to believe. The Mexican border was less than a day away. Then a flight, not yet booked, from Mexico City to London. 'Hey, Sal, gimme your phone for a minute.'

'It's in the glove,' he grunted.

Tyler reached in, found the smartphone, took out the sim card and replaced it with the one under his dressing.

'So you got some hot chick waiting for you?' the big man said, a grin looped over his pockmarked face.

'You could say that,' Tyler said, as he logged on to Facebook.

'Best fix yourself up before you see her,' Sal said. 'You look like you got sunstroke.'

Tyler flipped down the sunshade and checked in the small mirror. He looked like a Halloween creature. His skin was peeling, brown flakes revealing an angry mottled purple beneath, from his forehead down on both cheeks. The skin on his neck and shoulders was as scaly as a snake. But worst of all was his eyes. The whites were completely bloodshot, and made him look like a member of the undead.

'Gotta get me some sunglasses,' Tyler said. 'And we need to stop at a drugstore.'

'Sure thing. It better be me that goes in,' Sal said.

Just the few minutes standing outside in the Arizona sun pretending to throw up had given his body a huge dose of UV, more than it had needed to cope with in two years of incarceration. Without his goop, a dermatological steroid cream, he would stand out like a sore thumb. There was no chance of getting any, but total sunblock would help with the skin at least.

None of it mattered now for the long-term. Just so long as he lasted long enough to reach London, pick up the promised gun, and lure Jonathan Hale to his death.

Chapter Twenty-two

Zoe poked and prodded her cereal but didn't feel like eating any. Two days with no word from Tiffany, and no reply to any of her chatty messages. She had been boasting to so many friends about the arrival of her close friend the American clarinet prodigy that she was now really scared it wasn't going to happen at all. She would look such an idiot.

'You look miserable,' Lucy said, wandering into the kitchen in her pyjamas.

'I'm not.'

'You are too.' Lucy sat down and prodded her sister with a finger, trying to get a reaction.

'Why do you have to be so annoying?' Zoe said.

'I'm not, I'm a little angel. Margrethe said.' Lucy kicked her legs backwards and forwards under the table.

'She doesn't know you like I know you.'

Oliver finally looked up over the paper. 'Girls, do you mind.'

'I don't think Zoe's friend is coming to stay,' Lucy said.

Zoe kicked her, under the table.

'Ow, stop that. Daddy, can I have a boiled egg?'

Oliver looked at the clock and shook his head before returning to the newspaper. 'You don't have time. You've

162

got to be in school in twenty minutes. Have some corn-flakes. And get dressed!'

'If you do it properly, boiling an egg only takes three,' Lucy said. 'We did it in home economics.'

'It's three and a half, idiot,' Zoe muttered. 'And that doesn't count getting the water to the boil and the time taken to eat it.'

'She's dumped you, hasn't she?' Lucy said, with a big smile.

Zoe rolled her eyes. Her father was watching her now, indicating that physical retaliation would be a very bad idea. She looked down at her phone and went to Face-book for the tenth time that morning.

A message! Finally.

> Hi Zoe. Sorry for the delay 🐶 It's all fixed now 😄 Flying to LHR! 😺 🐧 arriving Friday 13.20. See you there!

Zoe was astounded. What? *This* Friday? Only a day and a half away.

'She is coming, on Friday. So there.' Zoe stuck her tongue out at her sister and waved the phone in her face. Lucy stuck her tongue out too.

'Hang on a minute,' Oliver said. 'Are you still expecting her to stay here?'

'Of course! We invited her.'

'*You* invited her,' Lucy corrected. 'I didn't.'

'Your mother is going to go into meltdown,' Oliver said. 'This is not a hotel!'

'It's all right,' Zoe said. 'I'll make up the room. Azalea is going to give her a lift from the airport. It will be fine.'

'You will be at school, as will Azalea,' Oliver pointed out. 'You told me she's got music exams next week.'

'So? She'll breeze them. And I've got a free period on Friday morning, and it's only clarinet practice in the afternoon.'

'How many times have I told you, it's a study period, not a free period,' Oliver said. 'And that's not the attitude I want to hear about the clarinet. Azalea wouldn't be as good as she is on the piano if she had your casual disregard for practice.' He pointed a finger at her.

'God, you are so boring,' Zoe said, standing up from the table, and heading out into the hall.

'It'll be me schlepping up to Heathrow, won't it?' Oliver called after her. 'Your personal bloody Uber, always at your beck and call.'

'Tch, kids today,' Lucy said, shaking her head.

Zoe thundered upstairs, scooping up the papers she needed, and dumped them into her satchel. She was still furious when she was ready to leave for St Cuthbert's. She popped her head back into the kitchen as if to say goodbye. 'Dad, I am not going to ask you to go to Heathrow. Azalea and I will sort it out between us.'

'You better had, because I'm not going. I mean it,' he called after her.

Given what was to happen, he sorely wished he had never said that. To have that time again to make a different decision.

–

Richard Tyler sat in his soft business class seat and watched the hazy suburbs of Mexico City recede beneath the wing of the British Airways jet. He was wearing a baseball cap, wraparound sunglasses and a Covid mask. Those three between them covered almost all of his face. His hands, which looked terrible, were in surgical gloves so the worst of the damage wasn't visible. He'd spent a half hour in the airport restroom, smearing as much of his exposed body as he could with sunblock and some nourishing skin rejuvenation cream he'd bought at duty free. He had no idea whether they would work.

For all that, Lady Luck had been on his side for a couple days now. The Mexican border had been no hassle at all. He'd hidden in the trunk of the sedan while Sal drove through at six in the morning. The federal border agents were far more concerned about who was coming *into* the USA, and what they were bringing, than about hassling those going the other way. As for the Mexican border guards, Sal said he'd not even had to stop the car, except when the immigration officer leaned out of her tollbooth and asked for a passport, which she stamped without formality. Airport check-in had worried him a little, with his skin so bad, a passport in his brother's name, and paying in cash. But after he had explained to the check-in agent that he was flying to London for treatment for skin cancer, she had accepted his documentation without further question.

Once the plane levelled off, a pretty flight attendant with the cutest English accent had asked him if he needed a drink.

'Sure. It's been awhile since I had some hard liquor,' he replied. 'What are they drinking in England?'

'Well, personally, I'm inclined towards a G&T before dinner.' He went along with that and she served him a generous measure of Bombay Sapphire in a real glass, with the mixer on the side. As he took the drink from her, she briefly rested her hand on his shoulder before passing to the next row.

It was the first time he could remember that any human had touched him affectionately. It gave him the itch. A desire that was well and truly awakened. Hale's daughter. Such an enticing prospect, and so close now.

—

Zoe was lying on the bed in Azalea's bedroom, watching her friend holding up a saffron dress.

'What about this?' Azalea asked.

'Too yellow,' Zoe said turning her attention back to phone. 'And too girly.'

'What does Tiffany wear?' Azalea asked, bringing out a conservatively cut blue flowered dress.

'I haven't asked her, and she hasn't said. She might be a grungy girl like me, T-shirts and jeans. That's what she is wearing in some of the photos.'

The door flew open, and Lucy leaned against the door frame with Socks in her arms, her face once again wearing the haughty expression of a Bond villain. The cat was wearing a helmet carved out of an orange, and was purring loudly. 'So, what conspiracy is this?' she asked.

Azalea, who hadn't seen this particular item from Sock's extensive millinery collection, burst out laughing. Zoe merely scowled at her sister. 'What are you doing here, trouble?'

'Can Socks do some more pictures for Instagram?'

'Not now.'

'But what about all his followers? They're expecting an update. I mustn't disappoint them.'

'Later, we're planning for tomorrow,' Zoe said.

'You've got to go to school,' Lucy said. 'You can't go gallivanting off to Heathrow at the drop of a hat.'

Zoe had heard this gallivanting phrase from her mother already a couple of times, and since it had been adopted by her sister had become heartily sick of it. 'Shut up, Lucifer.'

'Mummy says not to call me that.'

'She said it to Dad, not me. It's *his* name for you, little devil.'

'So are you really going?' Lucy asked Azalea.

'Well, we can't leave Tiffany all alone at the airport, can we?' Azalea said 'She'll be tired after a long flight, and she doesn't know her way around. It's an act of hospitality to someone from another country.'

Zoe scrutinised her friend. She often wondered if Azalea had inherited any of her father's lawbreaking attitudes. She wasn't sure she wholly approved of anyone being quite that nice and considerate.

'Can I come with you to the airport?' Lucy asked, her eyes at their innocent widest.

'No way,' Zoe said immediately.

'Lucy, you have to go to school,' Azalea said gently.

'Why is it only me that has to go to school?' Lucy asked tearfully.

'Don't cry,' Azalea said.

'Ignore her, she can turn it on and off like a tap,' Zoe said.

Lucy looked from one to the other, before settling her gaze on her sister. 'If you don't let me come, I shall tell Daddy.'

Azalea and Lucy looked at each other. The cat, finally fed up with his headgear, deftly clawed it off, then bit it before dropping it to the floor.

Chapter Twenty-three

Friday morning was always busy in the Barnes household. Jenny had to travel to Milton Keynes for an early meeting, and was gone by seven, and Oliver had a regular client conference call starting at ten, in fifteen minutes. He was just setting up when the landline rang. He reached across and picked up the phone.

'Oliver Barnes web design,'

It was Lucy's form teacher, Mrs Obasanjo. She told him his daughter had just tested positive for Covid and asked if he could come and pick her up from school. Oliver just managed to avoid swearing. He said he would do so once he'd finished his meeting.

He hung up and rubbed his eyes. Just typical. The primary school was only five minutes' drive away, but Mrs Obasanjo always seemed to assume that since he worked from home he could just drop everything to bring in forgotten games kit, an overlooked ingredient for home economics or the book that Lucy had left behind.

He picked Lucy up shortly after eleven. Despite the face mask she wore in the car she seemed extremely pleased with herself.

'You're not feeling ill, then?' Oliver asked.

'No, but better safe than sorry,' she said, another of her favourite adopted phrases.

'You know you have to go into isolation in your room?'

Lucy nodded.

'I'll bring you up some lunch, but you have to stay there, okay?'

'I'll catch up on my violin practice.'

Oliver was taken aback. She normally had to be dragged to her musical instrument, which he suspected she had only asked for in order to compete with her sister.

Indeed, for two solid hours after she had got back, she practised again and again and again the same beginner's piece until he thought it would drive him mad. Socks was nowhere to be seen. He often fled from the house at the first squealing note. At one p.m., Oliver took off the headphones he had used to drown out the squeaky practice while he tried to construct some dynamic web pages for a client. She still seemed to be playing. He went to the foot of the stairs and listened again. There was something about the distant quality of the violin that seemed wrong. Calling for Lucy, and getting no answer, he headed up the stairs and entered her room.

She wasn't there.

Lucy's computer was running, and the speakers were the source of the sound. He soon discovered that what he'd been hearing was a sound file recorded by Zoe of her sister's playing, set on repeat.

He'd been hoodwinked.

With a rising sense of panic, Oliver went into Zoe's bedroom, then checked out the rest of the house. No sign of Lucy. Her school uniform was dumped on the floor, so she was clearly wearing something else. He peered out into the front garden, and along the street. There were no children playing. Of course, these days there were never children playing in the street. That was something that had stopped in *his* childhood. He made his way into the back garden, carefully checking her favourite hiding places, including the shed and greenhouse. Finally, he reached the back gate, and looked beyond it to the palatial Edwardian home of Jonathan Hale.

He rang Zoe's phone but there was no reply. Then he rang Azalea's mobile, and left a message. He began to piece together what had happened.

For God's sake, he thought, she's only eight.

—

Half an hour later, Oliver Barnes was standing in Jonathan Hale's enormous kitchen talking to him and the au pair, Margarethe, who said: 'I saw Lucy here with Zoe, they were going out to the airport with Azalea. I thought it was all arranged.'

'Azalea should have been at school,' Hale said. 'But I just checked, and she called in sick. They've taken the Renault.'

'Zoe was so excited at the idea of going to meet her American friend,' Margarethe said. 'I understand that you really don't have the space, so Xolwa had offered to put Tiffany up here. She asked me to make up a room in the annex.'

'I didn't know about that,' Hale said.

'She said she mentioned it to you,' Margarethe said, then glanced at Oliver.

'Well, it was clearly planned,' Oliver said. 'I looked at Lucy's search history, and she'd been looking up how to fool a lateral flow test. Just a smear of orange juice does the trick, apparently.'

'Where are they picking this girl up?' Hale asked.

'Heathrow. They've been talking about it for days,' Margarethe said. She stared at Hale, clearly surprised that he hadn't picked up on the enthusiasms of his daughter.

'Well, I suppose we do have the space,' Hale said. 'Just a bit worried about Azalea driving on such busy roads so soon after taking her test,' he said.

'I'm sure she'll be fine,' Oliver said, though he felt less than sure of it.

'If I didn't have this client Zoom call in half an hour, I would go up to Heathrow myself,' Hale said.

Oliver looked at his watch. 'They'll probably be there by now anyway.'

'Do we have the flight number, or the terminal?' Hale asked.

'I'll look on Zoe's computer,' Oliver said. 'Seeing as she isn't answering my calls.'

He said his goodbyes, hugely relieved that at least he knew where his daughters were. Oliver strode down the formal lawns of The Cedars and opened the gate at the bottom, before crossing the stream and entering his own garden. His fear now turned to anger. One thing was certain, he was going to have to deal with his children's wilful defiance. Bunking off school, pretending to be infected with Covid, and lying to him. The biggest surprise was that Azalea had been roped in to all this. She seemed to be such a sensible girl. Still, one way or another, it would all be sorted well before Jenny got home this evening, thank God. He could only imagine her reaction. She would be incandescent, and judging by past experience, he would be first to get the blame.

Gillard punched in the code and entered the third floor of the CID building. Operation Whirlpool was still in monitoring mode, so he had agreed with ACC Anderson that he only needed to visit twice a day, while continuing to manage his existing caseload. Still, spreading him so thinly seemed like the perfect way to set him up to fail.

The NCA team here was a dozen strong, and from the look of it didn't have enough to do. The operation control room had two female officers, currently talking to each other, and six male officers, most of them standing around drinking coffee, laughing and joking. Amongst them was DI Colin Williams, who called him over to a terminal.

'Is there anything happening?'

'Not much on the voice traffic. Misbehaving teenagers, kids playing truant. So far so normal.' Williams said. 'But we've got some interesting results for Hale's web searches.' He offered Gillard a chair in front of a terminal. On the screen were lists of Google searches.

'He's certainly cranking up his laundering machine,' Williams said. 'A few searches on obscure legal rules in tax havens, quite a few lengthy logins to various bank and financial websites.'

Gillard noticed a large number of news searches on the word Tyler and the phrase North Bluff State Correctional, made at least a couple of times a week.

'He's quite nervous, isn't he?'

'For good reason,' Williams replied. 'I wouldn't want an enemy like Tyler.'

Gillard homed in on some of the financial searches. 'Has he made any significant sized transfers?' He knew there was an open-ended financial order covering a dozen bank accounts that the Hale family were known to have. The police could see all activity with only a short delay. But as the late Joe Kyrios had reminded them, the skill of the launderer is to have many more accounts than the authorities were aware of.

'There are some incoming payments, a few thousand here or there. Not sizeable enough to indicate illicit activity. It's notable that he's not been paying off his mortgage in full each month for some time.'

Gillard nodded. 'Kyrios guessed he'd be struggling for cash.'

'That's right, he needs money upfront.'

'Interesting,' Gillard said. 'I had one of my own DCs trace the route through Sunbury railway station that Hale took yesterday. We've got a bit of CCTV which shows that he walked past some low-rise office buildings and then disappeared left down a residential street. That doesn't seem to be much down there, unless he visited someone at home.'

'I could order another telegraph pole camera installation, in case he takes that route again,' Williams said. 'But it could be completely innocent.'

Gillard nodded. 'It's surprising though, isn't it, that none of the phones we know he has were activated during that journey.'

'Maybe he didn't make a phone call,' Williams said, suddenly looking up. A headphoned NCA officer inside the monitoring room was beckoning to them through the glass door. Gillard and Williams went through and closed the door behind them. The officer switched the sound onto loudspeaker. A woman was speaking.

'I told you about it, Jon. It's only for a couple of days and we've got plenty of space for the girl.'

173

'Well, I don't remember.'

'You don't seem to remember anything these days.'

There was a clattering of pots and pans, which drowned out the next few seconds of exchanges.

'I think you should see the doctor again. You're not right.'

'I'll be fine once we've scraped up enough to pay this mortgage back payment.'

The operative turned the speakers off.

'There's been a lot of this kind of thing this morning,' the officer said.

'Anything from the bugs in the cars?'

'Of him, no. We got all the details of his wife's hair appointments from her car. He uses the Maserati most, and thankfully the bug is now working.' He took off his headphones and laid them on the desk. 'Overall, it's been very quiet.'

'Who knows,' Gillard said. 'Maybe it's the calm before the storm.'

1.09 p.m.

Richard Tyler stood by the Heathrow Terminal Five baggage reclaim, his foot resting proprietorially on the edge of the carousel. Sal had done him proud. He had checked in one bag, with five changes of clothes, bullet-proof vest, toiletries, a wig in case he needed it, spare sunglasses and a thick scarf that he could wrap around his neck. There were half a dozen burner phones, still in their blister packs, and a box of cable ties. He would have preferred rope, but what the hell.

While he was queueing for immigration, he had opened Facebook messenger, and sent the final, really important message to Zoe. She might already be at the airport or close to it, and it had to be very carefully phrased to avoid spooking her.

> Hi Zoe, I forgot to mention I'm traveling with my dad. His flight got in earlier than mine. I'm still stuck in a huge immigration line because of Covid. It could be hours. 😩 Would you pick him up? He needs to run a couple errands. Thank you so so much I'm really looking forward to seeing you and your friend Azalea. 😊😇 love, Tiff xxxx

That message had gone fifteen minutes ago and there had been no reply. In an earlier message, Zoe had said she had a cardboard sign with the word Tiffany written on it in marker pen.

His bag finally appeared. He grabbed it and headed for the green line. He had nothing to declare except some murderous intentions. After exiting customs, he followed the sign to the pickup area within the short-stay car park.

What happened in the next few minutes, he had to get exactly right. It would still be easy to screw everything up.

The Renault was within Heathrow's road network heading for Terminal Five parking, while a procession of huge jets roared over their heads.

'Nearly there,' said Zoe. 'This is so exciting.'

'I can't believe you persuaded me to do it,' Azalea said. 'My dad is going to go crazy.'

'But didn't your mum say it was all right for her to stay with you?' Zoe asked.

'Yes, but I never mentioned that I was going to pull a sickie at school to fetch her. I think she thought that your dad was going to pick Tiffany up.'

'Well, you're all going to be in deep trouble,' said Lucy, shaking her head. She was sitting in the back seat with Socks on her lap. The cat was rarely happy about going in the car, which normally meant an unwelcome trip to the vets. It was only because Lucy was constantly stroking her that he remained calm.

'Not just us, Lucifer. Dad is not going to be impressed that you faked your Covid test so you can get out of school for a day.'

'For ten days, actually,' Lucy said, staring imperiously out of the window. 'Isolation is for ten days.'

Zoe turned round from the front passenger seat. 'You haven't got Covid, dimwit. You faked your test.'

'Yes, but I could still have it.' She began to cough dramatically, which made Socks' ears flatten in alarm, his eyes wide.

'We should probably put masks on before we meet Tiffany,' Zoe said. 'And I've got a big one for Lucy that covers her entire head.'

'I wonder if Tiffany likes cats,' Lucy said.

'She does,' Zoe said. 'And horses. She sent me a picture of her brother, who is quite a hunk.'

'Hunk just means big lump or piece,' Lucy said. 'So her brother is quite a big lump.'

Zoe rolled her eyes at Azalea, then said: 'I'm going to risk turning my phone on, in case Tiffany's left a message.'

She scrolled past the two angry texts from her father and didn't dare listen to the voicemail he had left. Once she tapped through to Facebook, she read a message from Tiffany left ten minutes ago.

'Shit, she's stuck in some huge queue, but her dad's got through,' Zoe said.

'What's this about her father?' Azalea asked. 'She didn't mention he was coming.'

'There's enough room in the car.' Zoe looked over her shoulder. 'If he doesn't mind sitting next to Miss Trouble here.'

'Jesus H. Christ, this is some weird shit,' said Lucy, yawning and stretching her arms. It was one of her current favourite phrases, picked up from TV.

'So how late is she going to be?' Azalea asked Zoe. 'We can't wait hours. Parking here costs a fortune.'

Zoe had decided to brave the message from her father. He was really angry, so she deleted it without hearing the end.

'Can't we just drive round and round?' Zoe asked.

Azalea shook her head. 'It's really strict, you have to wait in the underground short-stay, at a pickup point.'

Azalea picked up a ticket at the barrier, then followed the short-stay signs down a steep anti-clockwise ramp around a tower.

'This is like a big helter-skelter,' Lucy said.

'I just hope we don't get lost,' Azalea said.

Zoe messaged Tiffany asking for her mobile number, and giving her own. They trailed around to a dark and cavernous car park, thronged with traffic, and looked for available spaces. They went round and round looking for a spot. Eventually they found one, and Azalea got out of the car, holding up the cardboard sign. Zoe's phone rang, an unidentified number.

'Hi Zoe, it's Tiffany's father. Whereabouts are you, honey?'

There was something really cold and odd about his voice. The deep slow the way he said the last word made her shiver. 'Hi, Mr Dolan. We're on the second floor in the middle. Azalea's got our Tiffany sign. You should be able to see it.'

'Good thinking, sugar. I'm on my way up now. Now you just stay right there.' It sounded like an order.

'Shouldn't you wait for Tiffany?' Zoe asked him.

'It could be hours. Some electronic passport gates are on the fritz.'

'Will she be all right on her own?'

'It's all right, honey. Tiffany has been catching planes for years on her own. She's a big girl now.' His breath came unevenly and Zoe could hear the beat of footsteps on stairs.

'But why is she so late?' Something wasn't right. She had a feeling in the pit of her stomach. Zoe looked to Azalea for reassurance, but she was looking away at something.

And then he was there. A man in a baseball cap, wrapround sunglasses and a face mask making his way amongst the parked cars. He had a big black raincoat, with a wheeled suitcase to match, and he had his gloved hand on Azalea's elbow. They had a brief conversation, and Azalea headed away with him to join the queue at the payment machine.

'Where's Tiffany?' Lucy asked Zoe.

'Stuck in a queue,' Zoe said. She rang Tiffany's number, but it went to a robotic voicemail. As soon as she looked up, she saw Azalea and the man had returned. He opened the driver-side door, and said: 'You must be Zoe. I'm Tiffany's father.' Zoe could hear a hissing and turned to see Socks had backed away to the far corner of the rear seat, fur standing up, ears flat.

'Hi.' She could smell aftershave, but also some deeper odour, like the bins at the back of the school kitchen.

Socks was still hissing and trying to insinuate himself behind Lucy, his tail low and waving. Zoe's father walked around the back and lifted the boot lid so he could stow his luggage. When he slammed it closed, the car shook.

'What's with the cat?' he said accusingly.

'Lucy wanted to bring her,' Zoe said.

'That varmint looks rabid to me,' he said, walking around to the passenger side and opening Zoe's door. 'I'll ride in the front, honey.'

'Okay.' Zoe looked at Azalea, now back in the driver seat. Her eyes were wide open in silent alarm, trying to communicate something.

'Don't take all day about it, will you?' he said.

Zoe squirmed out and slid into the back, next to her sister. Azalea started the engine and eased the car out into the queue for the down-ramp to the exit.

'He smells funny,' Lucy hissed into her sister's ear. 'Socks is scared of him.'

Zoe reached for her phone, and with the practised fingers of a teenager, sent a rapid Facebook direct message to Tiffany.

He leaned over the back seat to her and his arm shot
out and snatched the phone from her. It was amazingly
quick. 'I'll take that, honey. Don't want you distracting
Azalea here.'

'You can't take my phone!' Zoe wailed.

'The hell I can't. I'll have yours too, sugar,' he said to
Lucy.

'I don't have one. I'm much too young,' she whispered,
holding the cat tightly to her chest. Her eyes were full of
tears. 'Are you going to hurt us?' she asked.

He laughed, slowly. 'Do what I say, and you'll be fine.
You've heard about Americans and guns, I guess? Well,
mine is in my pocket, and it's pointing at Azalea here.'
Zoe could see something bulging in his raincoat pocket
through the gap between the front seats. 'So just stay calm,
keep quiet, breathe nice and slow and we'll all be just
dandy.'

'You can't take a gun on a plane,' Lucy hissed to Zoe.
'You get searched and everything.'

Zoe put a finger to her lips and widened her eyes to
get her sister to shut up. They were in a queue to exit
onto a steep ramp, edging along at slower than walking
pace. There were cars everywhere, with people in them,
people who could help them. But if she jumped out,
what would he do to Lucy and Azalea? Socks had crawled
over the back seat into the luggage compartment to hide.
Zoe caught Azalea's glance in the driving mirror. She was
moving her lips ever so slightly as if trying to communicate, but Zoe didn't know what she was saying. They

were soon on the down ramp, circling down across an open area towards the canopied exit barriers. There was finally some daylight.

'Now take it real easy,' he said to Azalea. She buzzed the window down and reached out, her hand trembling. She dropped the ticket before she had chance to feed it into the slot.

'Okay. Open the door, reach out and pick it up real slow.' Someone behind was honking a horn. Zoe turned round and realised that now they were in daylight she could see people inside their vehicles. The man in the car behind was mouthing profanities. It gave her an idea. She felt in her pocket for the marker pen and reached down for the cardboard sign at her feet. Lucy was watching her, and Zoe put a finger to her lips in warning. Zoe popped off the cap and started to slowly and neatly write on the back of the card in large letters: 'Help. Kidnapped!!' Below it she wrote her home landline number. She was really scared the pen would squeak, but by moving slowly and not pressing too hard, it stayed silent. Besides, all his attention was on Azalea, who had now retrieved the ticket and had fitted into the slot.

'Try anything like that again, cutie pie, and I'll blow your fucking brains out,' he told Azalea, as the barrier rose. 'Now drive to the Premier Inn.' He pronounced it pre-mere.

Once they were out, Zoe placed the cardboard sign behind the rear seat headrest, and held it there with her hands, as if she was cupping her hands behind her head. A car with a large family in it overtook them, and the driver waved cheerily out of the window towards them before accelerating away. *He thinks it's just a joke.*

'Now kids, let's just keep calm. I know this ain't what you expected, but in an hour it will all be over and you will be fine, and I'll be away. You can then call the cops and have all the tearful reunions with your families. Do you understand?'

They assented in unison.

'There isn't really a Tiffany is there?' Lucy asked. 'And you're not her dad.'

'No, honey. Tiffany doesn't exist.'

'You're Richard Tyler, aren't you?' Azalea asked. 'My dad's enemy.'

'You got it, sugar.'

'Do you wash money?' Lucy asked.

He laughed loudly. 'No, cutie pie, that's what Azalea's pa does.'

'You've got funny skin,' Lucy said. 'What's the matter with it?'

Zoe grabbed her sister's hand and squeezed urgently. *Shut up, for God's sake.*

Tyler turned to look at her. 'I'm very sensitive to sunshine and heat.'

'Then why do you live in Arizona?' Lucy persisted. 'In Death Valley it's more hot than anywhere else, even in Africa.'

'Death Valley isn't in Arizona,' Zoe muttered. 'California.'

He laughed. 'Sometimes, honey, you don't get a whole lotta choice where you live.' He looked up as they went underneath a gantry. 'I never seen so many cop cameras as here. Every goddamn junction. It's like fucking North Korea.'

They'd been driving for ten minutes before Azalea said, 'I can see the Premier Inn, but we're on the wrong road.'

'Well, get us on the right road.'

Zoe interrupted. 'If you let me have my phone, I can open a map.'

'I'll do it,' he said. He pulled out Zoe's smartphone from his raincoat pocket. Zoe spotted Azalea's dumb phone in his other hand. Not a gun. She briefly wondered if all three of them together could overpower him. Probably not.

'Tap in your code,' he demanded, holding the phone for her. She unlocked the device, and under his watchful eye quickly pulled up a Google map on the area. She wondered if she could try to snatch the phone back and send her dad a quick text. No, that would still take too long. And he could probably kill Lucy with his bare hands. She couldn't risk it.

'You're pretty smart with this thing, aintcha?' he said. It was then that Zoe realised that their kidnapper was probably worse with phones than most of the adults she knew. *Of course, he's been in prison, maybe for a long time.*

–

At the same time, less than forty miles away at Mount Browne in Guildford, in the monitoring room of Operation Whirlpool, technician Paul Horncastle had just started his shift. He was listening in on headphones to a phone conversation. DS Lytton had just walked in, and on the screen noticed the jerky moving signals on seven of the twelve listening devices, indicating conversation. He put his hand on Horncastle's shoulder, who slipped off the headphones to talk to his boss.

'Quite some activity today, Paul,' Lytton said.

'Ah, not as much as it looks,' Horncastle said. 'Hale is walking around with his cordless phone in the kitchen and the hall, and we're picking it up on four different bugs, with varying levels of volume and clarity.'

'Anything interesting?'

'Well, not really. It sounds like a genuine property client. It's all too relaxed and chummy.'

'What about this?' He pointed to a very active display.

'That's the Mercedes. The voice pattern matches Xalwo Hale. The cell tower trace indicates it's her mobile, and she's somewhere near Woking station. I did listen in for a while, but it seemed to be a heated conversation between her and someone at the school about her daughter's attendance.'

'And this?' Lytton pointed at the remaining trace.

'That's the Renault, currently being driven by the daughter somewhere near Heathrow, according to our track of her phone.'

'Okay, no point listening into that,' Lytton said, tapping his colleague on the back and exiting.

What none of them noticed was a red dot which appeared on the Renault bug trace and move gradually rightwards with the signal. It was followed by several other dots, yellow, more red and blues. By the time Horncastle had returned his attention to the screen, the dots – which indicated the software had detected conflict or anger vocalisations – had fallen off the back of the trace.

–

With the aid of the phone, now back in Tyler's possession, the Renault was soon on the approach road to the Premier Inn. 'Head to the car park out back, and go right to the far end,' he instructed Azalea. 'Should be a red VW saloon parked there.' It was a big car park, and the furthest edge was 300 yards from the hotel building. It took a while to find. He got her to park next to the red VW, then took the Renault's keys from the ignition and pocketed them.

'Stay there and keep your mouths shut,' Tyler said. He opened the passenger door, and made his way to the other car, always keeping his eyes on them.

'He doesn't have a gun,' Zoe hissed to Azalea. 'It was your phone in his pocket.'

'Are you sure?' she said.

'Why don't we just run?' Lucy asked, reaching for her door handle.

'Because he'd catch you for sure,' Azalea said, reaching behind to pull the young girl's arm away. 'It's too risky.'

Zoe glanced at Tyler, who had briefly crouched, reached under the VW and retrieved a metal box the size of a cigarette packet. He slid the lid from the box, pulled out car keys and hit a fob. Orange lights blinked. Tyler returned to the Renault, pulled open the rear driver-side door and said, 'Okay little one, you come with me.' He unclipped her seatbelt.

'I won't, you're horrible,' Lucy said.

Tyler grabbed her face hard, his gloved hand squeezing her jaw to muffle her cries, and lifted her out of the car. 'One move from you two, and I snap her neck like a twig, understand?' He placed Lucy on the tarmac. She refused to stand on her feet, and just sagged like a puppet. Tyler glanced anxiously towards the hotel, and Zoe followed his gaze. There was another car manoeuvring at the far end, right by the hotel. He rapidly bundled Lucy under one arm, with his other hand across her face, opened the boot of the VW.

'Oh my God, he's putting her inside,' Azalea said.

Tyler slammed the lid and was back sitting in the front seat of the Renault with a sports bag in his hand a few seconds later.

'What are you doing to her?' Zoe wailed.

'I'm teaching her a goddamn lesson.' He leaned forward to examine the contents of the bag, propping his sunglasses up over his baseball cap as he rummaged.

Only then did Zoe get a glance at his eyes. They were completely red and horrible, like they were bleeding. He put his sunglasses on before turning back to them. This time he had in his hand a black pistol. 'See this, ladies? It's real, and it's loaded. I've killed a lot of people in my life, and I mean a lot, so I ain't afraid to add to the total. Just so you understand.'

It was only then that Zoe knew she'd been right that he hadn't previously been armed. But he was so scary, so powerful that they had believed. They had totally believed. And now he really did have a gun.

'Okay now we're switching cars. And you're gonna move together, slowly, and sit in the same places. It's a stick shift, so Azalea, you can drive. Zoe, bring my luggage. Bring nothing else. I'll keep the phones. Any questions?'

'What about Lucy?' Zoe said, as she emerged from the car.

'I'll deal with the little bitch, don't you worry.'

Zoe could hear her sister's muffled screaming and pounding the inside of the boot. She opened the Renault's boot, and Socks immediately shot out and hid under a parked car. I wish we could do the same, she thought. Zoe wound her window down so the cat could get back in when it wanted.

Tyler escorted Zoe first, the gun in his pocket digging into her side as she pulled his suitcase around to the back of the VW. She sat inside, in the rear passenger side as he instructed. The car felt cold and damp, as if it been there for days. Azalea was manhandled into the driving seat. Finally, Tyler opened the boot and the car shook with a blow. When Lucy's screaming abruptly ended, Zoe's began. 'Leave her alone! Please, let us all go!'

Tyler brought Lucy in, sobbing quietly, and dumped her on the seat next to Zoe. She had a big red graze on the left side of her face, and was as white as a sheet. Zoe grasped her hand, and cooed into her ear, like her mother used to do when Zoe had nightmares. And this certainly was a nightmare.

Azalea was trembling, and her skin seemed almost as white as Lucy's.

'Where is Socks?' Lucy asked tearfully.

'He ran away,' Zoe whispered. 'He'll be fine.'

'But he'll be lonely and lost!'

Tyler laughed. 'Stop it, sugar, you're breaking my heart.' Once the luggage was stowed and they were all sitting down, he said, 'You two in the back, hold out your hands.'

They did so, and Tyler grasped Zoe's wrists in one hand, and then bound them tightly with a thin plastic cable tie. He did the same with Lucy's.

'Ow, you're hurting me,' Lucy wailed.

'So sue me.' He gestured for Azalea to start the car. It coughed, wheezed and died. 'Not so much gas, honey, you're flooding it.' Her second attempt was no better, and the quick glance she and Zoe exchanged in the driving mirror showed that it was deliberate. In the end he exited the car, made his way round to the driver's side and roughly hauled Azalea out. He then got in and started the car himself, revving it hard before getting out and pushing her back in. Zoe looked at Azalea's face in the driving mirror and understood. She watched her gradually release the handbrake and then shift the gear stick into first.

'Keep it idling, don't rev it too much,' Tyler instructed. He was making his way around the front of the car, gun in his right hand away from them. When he was halfway round, Azalea gunned the engine and dropped the clutch. The car leaped forward, and it was only an extraordinarily quick reaction that allowed Tyler to jump, then roll across the bonnet to the passenger side. Azalea had her foot to the floor but was turning hard left to avoid hitting the row of parked cars opposite. Tyler had lost sunglasses and baseball cap but had his left hand on the passenger door handle and tugged it open. Zoe was amazed how quickly he moved, and could see he was going to get into the car which was pivoting around him. He was already halfway in when Azalea slammed on the brakes. The sharp top corner of the passenger door smashed the side of Tyler's head. She revved and dropped the clutch again, but this time he was able to throw himself in. Cursing loudly, he overpowered her in a moment, as the car grazed the opposite row of vehicles and stalled. The ensuing struggle in the front was brief and one-sided. He had his gloved hands on her long slender throat. She emitted an unearthly gasping sound.

'Stop, you're choking her!' Zoe screamed.

'You shut your mouth!' Tyler bellowed at Zoe, before turning his attention back to Azalea. 'If I didn't need you to drive, honey, I would take your sweet ass every which way right here, then soak you in gasoline and set you ablaze. But I can wait an hour for some fun.' Tyler kept the gun on them as he recovered his cap and sunglasses.

Lucy was crying softly, and Zoe could see she had wet herself. She herself was trembling, and angrily wiped tears from her eyes. It was like a horror film. The man's face was scabby and scaly, and where he had hit his head, there was a bloody mark, a flap of skin dangling the size of a thumb. She thought about her mum in some boring meeting, with no clue what was going on here. Her dad would be sitting at home working on his websites, just when she needed him most. She recalled her schoolfriends, and her clarinet, and all the fun times she'd had in her short life, and tears squeezed into her eyes. Was it going to end like this? At the hands of some American murderer. Had anyone seen the cardboard sign, and phoned the number? There had to be something else she could do.

–

Horncastle slip off his headphones. It was half two, and he was bored rigid listening live to Jonathan Hale's long business phone call. It was clearly unsuspicious and would be recorded anyway. There was nothing from Xolwa's Mercedes now, but as he checked the Renault trace, it was recording an unusual signal. AI had marked it as non-human, so he listened in. It sounded just like a cat mewing, in some distress. There were no human sounds. He checked across to the cell tower trace from Azalea's phone, and compared it to the GPS in the bug in the car. The car was static, and her phone was moving, half a mile away. Maybe the cat had been left in there while she went shopping.

He yawned and stretched his arms. Time to get a coffee. That would break up the monotony a bit. He thought better of it when he saw through the glass door that Gillard was in the operations room. Best look busy. He checked back to the main dashboard which oversaw the entire multi-channel input. The input summary showed the Renault marked urgent for oversight. AI had flagged up indicators in tension (red), swearing (blue) and screams or shouts; female/child (yellow). Frowning a little, he opened the trace to desk mic, and running back to the start of the colour codes, clicked on the first red dot.

'You can't take my phone!' a girl wailed.

'The hell I can't,' replied an American male voice. 'I'll have yours too, sugar.'

'I don't have one. I'm much too young,' came a younger-still voice, English like her sister. 'Are you going to hurt us?'

He laughed, slowly. 'Do what I say, and you'll be fine. You've heard about Americans and guns, I guess? Well, mine is in my pocket…'

The sample ended. For a moment he was alarmed. But then none of the audible traces matched Azalea Hale. He listened to a couple of other samples which had been flagged. She was on none of them. He sat for a minute, then he clicked his fingers. Of course, the system had been fooled by this before. It was a known bug to mistake recorded voices for real ones. Azalea must be listening to an audiobook, perhaps a thriller.

2.45 p.m.

Jonathan Hale walked back from the kitchen to his home office and set the cordless phone back on its rest. The Dubai client was coming good. He could probably bill him for twenty hours on the legal work as well as the ninety-minute call. The money wouldn't come in for a while, but it would be welcome.

He turned to his PC, opened Google and did his usual search on Tyler and the prison he was being kept in.

As usual North Bluff State Correctional Facility's own website was returned as the top item, but today there was a news result above it, an Associated Press item entitled 'Prisoner escapes while in medical transit'. His heart skipped a beat as he pulled up the brief story, now three days old.

> PHOENIX (AP) – Authorities are searching for an inmate who escaped while under escort from a state prison in Arizona early Tuesday.
>
> The 47-year-old felon, who has not been named, was being taken from the high security North Bluff State Correctional Facility to another complex for a medical procedure, an official at the Arizona Department of Corrections, Rehabilitation and Re-entry said.
>
> The circumstances of the escape have not been confirmed as yet, the official said, and declined to confirm local reports that the vehicle in which he was traveling was involved in an accident.

Icy fingers slid down Hale's spine. How old was Tyler? His recollection was forty-four or forty-five, but that was a couple of years ago. He went into the Arizona Corrections Department public database, searched on Tyler's name and initial, then clicked on the correct mugshot from the list of three R. Tylers listed. He was always amazed how easily one could find details of who was imprisoned in the US. When he was in prison in New Jersey the press had a field day digging up his personal details to put in their reports.

Tyler's record gave height, weight, hair and eye colour, ethnicity and expected release date, but not age. At the end of the record was a date box entitled 'last movement' intended to record the date the felon was moved to the current facility. Instead, this box was marked: *updating*.

Something about Tyler's status had changed.

A fresh search found another news item published a few hours earlier in an Arizona local newspaper, mentioning that three people had been found dead at the site of a road accident near Black Canyon City. Hale pulled up Google Maps and found that Black Canyon City was just twenty miles west of North Bluff State prison. It all made sense.

He stood up and made his way to the kitchen. *Be calm.* First, you don't know that it is Tyler. Second, even if it is, he's a fugitive in some of the most inhospitable terrain in the world, and the authorities would do all they could to recapture him. Third, Tyler would surely have lots of scores to settle locally before considering the complexities of trying to get a passport to get to him. Fourth, Tyler didn't know where he lived and wouldn't have had the resources in prison to find out. That scaffolding of logic lasted only a few seconds, before collapsing under the weight of his anxiety. Hale found his tablets, the ones he only took on his worst days. He swallowed one and gulped down some water.

The clock showed 2.55 p.m. Azalea should be back by now, with this American girl who was coming to stay. Strange. He picked up the kitchen phone and rang her mobile. It rang and rang, and then went to a message. He then rang Xolwa, who was in London with a friend, to have afternoon tea at the Ritz. 'Azalea called in sick, you know. She didn't have permission for this absence.'

'I saw her leave but had assumed she had permission,' Hale said.

'No, the form tutor rang me. I've left a couple of messages on her phone. She's probably driving. By the way. Azalea found my bag behind a sofa.'

'Your bag?'

'You, know, the white Birkin—'

'Glad to hear it. Look, Xolwa, there's one other thing...' Hale hesitated over whether or not to share his discovery that someone had escaped from Tyler's prison.

'—I've got to go, Jon, we've finally been called to our table. See you later. Bye!' She hung up.

--

Oliver Barnes was on his mobile in preparation for the Zoom call, so didn't pay attention to the ringing landline. Most calls on it these days were cold callers, and they never left messages. When he'd finished his work call, he just had time to prepare the slides for the new website review before the Zoom began. In his rush, he didn't think to go and listen to the message. If he had he would have heard:

'Oh hi, my name's Shelley. Look, this is probably nothing, but I've just seen a message about a kidnap scrawled on a piece of cardboard in the back of a Renault Megane.' She read out the registration number. 'It gave this phone number. I mean I hope it's not a joke or something. I saw two kids in the back, the older one holding the card against the window. Look, I just felt it was something I needed to do.'

She read out a mobile number to call her back on.

--

While Hale was speaking to his wife, the red VW was on the A40 heading for central London. Zoe looked out of the window, at all the other vehicles heading past, all those people with normal, safe, happy lives who had no idea what was happening in this car. Tyler had given Azalea directions and had looked up the postcode of the place he wanted to go on Zoe's phone. The phone had rung a couple of times, but Tyler let it go to voicemail.

'The place we're heading, ladies, is a piece of real estate that I own. They reckon it's been taken off me, but I have other opinions. I wanted to see what it looked like for real.'

'What's real estate?' Lucy whispered to her sister.

'House or property,' Zoe answered.

'That's right. I paid over thirty million bucks just for this one, and the British government took it for the DOJ. How is it they get to take all my money?'

'Isn't that the money you stole?' Lucy asked.

Tyler twisted in his seat to look at her. 'Honey, I never stole a dime. I was simply a businessman, providing the US consumer with something they were willing to buy. They were more than happy to pay the price I was asking. Whether they snorted it or not wasn't my business.'

'Drugs are illegal,' Lucy said.

'Let me tell you the golden rule of commerce, honey. The law has no business standing between a willing seller and a willing buyer. They will always fail. The best they can achieve is to jack the price up a bunch.'

Tyler was navigating, using Zoe's phone, and told Azalea to take the next turning, a slip road which rose to a roundabout jammed with traffic. They were immediately stuck in a queue. Tyler shifted the gun to his left hand and concealed the barrel under his right armpit, still pointing at Azalea.

'Okay, easy does it,' he said as they eased out into traffic, moving at a walking pace. He turned to look over his right shoulder at the two girls. 'Keep real cool, ladies. Heads lowered, eyes down.'

There were traffic cameras everywhere, and Tyler squinted up at them. 'Too much damn government in this country,' he muttered. 'Cops looking over your shoulder everywhere.'

'Can you let us go, please,' Lucy said. 'We won't tell anybody, honestly.'

'Sure you won't.'

Zoe turned to Lucy. 'We can't leave Azalea to face this on her own.' She offered her tied hands to her sister to hold in her own. 'We've got to be brave for a bit longer.'

'That's it, a bit of Dunkirk spirit,' Tyler said doing a terrible impersonation of a British accent. For some reason his mood seem to be improving. 'My mom was English. When I was seven, she brought me and my brother over to London. I guess we met a whole heap of relatives, but I don't remember that. I remember seeing the changing of the guard at Buckingham Palace. We went to that waxworks place...'

'Madame Tussauds,' Lucy interjected.

'Right. And we saw the jewels at the Tower of London. I thought it was really cool.'

'Did your mother die?' Zoe asked. She had decided it would be a good idea to be sympathetic and lull their captor into a false sense of security.

'Yeah, she did, when I was your age. She's buried in Highgate Cemetery in London. I'd like to go see her.'

'Was it cancer?' Lucy asked, having picked up on the new enquiring tone of Zoe's.

'No.' Tyler looked out of the side window.

'What was it then?' Lucy persisted. Zoe shook her head at her. *Don't keep prodding.*

He didn't answer. Zoe looked out of her window, and saw that Tyler was staring at a police car, parked at the roadside. A male officer was talking to a dark man with dreadlocks, while a female officer was taking notes. Tyler slid the gun inside his jacket, out of view. Zoe stared at the cop, trying to beam thoughts directly into his head. She wished she had her sign to hold to the window. Unable to think of a way of concealing it, she had left in on the back shelf of the Renault, innocent side upwards.

They finally slid past the patrol car, and Tyler seemed to relax a bit. 'Couldn't believe it when I heard that English cops don't carry. Is it true?'

'Some of them are armed,' Azalea said. It was a first sound she had uttered for some time.

'Crazy toytown country,' he said. 'My mom always wanted to come back and live here. She thought the weather would be good for me.'

'Does the rain stop your skin burning?' Lucy asked.

'It's the cloud cover. Lower UV. Not like Phoenix, where my pop lived. That's where I was stuck. For a long time.'

'Were you sad when your mum died?' Lucy asked.

'Sugar, I couldn't believe it. She was killed over here on a trip to visit her sister. In a hit-and-run. They never caught the guy. London cops never even tried.'

'That's terrible,' Zoe said.

'It's life. You never get a break when you need one. That's what my pop said, before he started on the bottle.'

'We could go to Highgate Cemetery,' Azalea said. Zoe glanced over and saw that the fuel gauge was only a quarter full.

'We ain't got time.' He sighed, then slapped the dashboard in anger. 'Goddamn Mickey Mouse country. Why don't they build some proper roads? There's enough traffic on this little alleyway for a freeway.'

'It's a typical Friday afternoon in London,' Azalea said. 'And there's roadworks. If it wasn't a pandemic, it would be even worse.'

Zoe could see that they were amongst some big posh houses, with grand old frontages protected by spiky railings. There were pedestrians walking briskly and quite a few cyclists making their way along the edge of the road. At a red traffic light one of them, a young guy with a delivery satchel, came up on the inside, right next to Tyler. Zoe hoped he would turn a look at them, and maybe spot the gun. She was practising mouthing the word 'help', but even before the lights changed the man had wriggled his bike through a gap to the front of the queue and ridden off.

'Has your brother got funny skin too?' Lucy asked.

'Wasn't born with it like me. Maybe he has now.' Tyler laughed. 'He died in a car crash a few years ago.'

'Is there any cure?' Lucy asked. 'Or will you always be ugly?'

Zoe glared at her sister, trying with her eyes to get across the fact that this wasn't some family friend who thought her bluntness was appealing. This was a man who by his own admission had killed repeatedly.

'Ain't never been pretty like you, that's for sure.'

Zoe was astounded that Lucy was getting away with this, and was convinced that at some stage her luck would run out.

After passing the roadworks, traffic eased and after twenty more minutes and a couple more turnings, Tyler looked at the map on the phone and announced, 'This is the road. Up here on the left.' It was a grand street, dominated by a very large double-fronted building, set well back behind iron railings amongst neglected gardens. The ground floor had eleven sets of floor-to-ceiling windows, a couple of which had been boarded up. A wide flight of stone steps ran up to the enormous sandstone portico, held up by Greek-style stone columns. Padlocked wrought iron gates guarded a driveway on the left between the house and its neighbour, disappearing into overgrown buddleia around the back of the property.

'Is this a museum?' Lucy asked. 'It's too big for a house.'

'Honey, the whole goddamn country is a museum. No, this is Imperial Hanover House, I bought it and I'm going to take possession right now.' He turned off Zoe's phone and pocketed it.

'We shouldn't leave the car here,' Azalea said. 'This is residents' parking.'

'I am a motherfucking resident. For the price I paid I can park where the hell I want.'

'It's just that you might get clamped,' Azalea said.

Tyler paid no attention. He was shuffling papers on his lap, ones that had come from the blue bag. They looked to be estate agent listings. Finally satisfied with what he'd seen, he turned his head towards the back.

'Okay ladies, showtime.'

-

Tyler took the car keys from the ignition, then bound Azalea's wrists with a cable tie. 'No one says a word until I say otherwise, okay?' He climbed out of the car, gun concealed in his raincoat pocket but still pointing towards Azalea. He made his way round the back of the car, until he was by the rear driver-side door, which he opened. He disengaged the seatbelt around Lucy and pulled her from the car.

'No, not her, take me instead,' Zoe called.

'Sugar, save the heroics, you're *all* coming with me. But the little one is my insurance for now.' Tyler took Lucy, and checking the street was empty of pedestrians, led her to the boot, which he opened. He brought out a small toolkit wrapped in a dirty cloth. 'Stick your arms out. Good. Now hold that for me.' The tools were balanced on her bound arms, but from a distance it just looked like she was carrying it. Tyler led her to the driveway gates.

'What can we do?' Zoe asked Azalea.

'There are passers-by, but if we talk to them he might shoot Lucy,' Azalea replied.

'Do you think he will release us, like he promised?' Zoe asked.

'I don't think so. I've been thinking about it. I think he'll use us as hostages to get my dad to come in here. He'll definitely kill him and maybe us too. I just don't know what to do.'

Zoe heard a metal squeak and turned to look. Tyler was easing the driveway gates open. He shepherded Lucy back to the car and dumped her on her seat. He then climbed back in the front passenger seat, passed the car keys to Azalea and used a pocketknife to slit the cable ties on her arms. 'Right, I need you to drive in and around the back.'

'I'm not very good at reversing,' she said, rubbing her wrists.

'Jesus H. Christ! Reverse the car in the street and drive in nose first. Do it, now.' He slapped the dashboard.

Azalea reversed against the traffic, until there was room to turn left into the driveway. The car rumbled down the driveway, until it disappeared into the shadows under the buddleias. It emerged at the rear of the house in a moss-covered parking area, the size of a tennis court and deep in the shadow of a huge sycamore. There were no other vehicles, just several wheelie bins and a four-wheeled commercial waste bin against an eight-foot-high high wooden fence, overgrown with ivy, which enclosed the yard. Above that protruded another six feet of shaggy leylandii hedge. The arching boughs of the sycamore almost reached the back of the house. Zoe looked around her, at this gloomy forgotten space overlooked by no one. If things were terrible in the car before, they were worse now.

Chapter Twenty-four

Gillard emerged from a first-floor CID conference room at 3.10 p.m. with a smile on his face and in urgent need of a proper non-machine coffee. He'd just finished a lengthy Zoom conference call with the Crown Prosecution Service over the Esher burglaries. Kieran Coughlan had, after interrogation, confessed not only to the break-ins he was investigating, but to nineteen others in Sussex and Kent over a three-year period. The crucial leverage Gillard had applied was the discovery in Coughlan's possessions of a distinctive item of jewellery, notified as having been stolen in Esher. With that and the evidence of the movements of his van captured on ANPR matching the pattern and timing of the burglaries, he owned up quickly. Gillard was relieved, because the ANPR and CCTV evidence that he'd used to browbeat Coughlan with during interview was in no way legally overwhelming. The CPS had just confirmed that to him, while simultaneously congratulating him on a job well done. He was expecting thanks too from his colleagues in Kent and Sussex for helping them to improve their burglary clear-up rate.

After a quick run down to the canteen for a big frothy cappuccino, Gillard returned to his desk, checked for messages, and then headed upstairs to see how the Hale surveillance was going. He took the stairs two at a time, daring to hope that if Operation Whirlpool had nothing to report, he might even be able to slip away on time for the weekend.

From a first glance through the glass door it was clearly not a hive of activity. Quite the reverse. He punched in the door code and stepped inside.

'Hello, sir,' said one of the female call handlers, looking up from what appeared to be a little web shopping.

'Any sign of Colin Williams?' Gillard asked her.

'No, he went off duty at three.'

'DS Lytton?'

'He should be around somewhere.'

Yes, he should be, Gillard thought. He could see technician John Horncastle in the monitoring room, feet up on the desk, reading something. When Gillard burst in, he jumped, dropping the leaflet onto the desk, and returning his feet to the floor.

'Gone quiet, has it?' Gillard asked, picking up the reading matter. It was a technical handbook for the monitoring system.

'Yes. Jonathan Hale is still at home, and from his conversations seemingly undertaking legitimate business.'

Gillard nodded. 'Any fresh web activity?'

'It's hard to distinguish legitimate and illegitimate activity, as they both centre around company formation in overseas territories. We're logging every corporate name that he refers to, and DS Lytton is trying to construct the relationships between these new companies, now that we can copy every file that he updates to the cloud. He's copying in ACC Anderson, as she had asked.'

'Excellent work. Where is Lytton?'

'As it was so quiet, he's gone to collect his son from school. His wife's car is off the road.'

'And will he be returning to finish his shift?'

Horncastle hesitated. 'I assume so, sir.'

'This place is beginning to resemble a holiday camp,' Gillard muttered. All these officers, who he could put to good use downstairs, were sitting up here wasting time.

Horncastle cleared his throat and turned back to his terminal. 'Hale is still searching on the web for Tyler and his jail on a regular basis. Apart from that I've got a list of the websites here, and the search terms used.' Horncastle pulled up a document.

'What's all this?' Gillard pointed to the summary dashboard, with its listing of red, blue and yellow dots.

Horncastle chuckled. 'Yes, it had me fooled for a minute. The daughter is out in the Renault Megane, apparently listening to some thriller or radio play. The system has registered the dialogue as if it's live speech. It's a known shortcoming. When we get release three of the software it should be better.'

'And this?' He pointed to a file showing new data. It was marked as unread since 10.58 a.m.

'That's just the household landline answer machine. Hale's got a separate landline for his own office.'

'And according to this, the messages haven't been picked up by the recipient either?' Gillard said, pointing at the screen.

'No. It's normally for Mrs Hale, or the daughter, and usually from the school or the shop where Mrs Hale works. There won't be anything of interest on there.'

'Indulge me.'

Horncastle switched on the desk speaker, selected the file and hit play. The first few messages were indeed from the school, asking to speak to Mrs Hale about Azalea's non-attendance. Then one from Oliver Barnes, asking if his daughters were there. It went on: 'Xolwa, I've just had a very odd phone message. It's probably nothing, but if you could give me a quick ring before three, that would be great.'

Gillard flicked through the duty clipboard, on which the movements of the Hale household were recorded. 'So, just to summarise: Hale is at home, his wife is in London in the Mercedes, and his daughter is in the Renault?'

'She's not in the car now. The last phone track we have for her is around Heathrow. The vehicle trace shows it's parked near a Heathrow hotel. She may no longer be in the car, but there is a cat there.'

'A cat?'

'Yes.' He highlighted the appropriate channel and hit play. For a while there was nothing, then the mewing of a cat could be heard. It stopped for a few seconds, then resumed again.

'The girl went to Heathrow to pick up a friend coming in from America.'

Something about this was nagging at Gillard. 'It all feels odd to me.'

'Look, sir, from conversations in the target house, we know a bit about the visiting girl.' Horncastle's tone betrayed a sense of impatience. 'She is fifteen, a top-notch clarinet player who might play in the school orchestra at St Cuthbert's. I take it you're not suggesting that she might be our unknown money laundering contact?'

'No, of course not. But we've got three girls, all of whom should be at school, seemingly absent simultaneously, and possibly together.'

'Well, I suppose we can check that,' Horncastle said, with an exasperated sigh. He clicked on the Renault's audio trace, dragged the slider back to the beginning, and directed it through the desk speaker. 'This trace begins from the first human sounds that were detected in the car today.'

> *Can I bring Socks? Can I bring Socks?*
> *No, you idiot.*
> *Please, he wants to come.*
> *All right, you can bring him if you like.*

'I recognise the two younger voices,' Gillard said. 'Lucy and Zoe Barnes, neighbours of the Hales.'

'Azalea was the last one to speak,' Horncastle said. He looked up at Gillard and his face changed shape. 'Oh Christ, oh no, oh no, what have I done?' His fingers flashed over the console too fast for Gillard to keep up with it. He adjusted the slider to bring up the conversation that had been flagged up by the system with the coloured dots. Over the desk speaker came an alarming exchange.

> '*You can't take my phone!*' a girl wailed.
> '*The hell I can't,*' replied an American male voice. '*I'll have yours too, sugar.*'
> '*I don't have one. I'm much too young,*' came a younger-still voice, English like her sister. '*Are you going to hurt us?*'
> He laughed, slowly. '*Do what I say, and you'll be fine. You've heard about Americans and guns, I guess? Well, mine is in my pocket and it's pointing at Azalea here. So just stay calm, keep quiet, breathe nice and slow and we'll all be just dandy.*'

'Hells bells!' Gillard exclaimed. 'Is there any visual in the car?'

'No, it was too risky. Even a tiny lens in the rear-view mirror mounting would be too obtrusive. Besides, they're not in this vehicle anymore.'

The audio recording was continuing, relaying a lot of background vehicle noise, and a rhythmic thump-thump echoing in the car. 'That's a multi-storey, probably Heathrow,' Gillard said. 'Ramps and drain covers. It's quite distinctive.'

Horncastle squinted at the time counter. 'At this point, the recording is more than two hours ago.'

'Right. Drop everything else. Find out where they are right now.' Gillard opened the door to the control room, and yelled across to the phone operator, who seemed to be packing her bag, ready to go home.

'Get me the emergency dispatcher, we've got an abduction.'

She jumped to it and put her headset back on. 'To the target house in Esher, sir?'

'No, not there. It's probably Met police. I'll get you a location ASAP, but I need the dispatcher on the line waiting. The next thing is I need all hands on deck here.'

'Righto, sir. I'll do an all-units alert.'

'Where the *hell* is Lytton?' Gillard asked.

'I don't know.'

'Call him, and Colin Williams.'

'He's off shift, sir.'

'I don't care, haul him back in ASAP. I need bums on seats and I need them fast.'

'Yes, sir.' The operator was already busy punching out numbers. Gillard took his personal mobile out, selected last call and hit dial. Sam. She'd be on evening duty in the Surrey control room a hundred yards away. He hoped to get her before she turned her personal mobile off in line with operational rules.

Horncastle called for Gillard's attention. 'Last location of Azalea Hale's phone was almost two hours ago, at Heathrow.'

Gillard had Sam on the line. 'Hold for a second, Sam.' He muted the phone, and called across to Rob Townsend, who had just come back into the office. 'Rob, we need to get an urgent trace on Zoe Barnes' phone.'

'Who?'

Gillard gave a brief summary of the abduction. 'Her phone should be one of those appearing on the mini cell site outside Hale's home, and will also have been at Heathrow at one p.m. today. Get me a list of all the phones which appear at both locations.'

'I'm onto it,' Townsend said, sitting at a terminal. Gillard, meanwhile, turned back to Sam.

'What's the matter, Craig? The switchboard's gone crazy here.'

'Do me a favour – this will be better coming from you. Ring Oliver Barnes and ask if he has had any contact from his daughters this afternoon. I need their mobile numbers.'

'Oh God, what's happened?'

'They've been abducted. Ask him about a phone message he had this afternoon.'

'What message?'

'I haven't heard it myself. Oliver Barnes left a message on Jonathan Hale's answerphone referring to it and I need to know what was said. Maybe it was the abductor making contact. Oh, and once you've made the call can you dispatch a family liaison officer in plain clothes to the Barnes household.'

'Yes of course. *Love you*,' she whispered at the end before hanging up, leaving him no time to respond. It seemed every phone in the Operation Whirlpool control room was ringing at once. The female operator had now been joined by a younger colleague, and they were busy dealing with calls.

'Sir, assistant chief constable, line three,' said the new girl, looking to Gillard.

'Tell her I'll call her back in a minute.' He knew that might cause him problems down the line but he had things he needed to do first. He sat at the nearest available desk just outside the monitoring room, and pulled up Google. He then searched on Richard Tyler, and hit news.

It was the first item. He skimmed through it, right to the background on the felon. Gillard swore under his breath and let his head fall into his hands. 'Pray God it's not him.'

Chapter Twenty-five

At exactly the same time Jonathan Hale, sitting in his home office, had found the same story.

PHOENIX (AP) – An inmate on the run from an Arizona state prison after killing two correctional officers and a civilian driver was late Thursday named as Richard E. Tyler. The Arizona Department of Corrections, Rehabilitation and Re-entry said that prisoner, 47, was being taken from the high security North Bluff State Correctional Facility to another complex for a medical procedure when the vehicle he was in left the road in what was initially thought to be a road accident.

Yavapai County Sheriff Dewey Donaldson yesterday morning confirmed earlier reports that bullet wounds had been found in each of the bodies found at the scene. 'We believe this was a planned ambush with another vehicle involved,' he said. 'We urge the good people of this community to be vigilant, keep their homes locked and not to approach Tyler, who should be considered armed and dangerous.'

Tyler was one of the three conspirators behind the L3 cocaine smuggling syndicate and was two years ago incarcerated for 130 years for multiple homicides, rape, and wire fraud. The trial hinged on British co-conspirator and money launderer Jonathan Hale, who turned state's evidence in exchange for a lighter sentence. Since incarceration, Tyler was involved in the 2019 slaying of North Bluff facility psychiatrist Kelly Ann Siley. After trial, his sentence was doubled to 260 years in lieu of execution.

A correctional official told the Associated Press that the fugitive has a distinctive scaly skin, caused by a sensitivity to sunlight, which makes him easy to recognise. Anyone who sees him should call the following number toll-free. 1-800-FUGITIVE.

Hale leaped up from the desk, and grabbed his phone. He was just about to ring Xolwa when he heard the distinctive note of her Mercedes parking at the front. He looked out of the window and rushed out to meet her.

'What is it?' she asked, seeing her distraught husband standing on the front doorstep.

'He's escaped.'

'Tyler?'

'Yes! Yes, yes!' Hale hissed. 'On Tuesday. Three bloody days ago. My God, what are we going to do?' He took his wife by the shoulders 'Is Azalea with you? She's not been returning my calls.'

'I thought she would be with you by now, with her American friend Tiffany. She went to Heathrow hours ago.'

Hale looked like he was going to faint, and put his hand up over his heart.

'Now, Jon, just hold on a minute,' she said, embracing him. 'Two and two doesn't make twenty. There certainly isn't any need to panic. Richard Tyler is almost certainly just skulking around in the Arizona desert hoping to avoid the helicopters. Azalea went to Heathrow with the two girls from next door to collect a fifteen-year-old American clarinet prodigy. I've seen her video. She is real. I mean, can Tyler even play the clarinet?'

'So why haven't we heard from her?'

'Maybe her phone's run out of credit, it's happened before. I'm sure I've got Zoe's mobile number somewhere. I'll ring her.'

Hale nodded, with his eyes closed. 'Yes, of course. She's pretty sensible.'

'Don't you think you should take one of the pink ones?'

'I've already taken one.'

'Maybe take another?'

'No, it'll zonk me out.'

Hale watched his wife swiping through records on her own phone. 'There it is. Zoe Barnes.' She rang but it went to voicemail, which turned out to be full. She then looked at the kitchen cordless, sitting in its charging base. 'Did you listen to the message?' she asked him.

Hale shook his head and reached for the play button. Before he got there, the phone rang. He saw it was from the Barnes family landline. He snatched it up 'Oliver?'

'Are Zoe or Lucy there with you?' Oliver asked, breathlessly.

'No, nor Azalea.'

He heard Oliver sob down the phone. 'I just had a call from the police. They think all three girls have been abducted.'

'Is it him?' Hale asked.

'Sorry, what?'

'Is it Richard Tyler?'

'They didn't say, but there is apparently a family liaison officer coming over. I've rung Jenny, she'll be home in a few minutes. Would you like to come over?'

Hale gasped. 'It's me he's after, Oliver. I just hope he's done nothing to Azalea.' His voice cracked when he said her name.

–

When the vehicle came to a halt at the rear of the building, Tyler took the car keys and pocketed them. He bound Azalea's wrists with cable ties, then leaned into the back of the car. He had his sunglasses propped over his baseball cap, and his red protruding eyes looked at each of them in turn. 'Time you all got fresh face masks.' He had in his hand a box of pale blue surgical masks, thoughtfully provided by the IRA man. He hadn't been wearing his since he got into the car, and it now dangled around his neck.

'Will you please let us go?' Lucy asked. 'You said you would.'

'So I lied. That's how you grow up, sugar. Gradually, you discover that there ain't no Santa Claus, that your parents lie, adults lie, and of course politicians and businessmen lie. Once you accept that, you're an adult.'

212

Zoe stared at this cynical man, a monstrous physical embodiment of his own bleak philosophy. He was right, in a way. She didn't feel like a child any more. When she thought back to her own bedroom, the toys and dolls she used to play with, the soft toys she had in infancy, it felt like centuries ago. She was responsible now not just for her own immediate survival but that of her younger sister. She fought against tears. Resolve, that's the word that was always used in school assemblies. I need to show resolve, she thought. And a cool head. She blinked away tears.

'A policeman we know is going to come and rescue us,' Lucy said.

'Is that so?' Tyler chuckled.

'A famous detective called Craig Gillard. He knows our mum and dad. He rescued his own wife when she was kidnapped.'

'And being a Brit, just armed with a nightstick and a stiff upper lip, I guess. Quite the hero. Now, open your mouth,' Tyler said to Lucy. 'I got a candy for you.'

'No.'

'Goddamn brat.' His gloved hand snaked out and pinched her nose. She squealed, trying to wriggle back away from him. Zoe leaned back, and kicked back at him, hitting him in the side of the head with her training shoe. The box of masks fell to the floor.

His backhanded slap was so powerful it knocked Zoe's head against the window. When she opened her eyes again, she was staring down the barrel of the gun. 'You wanna play hardball? That suits me just fine.' He cocked the gun with a loud click and held it against Lucy's head. 'You,' he said to Zoe. 'Scrunch up one of the face masks and put it in your mouth. Then do the same for your sister.' Tyler lifted the box of masks where Zoe could reach it. She did exactly as she was told, manoeuvring her bound wrists from the box to Lucy's mouth.

'Now lift your own face mask back up, over your mouth.'

With difficulty, Zoe slid the mask up and got it as far as her chin. Tyler lifted it the rest of the way with his free hand, the gun still pointing at Lucy's head. He lifted Lucy's mask over her nose and mouth, then went through the same process with Azalea, gagging her with a balled up face mask, and holding it in place with a second. He went round the girls in turn, twisting the ear loops to make the face masks tighter.

'Gee, isn't it nice and quiet now?' he said. Zoe watched as he clambered out of the car, and took a careful look around at the surroundings. Finally satisfied, he opened each of the car doors, and told the girls to get out. With bound wrists, it was a slow process. Zoe looked at her sister, whose eyes were brimming with tears, and was making a grizzling sound behind her mask. The poor kid was terrified. Her own cheek, bruised by the slap, was throbbing.

Tyler led them to a set of steps leading down to a basement level and a rear door, which was padlocked. With his toolkit, it was the work of less than a minute for him to prise off the hasp to which the padlock was attached from the door frame. A further few seconds work with a hammer and chisel, and the door relented.

'Welcome to my abode,' Tyler said, as he showed them into a dark musty corridor, with several doors leading off it on either side. He flicked a light switch and seemed to be surprised when a series of old-fashioned bare bulbs lit up dimly. 'Nice. Someone must be paying the bills,' he said. He beckoned with the gun for them to move ahead of him, which they did.

'I bought this place a couple of years ago, with the help of your weasel father, Azalea. Can you believe it cost me thirty million dollars? Jesus. He told me it could only go up in value. I kinda find that hard to believe,' he said, sliding a gloved finger along a picture rail, then examining it for dust.

He shepherded the girls up a flight of steps ending in a large wood panelled door. There was a big heavy fire extinguisher hung on the wall on either side, and various plasticised notices about how to use them. Tyler edged past them to open the squeaky door, which led out into a gloomy black-and-white tiled area in which their footsteps echoed. He found another switch, and they were suddenly bathed in the warm glow of a chandelier high above them. They were at the circular base of an ornate double staircase, with a curved stone balustrade that ascended to a vaulted ceiling at least three floors above them.

'Hey, that's more like it,' Tyler said. 'This is how I remember it from the brochure. There should be a ballroom over here.' He led the girls to a double door, turned the handle and led them inside. The room was huge, the size of a badminton court, with enormous floor-to-ceiling windows, curtained against the daylight. Tyler drew aside one curtain. Scattered motes waltzed in the sunbeams, above the puddles of light on the hardwood floor. There was dust-sheeted furniture left and right, around a large stone fireplace. Right in the middle on a wooden dais was a grand piano.

'Nice,' said Tyler, caressing it. 'Real nice.' He turned to the three bound and gagged girls. 'You know this place used to be the residence of some highfalutin European royals, kicked out of their own country, living the high life here in London.' He walked towards the fireplace and tore off several of the dust sheets. 'Come sit over here, make yourself comfortable.' Impersonating an English accent, he continued: 'Afternoon tea will be served by the butler, or maybe not.' He laughed to himself.

Shepherded at pistol point, the girls arranged themselves on a large settee, Lucy in the middle. Tyler then used cable ties to connect Zoe's right ankle to her sister's left, and Lucy's right to Azalea's left. 'Don't go away,' he said. They heard his footsteps disappear behind them out of the ballroom.

The moment he was gone, Lucy lifted her bound wrists, and over the course of the next minute pulled down her mask and plucked out the gag. 'We've got to do something,' she whispered. She had barely finished speaking before they heard footsteps approaching. Lucy pulled up her mask and sat on the expelled gag.

Tyler came back into the room pulling his wheeled suitcase and carrying the blue sports bag in his other hand. He glanced quickly at the girls, and then disappeared again, with the sound this time of ascending footsteps on the grand staircase. Lucy helped Zoe lower her mask enough to pull out the gag, and then turned the other way to do the same for Azalea. They then replaced their masks. A minute later Tyler returned again. He had ditched the raincoat, and now was wearing a black padded vest over a sweatshirt.

'Pure one hundred per cent Kevlar, don't you think it suits me?' He folded down the flap which covered his hips and groin. 'Stops bullets or your money back. I guess not too many folks get the chance to get a refund.' He chuckled. 'Right, ladies. Seems there's no hot water, so my plan to take a nice long soapy bath with Azalea here will have to wait. Shame.'

Zoe heard Azalea groan and in her peripheral vision could see she was trembling.

'I was hoping to tell her father all about it, but maybe I should just call him up anyhow.' He knelt down in front of Azalea, pulled her mask down and said: 'Hey, what happened to the gag?'

'I swallowed it,' she lied. 'I was choking.'

Zoe was expecting Tyler to hit Azalea for this, but he merely laughed. 'Well, I reckon you'll be just fine for some of the other stuff I'm going to get you to do.'

'Just let us go, we won't say anything,' Azalea murmured. The other two girls nodded their heads in vigorous agreement.

'No can do.'

'You promised.' This was Lucy from behind her mask.

'Jesus, you too?' He pulled down her mask and confirmed the gag was gone. He took out a wicked-looking knife from a pocket in the vest, cut Lucy's wrist bonds, turned her over and with fresh cable ties bound her hands behind her back instead of in front. He did the same with Zoe. He found the gags they had spat out, then pushed them back into their mouths. This time he twisted the face mask loops so tightly that their ears hurt. Then he pulled Azalea to her feet, cut the ties that connected her legs to Lucy's, removed her gag and retrieved her mobile from his pocket.

'Time to phone your weasel father,' he said. Tyler turned on the device, then took out the gun and pointed it at Lucy's head. 'All right, listen up. This, word perfect, is what you're gonna say.'

Chapter Twenty-six

It took fifteen minutes to bring the Operation Whirlpool control room up to ten officers. Five NCA officers including a contrite DS Lewis Lytton, three phone operators and two monitoring technicians. Gillard was just briefing them on the latest developments when he was interrupted by the arrival of Assistant Chief Constable Stella Anderson.

She said nothing but was looking daggers at him. He hadn't returned any of her five calls.

'All right everybody, here's where we are,' Gillard said. 'We're suspending Operation Whirlpool, but devoting the unique resources we have trying to track down the three abducted young women: Azalea Hale, seventeen, Zoe Barnes, fifteen, and her eight-year-old sister Lucy. We don't know where they are, but we have pointers. We have Azalea's car, apparently abandoned in the car park at the Premier Inn Heathrow, with the Barnes family cat inside.'

There was some murmuring amongst the officers.

'Yes, you heard me right. A cat. Anyway, Met Police CSI is on the spot, and we're hoping for some fingerprints and DNA evidence which could point us in the direction of the abductor. There is also an armed response unit, and an experienced siege negotiator on standby, when we know exactly where to send them. We've just got a trace from Zoe's phone, last triangulated to Marloes Road, Kensington. As it wasn't one of the tagged devices, there's a twenty-minute lag. The speed of cell-site handoff shows it was a moving vehicle and we cannot be sure this was the final destination. Azalea's phone has been off since Heathrow. We have, however, located the phone that Zoe was calling, one that she thought belonged to her American friend Tiffany Dolan. We believe that this phone belongs to the abductor, but is also off now.'

'And we don't know who he is?' asked one of the NCA detectives.

'Well, we know who Jonathan Hale thinks he is. Richard E. Tyler, who three days ago escaped from North Bluff State Correctional Facility in Arizona. Thanks to our listening devices in Hale's home, we are getting some measure of the terror that has gripped our former money launderer. For those of you who didn't attend Joe Kyrios' presentation, I've saved a quick web search to the system, on Tyler's background history and character. It's pretty grim reading.'

One of the three call handlers was busy on an incoming call, and now looked up. 'Sir, if I can interrupt. I just had a message back from the US Department of Homeland Security. They confirm that Richard Tyler's passport is in the possession of the authorities, that no flight manifest from any airline leaving the US in the last week had anyone by that name aboard, and the biometrics confirm it.'

'All right, so we keep an open mind…' Gillard said.

'One more thing. No one by the name Tiffany Dolan was on any flight from the US to Britain either.'

Stella Anderson spoke. 'Has anyone told Jonathan Hale that his daughter is missing?'

'He heard from Oliver Barnes,' Gillard replied. 'We overheard that call. A family liaison officer is already at the Barnes household.'

'It's very important, DCI Gillard, that at no point is Hale made aware of how exactly we know so much about what he has said and what he's done. While this may yet turn out to be a tragedy, we do not want to blow the cover of the surveillance operation. It is understood?'

'Yes, ma'am.' He paused and then asked: 'There is one crucial thing you can do for us, ma'am. I understand you were on the operation which seized the properties which Richard Tyler acquired in London. We need the addresses.'

'Why? Most of them have been sold now, or are in the possession of the Crown.'

'Look, if it is Tyler, we are trying to figure out where he would take hostages. Our counterparts in the Department of Justice claim that Tyler hadn't ever left the US, at least as an adult. Given that we're struggling to identify any UK-based contacts, we have to assume he is on his own, a stranger in a strange land. Where would you go? To me it would be somewhere defensible, where he knows the layout, in case there is a siege. When Hale went to visit him in the US, he would probably have taken estate agent listings for the property he'd bought.'

She nodded. 'I see what you're driving at, Craig. I'll get someone onto it.'

–

Jonathan and Xolwa Hale were standing in Oliver Barnes' living room with police family liaison officer Gabby Underwood. She had tried to be as reassuring as she could but had very little information to give.

'Where are they being taken?' Xolwa asked.

'We don't know yet,' she replied. 'As soon as I have any information—'

'He wants me, you know,' Hale said. 'He is using the girls to get to me.'

'Who?' she asked.

'Richard bloody Tyler, who do you think?' Hale said, rolling his eyes at Oliver, who shook his head in sympathy. Gabby had only been rapidly briefed a couple of minutes before arriving. She knew that it was often police practice to keep the family liaison officer in the dark so that family members could not extract information that they shouldn't hear. But in this case, she felt particularly ignorant, and foolish with it. You can't reassure if you know less than everybody else.

Jenny Barnes, whose car had arrived a minute ago, burst into the room, and flung herself into her husband's arms. 'I can't believe this has happened,' she sobbed. 'I was called out of a meeting and came as fast as I could.'

Jonathan Hale then summarised the situation, most of which Jenny had already heard on the phone from her husband.

'We are doing everything we can,' Gabby said, with as sympathetic a smile as she could muster. 'This is a fast-moving inquiry, and significant resources are being deployed.' She wondered how many times she had repeated these standard police cliches to worried families.

'You do know that this Tiffany Dolan doesn't exist, don't you?' Oliver Barnes said to her.

Gabby looked blankly at him. 'I'm sorry, I don't know who you mean.'

'Come with me,' Oliver said, leading them all into his home office, where he sat at a computer screen. He clicked on an icon on his desktop, which opened the video and showed a young woman playing the clarinet. 'This is supposedly Tiffany Dolan,' he said, pointing at the caption underneath. 'And there are a few more stills, from the same video, on an Instagram page in her name. While I was waiting for Zoe to ring home I did a little bit of research on who she'd gone to fetch. I started with a reverse search on the image.'

'What's that?' Xolwa asked.

'You simply right click on any picture, and select reverse image search, like this. It shows you where the image first came from. And as you can see in this case, it's from a video on YouTube.' Oliver clicked through to the source, and found a website linked to the name Natalia Petrov. 'She is the daughter of a member of the Moscow Symphony Orchestra and now runs an online music business. She is not Tiffany Dolan.'

Xolwa pointed at the screen. 'You're saying that somebody used this video, created a name to go with it, and then pretended to be that person.'

'But why?' Jenny asked. 'I don't understand.'

'To get at me,' Hale said.

'Zoe was easy meat because she is a clarinetist herself, though not this good,' Oliver said. He searched for Natalia Petrov and then clicked on her website. There were dozens of images and video clips of a woman who, in her youth, looked identical to the picture of Tiffany Dolan.

Jenny shook her head. 'Zoe drove us all batty going on about this virtuoso American girl who was going to come over and see her. She's a bit of an outsider at school, and it made for a great social bragging point.'

'But why did Tyler go for your daughter, rather than directly going for Azalea?' Xolwa asked.

'Simply because he couldn't *find* Azalea,' Hale said, glowering at his wife. 'That's *exactly* why, despite your pleas, I wouldn't let her have a smartphone, and *exactly* why I wouldn't let her have any social media accounts. I was making sure she couldn't be found online.'

Gabby could see that this was the continuation of a domestic bone of contention.

'Not quite true, Jonathan,' Oliver said, opening another icon on his desktop. 'This is one of the few pictures of Azalea online, with Zoe and other members of the school orchestra, from the orchestra website, and it was used by the local press.'

'But it doesn't even give their surnames, just an initial,' Xolwa said, peering at the photograph. 'How did he know?'

'It's an unusual forename,' Hale said. 'When I was working with Tyler, I probably mentioned my pride at Azalea's piano and cello progress. It was probably the only search term he needed.'

'Internet access isn't allowed in US jails,' Oliver said. 'So someone on the outside must have done it for him.'

They all nodded. And then Hale's mobile rang.

'It's Azalea's number,' he said.

–

'It's me, Dad.'

Azalea's voice sounded shaky, and there was an echo which made it seem like speakerphone.

'Oh my God, thank goodness,' Hale breathed, putting his mobile on speaker. 'Where are you? Are Zoe and Lucy with you? Is everyone okay?'

There was a slight pause. 'We're fine. Dad, I need you to come and give us a lift home. I'm only going to say this once, so please write it down.'

Gabby Underwood indicated she would take notes and got out her pen.

'You have to drive to central London, get on the A3. Take your phone with you, and you will be called again en route in exactly thirty minutes. Do not contact the police... our lives depend on it.' Her voice broke on the last phrase, and she could be heard sobbing.

Another voice came on the line. 'Hale, you miserable piece of shit, this is your destiny. Do something heroic for once and save the lives of these three innocent girls. By the way, if I see a blue light, hear a siren, see a cop, it's the cute little one who gets shot first. I mean it. Try to weasel me, and little Lucy's body gets tossed out of the window. And I'll still have two to negotiate with.'

The line went dead.

'My baby, my poor baby,' Jenny Barnes shrieked, and fell to her knees. Oliver and Jonathan moved her gently back to the lounge and laid her on the sofa. Gabby Underwood did her best to comfort her. Jonathan looked at them both, and at Xolwa. 'I suppose I better go,' he said, blowing a sigh. He went out of the room.

Gabby was tapping out a number on her phone.

'Don't you dare!' Oliver shouted, grabbing it from her. 'You heard what he said, that's my daughter.'

'I do understand that,' Gabby said levelly. 'But there are already huge police resources devoted to the abduction. I'm only passing on the message that they need to keep out of sight.'

Eventually, Oliver returned the phone.

'Get me Gillard,' Gabby said, when her call was answered. 'I don't care if he's in a bloody meeting, pull him out. He needs to hear this.'

Chapter Twenty-seven

'Was there any clue on the call as to where Tyler was?' Gillard asked. He was talking to Gabby Underwood from the middle of the Operation Whirlpool control room.

'No. It was on speakerphone, seemed like an echoey room.'

'So they're not in a vehicle?'

'No, I don't think so. It was too quiet.'

'Could you hear traffic in the background? Could you hear aircraft? I mean could he still be in the vicinity of Heathrow?'

'Perhaps some traffic. I didn't hear any planes.'

'How long ago did the call come in?'

'Less than five minutes.'

'Hold on.' Gillard muted the phone and called across to the monitoring room where Horncastle was busy on headphones, making notes. 'John, have you got audio on Hale's mobile?'

'I'm just listening to it live now,' he said. 'We're also getting some audio input from one of the vehicles—'

'John, go back five minutes on the mobile, to Hale's conversation with Tyler. Get me an analysis on the background sounds. And any clues from what Tyler says as to where he might be.'

'I'm onto it,' Horncastle said.

Gillard clicked his fingers. Of course, why hadn't he thought of this before? Jonathan Hale himself would be the perfect person to know where Tyler might go. He was the man who had supplied the damn properties. He unmuted the call to Gabby. 'Is Jonathan Hale with you? I could do with speaking to him.'

'I'm afraid he's just gone, while I've been talking to you. He's driving up to London, as instructed.'

'What?' Gillard said. 'On his own?'

'No. With Oliver Barnes. He's taken a pale blue Maserati, regist—'

'It's all right, we have the number.' Gillard thanked her and hung up. He looked heavenwards, blinking at the ceiling. Things were moving too fast. Somebody should be tailing Hale. He shouted for one of the NCA officers, a whip-thin DC called Critchlow, to arrange it. 'Check ANPR on the A3. We need to follow a pale blue Maserati.' He gazed down at the clipboard where Hale's vehicles were detailed, and then read out the number plate.

'Sir!'

Turning around, Gillard saw Lewis Lytton at the far end of the control room, just finishing up a phone call, and standing to speak to him, the handset still in his hand. The rapid movement made his short dreadlocks bounce. 'We've identified the vehicle Tyler switched to, it's a red VW Golf saloon.' He read out the registration number. 'It's a false plate.'

'Take it across to Critchlow, he's co-ordinating CCTV and ANPR.' Gillard pointed out the officer's location. 'Where did we get this from?'

'The CSI unit there. It's from CCTV overlooking the Premier Inn car park at Heathrow. The Renault went in at 14.09 and six minutes later the VW exited.'

'How do we know it's that vehicle they're in?' Gillard asked. 'These car parks can be busy.'

'Because it's stolen, I suppose,' Lytton admitted.

'Sergeant, do you imagine that this is the only stolen vehicle near the airport? It wasn't dubbed Thief Row Airport for nothing. All right, get them to email us the footage ASAP, I want to see if there is a view into the vehicle itself.' Gillard raised his voice further, addressing the roomful of officers. 'Remember, people, that if that vehicle was prepared and left for Tyler, then it proves he *does* have someone on the ground here. Let's not make assumptions.'

Gillard called across to Research Intelligence Officer Rob Townsend, who had a phone to each ear. 'Come on Rob, I need that trace on Zoe Barnes' phone, quick as you can.' Townsend acknowledged the request with a nod.

Behind Gillard, a receptionist waved for his attention. 'Sir, Met Police silver commander on the line.' Gillard took the call, knowing that having called in a huge level of resources for a potential siege, senior officers would now be growing impatient to know where they would be deployed.

'Simpson here, Gillard.' DCS Alan Simpson was known throughout the Met as the coolest head in a crisis. He was nicknamed Blofeld for the soft but menacing tones in which he addressed subordinates. Who knows, maybe he owned a cat too. There was one going spare if not.

'Sir, we're just trying to pin down confirmation of the vehicle Tyler used,' Gillard said.

'Good, good. I've assembled a team with a hundred officers including siege negotiators, two firearms units and a command van at Paddington Green, which are ready to move at a moment's notice.'

'That's brilliant, sir.' In Gillard's mind the unspoken question was why Stella Anderson, technically the senior investigating officer, wasn't taking these calls. A silver commander was the tactical head in any major operational incident, and would normally liaise with those of Anderson's rank.

'Can't get hold of ACC Anderson,' Simpson said, as if reading his mind. 'Is she there with you?'

'No, sir. She left a few minutes ago.'

Simpson sighed. 'Well, keep up the good work. If you see her, tell her to call me as soon as she can.' He cut the line.

Gillard looked up to see that DI Colin Williams was just coming in. 'Don't take your jacket off, Colin. I want you to follow a red VW. DS Lytton will give you the details.'

Finally, almost dizzy trying to keep so many operational balls in the air, Gillard responded to John Horncastle, who was frantically waving to him from the monitoring room. He made his way into the glass office and shut the door behind him to keep out the growing hubbub.

'I've got live audio from inside Hale's Maserati. I think you better listen to this,' Horncastle diverted the audio feed to the external speaker.

'—and it's very brave of you, Jon.'

'I don't have any choice. I've been thinking about this since the moment I got out of jail. I've made my peace, and I'm entirely ready to give up my life to save my daughter.'

'I would do the same for mine.'

'You may yet have to do it, Oliver. Who knows? There comes a point in life when you have to put theory into practice.'

229

The Maserati was eating up the journey to London. Jonathan Hale kept his eyes to the road, flashing everyone ahead of him in the fast lane. Oliver's attention seemed to be glued to the speedo, which was registering 120 mph.

'Oliver, when he rings in a minute, I'll handle the call on speakerphone. No need for you to answer it.'

'You'd better slow down then,' Oliver replied. 'If we have an accident, more people will die than just us.'

Hale eased back until they were doing under a hundred. Traffic on their three-lane carriageway was manageable. The other side, weighed by Friday's late afternoon traffic streaming out of London, was moving at a crawl. Commuters on their way home, with dull, safe and predictable lives. How he envied them.

'I'm not doing any more of it, you know,' Hale said.

'More of what?'

'Money laundering. I recently sold someone a kind of starter kit, all the instructions you need to create the various international bank transfers to hide a flow of money. But I don't want to get my hands dirty actually doing it anymore.'

'That's good to hear,' Oliver said. 'I don't know why you ever did it to start with. You were well enough paid as a property lawyer, weren't you?'

'It's greed, Oliver, and it's also a game. An intoxicating, addictive, adrenaline-filled game. To outwit the forces of law and order, and to be handsomely paid for doing so.'

'But you were always bound to be caught,' Oliver said.

Hale laughed. 'The first time, yes, I was nervous. The second time, when some big bucks came in, I realised that it wasn't that dangerous. I knew I was good. By the time I been doing it for five years, I was a master of the universe. I was bloody invincible.'

He pressed the accelerator to the floor, and the car raced past a line of traffic. Oliver sank even lower in his seat, one hand braced on the dashboard, the other on the door handle.

Hale's mobile, in the hands-free cradle, buzzed.

A withheld number.

It had to be him.

–

It was the first half minute in an hour that Gillard had for himself. He was standing at the third floor CID urinal, trying to pee and check messages at the same time, when the mobile rang.

Stella Anderson.

It was enough to inhibit his flow. 'Yes, ma'am?'

'It's taken quite a while to get it together, but I just emailed you a full list of all the properties Hale acquired, or tried to, for Richard Tyler. There's three or four of them in west London.'

'Excellent, thank you. Where are you, ma'am? I've had Blofeld on the line asking for you.'

'I'm at East Surrey Hospital. My mother has had a stroke, she may not survive.'

'So sorry to—'

'I've been on the phone continuously, so if he tried to reach me...'

'I understand, ma'am. I'll let him know.'

'I have no siblings to help me. My mother has no one else.'

The self-justification continued for a couple more minutes, time that Gillard knew for both of them should be spent elsewhere.

'Must go now, ma'am. Fingers crossed for your mother.' He ended the call. Second-guessing her difficult decision was way above his pay grade, but Blofeld would undoubtedly make his opinions known.

He finished up, rinsed his hands and wiped them on his trousers. No time for the gutless dryer. He strode back to the office to see a group of officers gathered round Horncastle's desk.

'We've got Tyler, live, giving Hale directions,' Horncastle said.

Gillard came over and listened in.

'*Where are you?*' Tyler demanded.

'*Crawling in traffic on the A3 near Richmond Park. Put Azalea on the line.*'

'*Hold on,*' Tyler said, turning away from the phone. '*Give him a shout, honey.*'

'*We're okay, Dad.*' The phone seemed to be on speaker.

'*Azalea, where exactly are you being held?*' Hale asked.

'*I'm doing the talking, Hale!*' Tyler bellowed. '*Right, that's it. She's getting a bullet.*'

'*No, no, no. Please, I'm sorry,*' Hale pleaded.

'*Three, two, one.*' Tyler said.

A bang, then a girl's scream. The discharge from the gun was unmistakeable. Hale's cry of anguish was not the only one. Azalea could be heard sobbing freely. It didn't sound like she'd been hit.

'*Head for Hammersmith, then on into Kensington,*' Tyler said. '*Next time it's for real.*'

He cut the line.

'Right,' said Gillard. 'Get those direction details to DCS Simpson.'

'Guy sounds like a maniac,' Horncastle said.

'You don't know the half of it.' Gillard had just been emailed by a DOJ official in the US who said that Tyler had been heading to a skin cancer appointment when he'd escaped. 'He's dying, so he has absolutely nothing to lose.'

–

Tyler hung up, and gazed at Azalea, who was sobbing uncontrollably. 'Let that be a warning.' He looked at the hole in the wood panelling that the bullet had made and stowed the gun in his waistband.

'Right, I've got thirty minutes to play with you girls. What d'you reckon?' He looked at the grand piano. 'Say, Azalea. Play for me.'

Azalea looked at Zoe, and then at her captor. 'You have to untie me. Feet as well as hands.'

'Stop jerking me around,' Tyler said. 'You play the piano with your feet?'

'There are pedals.'

'I didn't ask you to ride it round the room. Just hit the goddamn keys.' He picked her up over his shoulder and carried her to the piano stool, then dumped her onto it. While she was sitting, he cut the cable ties on her wrists. She rubbed at the deep indentations.

'Play me something, for my mother.' He waved the gun at her, as if it was a conductor's baton.

Azalea tapped a few keys, and to Zoe it sounded to be reasonably in tune. Then she began to play Debussy's 'Clair de Lune'. The slow plaintive chords filled the ball-room, and even though Azalea made more mistakes than Zoe had ever heard from her, the rhapsodic beauty of the piece seemed to pluck them from their captivity. Zoe thought about her family, about her mother and father, but most of all about Lucy, her annoying but beau-tiful little sister, who picked up magpie phrases of other people's conversations.

At the end, Tyler clapped with enthusiasm. 'That was way cool,' he said.

'I could play better with the pedals,' Azalea said.

'Okay okay, I got a soft heart.' He brought out the knife and asked her to stretch out her legs towards him from the footstool. She did so, and his bulbous red eyes feasted on her long slender calves. He took off his gloves, revealing hands the texture of raw meat, and ran them up her legs, to her knees and then a little beyond, under the hem of her dress. Azalea was softly pleading, face screwed up anguish. 'No, please don't, please don't.'

'Are you gonna play nice with me?' he asked softly. 'Or d'you like it rough?' He cut the cable tie around her ankles, then glanced at Zoe and Lucy, looking daggers at him.

'I don't like an audience,' he muttered. He dragged Azalea to her feet and pushed her at pistol point ahead of him. 'Carry this,' he said giving her the wheeled suitcase. 'We got a nice choice of bedrooms upstairs. I'm gonna describe what we get up to to your pa before I blow his miserable brains out.'

Chapter Twenty-eight

It had taken a precious forty-five minutes to trace Zoe Barnes' phone, but once the data was in, Gillard matched it up against the newly constructed map of Tyler's former properties. Gillard and DC Townsend were sitting side-by-side at a computer terminal, looking at what it showed them.

'The phone seemed to be in a vehicle,' Townsend said. 'It reached here, Marloes Road, Kensington, and was then turned off for more than half an hour. It hasn't been turned on since, but Azalea Hale's dumb phone has. It was briefly turned on to call Jonathan Hale, and we traced that call to the Marloes Road area too.'

'...Which is where the most expensive of Hale's property purchases for Tyler is located,' Gillard said. 'Imperial Hanover House, 196 Marloes Road, to be precise. I've just tipped off the silver commander, and they are cranking up the big siege engine. We are getting a floor plan emailed from the estate agency which had been trying to sell it.'

'What about Tyler's threats?'

'To kill the youngest girl? I wouldn't doubt it for a second. He'll keep them all alive only so long as he can trade them for something.'

Azalea made her way up the broad carpeted staircase, carrying Tyler's heavy suitcase. Although she was terrified and shaking, all her senses were heightened. The stench of him was still there, but there was a mustiness about this cavernous home too, redolent of damp and rotten wood. The faint drone of traffic could be heard above the heavy breathing of her captor, and his footsteps behind her as they reached the first landing which branched out into gloomy wood-panelled corridors left and right. Tyler directed her to climb the next flight, which curved back and around the grand atrium of the stairwell. She was halfway up, level with an enormous chandelier, when she wondered if she could swing the case, and knock him down. He was following on her right, one stair below, and she was carrying the luggage in her left hand. In her peripheral vision, she could see the gun, pointing at the small of her back.

'This is getting heavy,' she said, switching the bag to the other hand. They were now two steps from the second landing.

'Nearly there,' Tyler said. 'Got a choice of six luxurious bedrooms. I can't wait to get going.'

Something snapped insider her. She swung the suitcase at him, but it was too heavy to move fast, and by the time she had let go, he had stepped further to the right. The heavy plastic case slid, then tumbled, down the stairs, coming to rest intact on the first-floor landing.

'Bitch.' The pistol slap he gave her came out of nowhere, the metal agonisingly impacting her ear. It caught her off balance and she stumbled backwards, only just managing to steady herself against the ornate wooden banister.

'I've just about had it with you,' he hissed, pressing the gun to her throat. 'Unfortunately, necrophilia is not my thing, so I ain't killing you for a few minutes yet. Now go and fetch my luggage.'

Azalea descended the stairs, her ear throbbing, and acutely conscious that the pistol was aimed at her. She picked up the suitcase and lugged it back up the stairs to the landing. Tyler had found another light switch, illuminating a narrow wood-panelled corridor heading off to the right. At the first door on the right, he turned an ornate brass handle, and pushed her into the room. It was a sizeable bedroom, with a large divan bed and bare mattress. Mullioned windows looked out over the front. Tyler turned on the light and quickly closed the curtains.

'I've got a little phone call to make to your miserable jerk of a father,' Tyler said, checking his wristwatch. 'Now, sugar, just lie on the bed and relax. I won't be long.'

He extracted Azalea's phone from his pocket, turned it on and hit 'redial'.

–

The Maserati was struck in a traffic jam near Hammersmith Bridge when the call came through. Hale could see that it was from Azalea's phone.

'Hello,' he called to the hands-free device.

'Listen carefully, Hale,' Tyler said. 'You are to come to 196 Marloes Road—'

'Imperial Hanover House. I knew you couldn't resist,' Hale said. 'I should be there in ten minutes. Put Azalea on the line. I need to know she's okay.'

'She's on the bed here just waiting for me,' Tyler said. 'Beautiful bodywork, I have to say. I was hoping to have been able to give you my road test review of her by now, but the logistics have been a little tricky.'

'I'm here, Dad,' Azalea shouted.

'Thank God,' Hale breathed.

'He ain't gonna help you,' Tyler said laughing. 'Boy, Hale, I got a real itch for this girl of yours.'

'You leave her alone!' Hale shouted.

'The sooner you get here, the sooner her torment ends.'

'You won't get away with this, you know,' Hale said.

'Of course I won't. I've got skin cancer and I reckon it's pretty far spread by now. I missed my appointment to come see you. But you know what? I don't care. So long as I make your head explode like an over-ripe melon, I'll die a happy man. By the way, if I see a cop, you do know what's going to happen, don't you?'

Hale and Oliver Barnes looked at each other. Their faces were white.

'I said, don't you?'

'Yes, we know.'

'Who the fuck is *we*?' Tyler asked. 'I said come *alone*.'

'Oliver Barnes,' Oliver said, leaning forward towards the device. 'I'm Zoe and Lucy's dad.'

'Who's driving?'

'I am,' Hale said.

'Anyone else apart from you two?' Tyler demanded.

'No,' Hale said. 'And no one else knows we're here.'

'Well, Hale, when you get here, drive into the back yard and hit the horn. Remember, Oliver, the life of your cute little Lucy depends on there being no cops around. What's the vehicle?'

'Pale blue Maserati Ghibli,' Hale said.

'Jesus. Bought with my money, no doubt.' Tyler cut the call.

—

Gillard, standing beside the seated Horncastle, had caught every word of the call on the desk speaker.

'How far away is the Maserati?' he asked Horncastle. The monitoring technician clicked on the icon which monitored the GPS tracker built into the Maserati's driving mirror.

'Ten minutes, depending on traffic.'

'I think I better speak to the silver commander.'

Gillard stood away and rang DCS Simpson. He updated him on the latest overheard conversation within the Maserati, and the call from Tyler.

'It's going to be tricky,' Simpson said. 'We are sealing off both ends of Marloes Road to traffic, away from the view of the house. We're contacting residents in homes overlooking the target building, with a view to getting snipers set up there. Two mobile firearms units have arrived and just switched to unmarked vehicles. I've got a call in to the Home Secretary for permission to shoot to kill.' The commander was in full Blofeld mode, menace oozing out with every soft word. 'We can't take any chances with him. By the way, I still haven't heard from ACC Anderson, is she there?'

Gillard looked out into the control room. 'No, sir. She's apparently at East Surrey Hospital, her mother has had a stroke.'

Simpson said nothing for a moment. 'She's supposed to be SIO, at least for your end of it.'

'I think we're managing, sir.'

'Look, I could also do with someone here who knows the hostages and can identify them, both by voice and sight.'

'Oliver Barnes, the father—'

'No, I mean someone I can use operationally here, and who can go in with the assault team should it be necessary, to keep them calm.'

'I have met two of the girls, sir, and I've been monitoring their voices.'

'Right. I need you here in ten minutes, so it'll have to be by chopper. I take it Mount Browne has a helipad?'

'Yes, sir.'

'Good.' Simpson ended the call, leaving Gillard staring at the receiver.

Horncastle stared at him in admiration.

'How can you encircle a hostage taker without him knowing?' The technician asked.

'In the end you can't,' Gillard said. 'He's going to find out.'

He thought of the two Barnes girls, full of life and character, and wondered what must be going through their minds, and that of their parents. Even Jonathan Hale, money launderer though he was, did not deserve to have his daughter endure this.

Five minutes earlier

Zoe and Lucy watched from the sofa as Tyler climbed the stairs with the gun pointing at Azalea. The moment he was out of view, Lucy tried to signal something to Zoe with her eyes. She crawled caterpillar-like, face down across Zoe's lap, with her hands sticking out behind her, waving and stretching her fingers. Zoe got the idea and lowered her head until Lucy's fingers could reach her mask. Once Lucy had a grip, Zoe lifted her head, the mask pulled down over her chin. She then put her mouth onto Lucy's stretching fingers, so her younger sister could pull out the gag. They wriggled into reversed positions and got rid of Lucy's mask and gag. They then heard the clatter of luggage sliding down the stairs, the sound of a blow, and Tyler's threat to kill Azalea. They waited until the sounds receded before taking the next step.

'We can escape,' Lucy whispered. 'I saw this video on the Internet. Sit down on the floor.' Zoe did so. Lucy then sat behind her and pushed her bound legs towards her sister. 'Feel for my shoelaces,' she said. Zoe's fingers stretched out behind her until she could feel Lucy's trainers. She pulled at the bows and then at Lucy's instruction threaded one lace through her own wrist bonds. It took several attempts. 'Now tie it to the other shoelace,' Lucy said. 'It's got to be a good strong knot.' Once she was satisfied, Lucy sawed her feet backwards and forwards, the laces abrading the plastic edges of the cable tie. It gave way in less than five seconds. Now, with Zoe's hands free, it was relatively quick to release themselves from all their bonds using the same technique.

The two girls went over to the blue sports bag and looked inside. There was a brick-sized box of cable ties, a cardboard box which turned out to be full of bullets, and a small wad of £20 notes.

Zoe had an idea. She took off her training shoes, removed her socks and filled them with bullets, tying a knot hard above them. She then swung around the sock above her head. 'That would give him a headache,' she said, putting her trainers back on her bare feet.

'Let's go upstairs and save Azalea,' Lucy said.

The two girls crept out of the ballroom and padded silently up the heavily carpeted stairs. They could tell Tyler's whereabouts from his muffled voice, well above them. When they reached the second floor Zoe signalled to her sister to hold back and hide, while she made her way along the corridor. She heard Tyler speaking to Azalea, in the first room on the right, which would look out over the street. She crept up to the door and put her ear against it until she could hear the phone call Tyler was now making, seemingly to Azalea's father.

–

As soon as Tyler hung up, Azalea could see that he was looking at her with hungry eyes. She had her back against the full-length curtains and was trying to feel if there was a window catch.

'Get away from there,' Tyler barked. As she stood away, he opened the curtains and peered out. 'Ain't no traffic. What's going on?'

'It's probably just traffic lights for roadworks,' Azalea said.

'Yeah, or maybe it's cops.' He was still peering through the window, the gun held loosely in his right hand. She thought about trying to grab it from him but recalled how immensely strong he was. She was trembling like a leaf, her face still throbbing from when he'd pistol-whipped her and her throat was bruised from the struggle earlier in the car. She had absolutely no doubt that he would kill her, Zoe and Lucy the moment it suited him to do so. She didn't dare think what he was planning to do to her in the meantime. Hoping for rescue, she couldn't imagine how it could happen. If he was going to kill Lucy the moment he spotted a policeman, there was little hope.

Finally satisfied that there was nothing to see, Tyler turned to her, pointed the gun and said: 'Okay, honey take your clothes off. This is the moment you've been waiting for.'

He slid off the bulletproof vest, undid his shirt with one hand, the gun still pointing at her. His torso was reptilian, dry and scaly, pitted with scabs. Just the thought of what would come next made her heave. She made no move to remove her dress. The gunshot took her by surprise, a deafening sound which prompted an involuntary jump and a scream of panic from her. She felt no pain, and opened her eyes to see a wisp of smoke from the barrel, the taint of the discharge in her nose, and a hole in the wall to her right.

'I'm not going to tell you again. And if I have to waste you, I'll just do to your friends what I was going to do to you. So think on.'

Azalea started to undress. She felt she had no choice.

'Do it slow, do it seductive,' he said. 'This is your big moment. Entertain me.'

She was down to her underwear, shaking uncontrollably.

'Now the rest.'

'I've got my period,' she said. It was a last desperate lie. As Tyler was considering his response, something happened to distract him.

A car horn, nearby.

Five minutes earlier

Jonathan Hale and Oliver Barnes stopped fifty yards short of the police cordon at the junction of Scarsdale Villas and

Marloes Road. There were two patrol cars, a riot van, a large satellite truck, and at least thirty officers.

'Oh shit,' Oliver said. 'What are we going to do?'

'They got to let us through,' Hale replied. 'Once I offer myself as a hostage in exchange for the three girls. That's what Tyler wants, and if he gets what he wants, they'll be safe.'

A uniformed Asian officer with silver bling on his shoulders was approaching the car on foot, followed by a man in plain clothes, of formidable size and bearing. Hale buzzed the window down and greeted them casually. 'What's the hold-up here, officer? We have an urgent meeting in Marloes Road.'

Oliver was astounded at the coolness that Hale was now showing. His voice betrayed no hint of emotion, merely the confidence of the well-paid City lawyer. It could only be that he had accepted that he was going to die. That was a stage beyond where Oliver was.

'Just stay there, Mr Hale,' the uniformed officer said, turning away to make a quick call on his radio. When he turned back, he said, 'Mr Hale, I'm Inspector Dev Mehta, speaking on behalf of DCS Simpson, silver commander for the operation. We don't have much time, so listen carefully.' He then leaned into the car and addressed Oliver. 'We are assuming Richard Tyler does not know what you look like, Mr Barnes. So we would like you to switch with DC Gregory Marshall here.'

'Look, both my daughters are in there,' Oliver said. 'They need me.'

'I understand your feelings, Mr Barnes, but you are not equipped to face an armed and desperate kidnapper. DC Marshall is a martial arts expert and a pistol marksman. He will be carrying a concealed weapon.'

'Sounds like a plan,' Hale said, turning to Oliver. Marshall moved forward and opened the passenger-side door to let Oliver out.

Oliver was reluctant to leave, even though he could see the logic. 'You won't forget what Tyler said about killing Lucy if he sees a policeman,' he said to Mehta.

'Tyler will not see a policeman. Both occupants of the car will be wearing lightweight body armour. In your case, Mr Hale, I would suggest concealing it beneath shirt and jacket,' he said.

Hale got out and followed the instructions he was given, stripping rapidly to the waist, donning the light-weight vest and tucking the long Kevlar flaps into his trousers. He then put his long-sleeve shirt over it and donned the jacket.

Two minutes later he was ready to go. He made a last-minute phone call to Xolwa, who was in floods of tears.

'Darling, I'm going in now. In case I don't get out, I want you to know that I've always loved you. That everything I have ever done, both the good and bad, has been to give you and Azalea a more secure future. I am just profoundly sorry that I've put her in such mortal danger.'

'I love you, Jon,' she said.

Mehta was tapping his wristwatch.

'I've got to go now, love. Wish me luck,' Hale said, then ended the call and nodded at the officers at the cordon. The plastic barriers blocking the road were drawn apart, and the Maserati eased slowly forward. Hale drove steadily, past the Senegalese embassy and the Devonshire Arms, until he could see the Edwardian façade of Imperial Hanover House. Directed by Marshall, he slid the car down the open driveway to the left of the house.

'Don't look in his direction,' Marshall said, as they glided past an armed officer hiding in the pillared portico of the house next door. He was wearing full body armour and helmet with a bulky rifle and scope. Hale brought the vehicle round the back into the gloomy parking area, and stopped next to a red VW. He felt an icy fear in the pit of his stomach. Reptile had been terrifying enough even when they were working on the same side, but here he was about to confront the man who'd become his personal nightmare. The man who was holding his precious daughter at gunpoint.

Hale pipped the horn as he'd been instructed, and then sounded it again loudly.

'Play it cool,' Marshall said to Hale. 'If we can get within a few feet, I'll be able to bring him down quickly.'

The phone rang in the car. The screen indicated it was Azalea's number. 'Answer it, but play it steady,' murmured PC Marshall.

Hale's throat went dry as he gestured with his hand to pick up the call hands-free.

Chapter Twenty-nine

The South-East Air Support helicopter could be heard approaching Mount Browne two minutes after Simpson's call. Gillard barely had time to grab his stab vest and take a gulp of coffee before he was running out of the CID building onto the grass. The dark blue and yellow chopper hovered just off the ground long enough for one of the aircrew to pull Gillard in, then departed with a thunderous roar. The co-pilot gestured to Gillard to buckle the seat-belt and put on his helmet so he could converse with the pilot through the mic. Gillard waited until the pilot had finished his air traffic control notifications before asking how quickly they would be there.

'With a south-westerly behind us we might get it down to eight minutes,' he said.

Below him the leafy shire of Surrey looked pristine in the late afternoon sun. Cattle and sheep looked tiny in irregular-shaped fields, a hundred shades of green, bounded by soft hedges. Soon the greenery gave way to the broad quicksilver arc of the M25, pierced by busy arterial roads, spokes to the hub of the metropolis. The rural gave way to the suburban, swathes of houses ever more tightly packed as the helicopter thundered on its way.

Gillard tore his gaze away from the view to text Sam with the news that he was heading off to a siege in Kensington. Although her personal phone would be off, she would have at least heard the chopper arrive, and there was a good chance someone in the control room with her would have spotted him running across the grass. He didn't mention that he might have to go into the house with the assault unit. It sounded dangerous, and felt worse, suicidal even. He tried to keep in mind the statistics: any officer was much more likely to be stabbed while making an arrest or injured in a road accident in the course of ordinary duties then gunned down at the back end of an assault squad. Especially as he had been promised body armour.

But his fast, shallow breath and surge of adrenaline told him otherwise. He was scared.

As the helicopter roared across west London, his thoughts turned to the hostages. Azalea Hale, a gifted pianist and cello player. Zoe and Lucy Barnes, two normal but utterly charming children, full of life and energy and hope. He would do anything he could to save them.

The chopper flew in over Kensington and touched down on the tarmac inside a police cordon. On one side were gathered hundreds of people behind the blue police tape, on the other a half-dozen police vehicles and at least twenty officers.

The moment he stepped out, someone handed him a bulletproof vest.

–

Tyler heard the horn and winked horribly at Azalea. 'Saved by the bell, yeah?' He took her phone from his pocket and tapped a few buttons. While it was ringing out he looked meaningfully at Azalea and put a finger to his lips. She had no intention of making another sound. Tyler had proved that he was capable of anything.

'Hale, you miserable piece of shit, where have you been?'

Azalea couldn't make out the answer from her father.

'Stay there in the car. Don't play any games or we've got one dead girl.'

Tyler hung up. He took a bunch of cable ties from his pocket and seized Azalea, tying her wrists to the pipes each end of a substantial old-fashioned cast-iron radiator. She was left sitting on the floor in bra and pants, arms held wide, shivering against the cool metal. He began to dress himself, starting with the bulletproof vest, then a shirt, followed by a sweatshirt and shoes.

'Don't go away,' he warned as he made his way to the doorway. 'I'll be back in a minute, and then we'll have some fun.'

He tucked the gun into his waistband, opened the door into the corridor and stepped out.

–

Crouching in the corridor outside, Zoe heard Tyler coming to the door. It opened, and he stepped through looking the other way, towards the stairs. She stood and swung the bullet-filled sock with all her might. 'Murderer!' she screamed. 'I hate you!' Tyler's shoulder broke the force of the blow, which then made only a glancing impact on his face. He yelled in pain, lurched sideways and banged his head on the door frame. Zoe swung again, but this time his right forearm blocked the blow, his left propping him up against the door frame. She screeched, moving her arm back for another attempt. Tyler's right leg kicked out and caught her painfully on the thigh, the power of it almost knocking her off her feet. As she stumbled against the far side of the corridor, she could see him going for the gun in his waistband.

She hurled the sock towards him with both hands and let go. This time it did hit him full in the face, and she heard the crack of bone as he staggered backwards. Her courage now deserted her. She fled towards the stairs, running down two at a time, hand on the banister. She reached the first-floor landing, not daring to look behind her, but heard Tyler's yells as he reached the top of the curving stairs.

'I'll fucking dismember you all,' he roared, as he began to thunder down. She sprinted off right, taking her out of Tyler's view, into the corridor beneath the one where she had lain in ambush. She had left Lucy hiding in an empty linen cupboard on the higher floor, having begged her to stay quiet and not to move. She was well hidden at the back, behind a hot water cylinder, and had the other bullet-filled sock.

Zoe sprinted along the corridor, which had two doors on each side, and ended in a fire exit. She ran for this door and turned the handle. Locked. Glancing behind, she could see Tyler just getting down to her landing. She shrank into a doorway on the left, which was just deep enough to keep her from view. She could hear Tyler cursing to himself, as he tried a couple of the doors nearer his end. They sounded to be locked. His footsteps then receded, and she could hear nothing for a while. She risked a glimpse and could just see Tyler in the opposite corridor beyond the stairs, going into a room on the right.

–

Jonathan Hale sat in the Maserati with DC Marshall, who showed him the iPad he'd been staring at. On it was the floor plan of Imperial Hanover House. 'It's a big place, three dozen rooms or more, arranged over two wings,' Marshall said. 'When you are called in, just talk to him from cover and I'll do the rest.'

'He'll just shoot me. That's what he said he'd do.'

Marshall cocked his head to indicate ambiguity. 'He'll need to negotiate a way out, they always do. And if he does fire, don't be a hero. Just play dead.'

'I doubt whether any playing will be involved,' Hale muttered.

Marshall held up a finger to ask for silence. 'Let's just have a listen.'

Hale buzzed down the windows. There were no sounds bar the distant drone of traffic and the cooing of pigeons in the sycamores. Marshall told Hale to close the windows, then took his radio out, turned the volume right down and turned it on. He called in their position.

'No sign of Tyler, over,' Marshall said.

'Okay,' said the call handler. 'Silver commander instructs you to hold your position. We're patching you into the NCA monitoring room.'

'Roger that.'

Lytton then came on the line. 'We have rough traces on three mobile phones indicated still in the building. Two belonged to the captive girls, and the third we believe is a burner phone belonging to Tyler. Our expectation is that he has all three on him.'

'Should I go in?' Marshall said. 'I've memorised the layout.'

'Not yet. Silver commander is still working to get more line of sight to the building.'

'I want to go in,' Hale said. 'My daughter is in there. He could be doing anything to her!'

'Don't—'

The ringing of Hale's phone in its cradle interrupted.

'Hello?' Hale answered, forcing Marshall to hurriedly switch off the radio.

'It's me,' said Tyler. 'You better both still be in the car.'

Marshall mimed calming hand movements.

'We are. Let me speak to Azalea,' Hale asked.

'In a minute,' Tyler said. 'Put both hands on the wheel where I can see them.'

Hale looked at Marshall, who nodded his approval, then did so. Marshall undid his seatbelt, pulled out a small black pistol.

It was the last thing he ever did.

The gunshot was deafening, and was followed by a second and then a third. Hale couldn't suppress his shout of terror. He turned towards Marshall and screamed again. The policeman was slumped forward over the dashboard, a neat bloody hole in the top of his head. There were three bullet holes in the car roof, and in the three beams of sunlight wisps of smoke and dust circulated.

Tyler's voice came through the hands-free phone 'Hale, put your goddamn hands back on the wheel.'

Hale's arms shot back to the wheel. 'You *killed* him.'

'Just another dead cop, get over it.'

Hale considered contesting the assertion but decided against it.

'Hale, I warned you, but still you tipped off the cops, you piece of shit.'

'I didn't.'

'Listen, I watched a van stop across the way. Out came three big guys with a military bearing, clean overalls and brand-new toolboxes. Not a beer gut, sagging pants or paint stain between them. They hurried into the big house opposite. Do they think I'm stupid? I can smell cops at half a mile, even British ones. And the guy in your passenger seat was a cop. It was too good an opportunity to get someone close to me.'

'What about Azalea? Let me talk to her.'

'Sure, come on in. I've finished with her now. In fact she's not much good to anyone.'

Hale made an involuntary cry. 'You *bastard*! I'm going to kill you!' he growled.

'The basement door is open, so come get me. By the way, tell your cop friends that the entire house is booby-trapped with explosive devices.' Tyler ended the call.

Tears slid into Hale's vision as he thought of his beautiful daughter. He wiped them away angrily and reached down into the passenger footwell. He slid the dead cop's fingers from the pistol. He had never used a gun of any kind, ever. Invited by clients to grouse shoots in Scotland, he had always used an excuse to avoid them. A pointless projection of masculinity, was how he had viewed such weapons.

But he was glad of this one, now.

He slipped the gun into his jacket pocket, opened the Maserati's door and sprinted for cover to the back of the house. Looking up he saw a couple of slender wrought iron balconies projecting from the second floor. That must've been where Tyler stood to shoot Marshall. He made his way down the staircase and pulled open the basement door. He took in the low corridor, dimly lit by naked lightbulbs, and made his way to the door at the end. When he eased it open, he realised.

A stairwell, black and white tiles, and a double balustrade. From the dream.

This was the place and the time of his destiny. Right here, right now. He would die to save his daughter. The premonition would come true. He felt his legs turn to water, and he took a deep breath. He fought off the fear, and gritted his teeth. *Azalea, my sweet precious love, I'm here for you.*

Chapter Thirty

Gillard was taken by Inspector Mehta to a long-wheelbase van bristling with satellite dishes and aerials, Silver Command HQ. Inside were DCS Simpson, plus three other officers, most wearing headphones, crammed in with monitoring equipment. They looked preoccupied, and before Mehta could make the introduction, Simpson held his hand up.

Three shots could be heard, then an exchange between Hale and Tyler, which had been patched through from the monitoring room feeds. One of the officers made repeated radio calls to Marshall, getting no reply.

'We must assume he's down,' Simpson muttered, before turning to Gillard.

'Can anyone see the sight of the firing, sir?' Gillard asked.

'Not yet. We have operational difficulties. No line of sight to the rear of the house because of the trees. We have three marksmen on the third floor of Cavendish Mansions, on the opposite side of Marloes Road. We are getting two armed officers on the roofs of each of the adjacent houses, but I suspect they give no view of the principal windows front or rear. The drone surveillance unit is stuck in traffic at Marble Arch. We have got a request in to the security services to assemble a team who can remotely take control of any mobile phones there in Tyler's possession. I just need more time.'

'Should I ring Tyler?' Gillard asked. 'That might give us some time.'

'I would prefer to start negotiations when we have the full ring of steel around him.'

'But Hale sounds like he's going in now, sir. It would be a useful distraction.'

'Gillard, have you been on the siege negotiator course?'

'Yes, a few years ago. The important thing is I have met the two younger girls, Zoe and Lucy Barnes, and they also know me.'

'All right,' Simpson said. 'It goes against my better instincts, but my biggest fear is how we explain the deaths of three innocent schoolgirls to the great British public. Anything you can do to prevent that would be welcome.'

'I will do my best, sir,' Gillard said.

—

Tyler closed the back bedroom window from which he had shot through the roof of the Maserati. His instincts were always spot-on. The passenger was bound to be a cop, and that just left Hale himself. He opened the door and checked carefully to either side before emerging into the corridor, and then heading to the landing immediately above the door from which Hale would emerge. Blood was still seeping from his nose. He could hear it click as he prodded it, and his face was in agony. Maybe she had busted his eye socket as well. At this stage it didn't matter. He didn't have time to track down the little bitch, when the whole purpose of his trip was within his grasp. He'd escaped from a maximum security jail in Arizona, crossed the border to Mexico and flown right across the Atlantic Ocean for just one purpose. To get revenge on a snitch. To kill Hale, preferably slowly, to see him writhe in agony. Popping his kneecaps and elbows first, IRA punishment style, would do the trick. Yeah, he still had enough ammunition. The Glock held seventeen and he'd fired maybe five, and he now had a bloodstained sock of extra ammunition in his pocket should he need it.

He knew he wouldn't be getting out of here alive.

As long as he got even, he'd die a happy man.

The sound of a creaking door below him indicated the arrival of Jonathan Hale. He cocked the weapon, leaned over the stone balustrade, and waited.

–

At the same time, a floor above him, Lucy Barnes was emerging from a linen cupboard into a carpeted corridor. She was frightened and lonely. She desperately wanted to find her sister and Azalea. She also thought about poor Socks, who had run away from the other car all on his own, such a long way from home. Lucy had been very reluctant to be hidden away in the first place, not knowing what was going on. She regretted it especially when she'd heard Zoe's shouts just a few yards away. It sounded like she had been fighting the man, perhaps hitting him with the sock and then running away down the stairs. She had heard Tyler run away after Zoe, shouting after her. She didn't dare think what might have happened if he'd caught her. She began to cry when she heard the distant sound of three gunshots a minute ago, and that was when she really decided she must come out.

Zoe might need me.

There was nobody in the corridor, but there was definitely noise from the floor below. Man-sized footsteps, and the click of metal. She ran as softly as she could back to the door which Zoe had been listening at. It was closed, and there was a bloody handprint on the frame. She could hear soft crying from within, and a kind of metallic ringing sound. The voice was Azalea's. Stealthily she turned the handle of the door and pushed it open. Azalea was tied to the radiator, wearing only her underwear, and the noise had been the sound of her pulling at her bonds against the heavy metal.

Lucy rushed in with a finger to her lips. 'Oh Lucy, it is so good to see you,' Azalea whispered. 'He left his knife just there, on the bed.'

Lucy grabbed it and began to saw away at the plastic cable ties on Azalea's wrists and ankles. It took less than a minute to free her. Azalea grabbed at her clothes and trainers, but Lucy hissed: 'There's no time. Come to my secret room to dress, he won't find us there.' Azalea bundled up her clothes and followed Lucy to the linen room. Azalea was keen to hear how Lucy had found a way to escape the cable ties, and what they had discovered about Zoe's attack on their captor.

'And we've got his knife now,' Lucy said, holding it up.

–

Jonathan Hale eased the heavy door fully open and surveyed the tiled lobby, which stretched away to the front of the house, lit by high windows. There was no sound but the distant drone of traffic. He was too scared to step out into this exposed space, in which he would be vulnerable to shots from above. No need to accommodate destiny. He could still try to ease the odds his way.

258

Slipping the gun into his right jacket pocket, he rang Azalea's phone. He could just detect its familiar buzz, just a few feet above him, before being turned off. He pocketed his own phone, now slick with sweat from the palm of his hand, and brought out the gun. He reckoned he knew where Tyler was, but then Tyler had a pretty good idea from the open door where he was.

'Tyler, I know you're up there!' he shouted.

There was no reply.

'Let Azalea come down the stairs, Tyler. I need to see she's alive.'

'I've got her right here, come out and take a look,' Tyler said.

'I need to see her first, send her down the stairs.'

'She's tied up, she can't move. Come take a look.'

–

'That's my dad,' Azalea hissed to Lucy. 'I recognise his voice.' She was now fully dressed, crouching next to her young neighbour in the linen room.

'But where are the police?' Lucy asked. 'I want Zoe to be safe too. Where is she?'

'I don't know. We should probably stay hidden if the police are coming so we don't get shot by accident, but I can't bear to think of my dad in danger. He thinks Tyler still has us captive.'

'I've got an idea,' Lucy said. 'We could go back to the room you were in and shout for help out of the window.'

'That's a good idea,' Azalea said. 'Tyler sounds like he's at least a floor below us.' She made her way over to the door, then out into the corridor just in time to hear Tyler say:

'*She's tied up, Hale, she can't move. Come take a look.*'

'Dad, don't come in, it's a trap!' Azalea screeched. 'We've got away from him.'

Tyler's roar of fury was immediate, and followed by the thunder of feet up the stairs.

–

For Jonathan Hale, Azalea's shout was a clarion call. The bellowing overhead and the thunderous footsteps of Tyler's pursuit of his daughter overcame his terror. He could save her! He had to save her. He jumped out into the lobby, immediately turning and raising the gun in both hands, scanning the balustrade for his enemy.

They saw each other at the same time. Tyler was halfway up the next flight of stairs to the second floor, leaning over, the gun pointing at him. Hale only got off one shot to Tyler's first three, a deafening fusillade. Hale felt an immense blow to the chest that knocked him off-balance, then another a second later which smashed into his shoulder like a thrown brick. Breathless and dizzy, he twisted towards Tyler, who was now behind and above him, high on the stairs.

'You're gonna die, Hale,' Tyler said, both arms on the gun pointing down at him. The final bullet hit him in the head, like an icy lance, just as he fired his own shot. As he fell to the floor, the chandelier swinging gently above him dropped crystal glass like raindrops all around him. His last thought as consciousness slipped away was: *I'm dying. I've done my best, Azalea. I just hope it's enough.*

–

Taking Lucy by the hand, Azalea ran back into the room where she had been held captive against the radiator. Shots rang out: four, five, six. She heard her father's cry of pain, and the raining of broken glass onto the tiles.

They slammed the door on the awful sounds. But there was no key to lock it. As the heavy footsteps came closer, she manoeuvred the heavy divan bed so that it blocked the door. Lucy ran to the window, pulled back the curtains, and stood on the radiator so she could reach the latches. She pushed open the window, and immediately started yelling.

'Help! Help! Help!'

Far away, in a building across the other side of Marloes Road, she could see men in dark clothing and helmets with rifles. She waved at them.

—

Zoe had hidden in a second-floor rear bedroom for ten minutes. Looking out of the window, she couldn't see any way of escaping. It was at least a thirty-foot drop to the hard surface of the car park. The two parked cars were too far away to the left for her to jump onto. There was no outside ledge, and the nearest drainpipes were too far away to reach. The worst news of all was that she couldn't see anyone else. No policemen, no rescuers, nobody.

With the first sound of gunshots she realised she had to go out into the corridor, and take her chances. She couldn't bear it if Azalea or her sister were hurt. She wished she had kept hold of the sock full of bullets. The bedroom was completely bare. Even the built-in cupboards were empty.

Finally, she eased the door open and, after listening carefully, stepped out.

'Finally, the little bitch is caught.'

Tyler's gun was pointing right at her head.

–

Gillard stood outside the command van, with all hell breaking loose inside. He had rung all three mobiles he knew were inside Imperial Hanover House: Azalea's, Zoe's and Tyler's. Each was turned off. The message boxes were full on the girls' phones, so he left a short message on Tyler's. Before he'd finished, he was called back in by Simpson.

'Gunshots in the house, and two of the hostages are visible at a third-floor front window, waving and shouting for help. We haven't spotted Tyler himself, and we fear this could be a ruse.'

'You mean he's not with them?' Gillard asked.

'Hold on. Azalea has just shouted that they are barricaded in the room. Tyler is apparently in the corridor. He claims there are boobytraps.'

'What about Zoe Barnes?'

'No information. I take it you didn't get through to Tyler?' Simpson said.

'All the phones are turned off.'

'Right, I just can't wait until everything is set up, the assault teams have to go in now. We can't wait for the bomb disposal team. Mehta will kit you out. Go, and good luck.'

Gillard stepped out of the command van and was offered a helmet and a flak jacket. He had barely got into the latter when his mobile began to ring. He glanced at it, and his heart skipped a beat. 'Tyler is ringing me.'

Simpson joined him outside the van to listen.

Chapter Thirty-one

'Are you Gillard?' Tyler said. He was standing outside the barricaded door, with Zoe bent over in a headlock under his left arm, the same hand holding the phone. In his right hand was the Glock, its tip resting against her temple.

'Yes.'

'Well, here's a newsflash. I already killed Hale, so objective number one is reached. I got a little hellcat here who wants to speak to you. Give him your name, honey,' Tyler said, tapping speakerphone.

'Zoe Barnes,' she croaked.

'Zoe, we're going to do everything we can—'

'Listen, cop. I can hear your goddamn SWAT team downstairs. Get them out right now or the girl gets a bullet.'

'Tyler, just stay calm. No one else needs to be hurt. So long as the hostages are unharmed, we are willing to discuss your demands.'

'Don't bullshit me. Call them back NOW!' He cut the call and pocketed the phone. Still holding Zoe tightly by her head, he kicked at the door. It moved an inch or two and was then pushed closed again.

'Open it now, or I shoot Zoe. I am not fucking joking.'

There was the sound of furniture being shifted. Then the door opened.

'I'll get the assault team to hold on the ground floor. You go and join them,' Simpson told Gillard. 'I'll be able to see through your bodycam and microphone, so make sure they are switched on. Just speak to the man face-to-face if you can.' The silver commander disappeared inside his van. Gillard was still thinking about Zoe, the cheeky fifteen-year-old, with Tyler's gun against her head. Had he said the right thing? Was there anything more he could have done?

A female officer in flak jacket and helmet arrived to guide Gillard into the target area. She introduced herself as Sergeant Grace Sparkes, then took one look at him and said: 'Sir, your helmet's too loose.' She slid the catch until the strap was tight under his chin. He followed Sparkes as she jogged along the pavement on Marloes Road until they came into view of Imperial Hanover House on the same side. 'Stay low now, we're in view.' Using a garden wall as cover they crouched and shuffled forward, until they reached a more sizeable hedge, and could move more rapidly. Gillard could now see the driveway to the left of the house, and the two marksmen now crouching in the portico of the neighbouring building. Gillard could hear various messages crackling on the radio connected to his flak jacket, one of which sounded like it was from leader of the assault team.

Bravo squad now in position at the base of the main staircase. No contact with target.

Hold position and await further instruction, came the reply.

Sparkes turned to Gillard and said, 'This is open ground, so we'll be taking it at a run when I get the say-so.' She then called in on her radio.

'Delta three, permission to advance, sir.'

Okay, Delta three, sharpshooters report no sign of target. Hostages no longer visible.

Sparkes sprinted up the drive, leaving Gillard struggling to keep up. They were almost level with the house when they heard the sound of a window opening at the front. They immediately dived for cover at the side of the house.

–

Tyler kept the gun pointing at Zoe's head as he walked her into the room, still in the headlock. Azalea and Lucy were staring at him. 'Shut the curtains and get away from that window,' he said. They complied. 'You're coming with me. Walk ahead and don't try any funny business. This trigger finger is getting kinda itchy.'

Azalea and Lucy walked ahead of him as he led them to the furthest end of the corridor. He got them to open a door on the right, which led to a narrow staircase. He urged them on, going up towards a small room with a sloping ceiling on either side. He virtually dragged Zoe up the stairs, still with the gun to her head.

'Okay, ladies we're going out on the roof. But not yet.' He threw a bunch of long curtain cords at them, together with some cable ties. 'You,' he said, pointing at Azalea. 'You got some work to do.'

–

PC Chris Smith was looking through the telescopic sight on his AR15 at the front of Imperial Hanover House. Curtains were now drawn out the window where the two hostage girls had appeared. But there appeared to be activity at a gable window in the mansard roof. Looking closely, he could see the double casement windows were being opened from the interior. The face of a teenage girl appeared, with someone behind her. He reported it immediately to the command van. After a short crackle there was an immediate reply.

Silver commander to Alpha Seven. That is Zoe Barnes. Can you see Tyler?

Yes, but no clear shot…

There was an interruption on another channel. *Alpha Four to Silver One. White male behind hostage three.*

Through the scope, Smith could see that Zoe Barnes was shuffling out from the dormer window onto a narrow ledge, arms tied behind, her face dissolving in tears. It was a good sixty feet above the paved margin around the front of the house, and she moved very slowly. Some kind of braided cord was tied tightly around her waist and led back into the room. She moved a few inches to the left, clearing a view into the window, where Azalea Hale, similarly bound, was now beginning to emerge. The older hostage moved very carefully around to the right on the ledge, the cord from her waist also leading back into the room. Finally, Tyler emerged, with young Lucy Barnes roped to him in the same fashion, and wailing in distress. Three terrified hostages, each with their arms tied behind them, each bound directly to their captor by five feet of what looked like curtain cord.

The radio was a cacophony of marksmen notifying that they had a clear head shot to the target. The reply from the silver commander was immediate. *Alpha squad. Hold your positions. Do not fire. Repeat, do not fire. The safety of the hostages is paramount. Bravo squad, advance cautiously to the third floor. Do not attempt to reach the roof level until I give the word.*

Smith could see why. Tyler had rigged up the hostages so that if he fell, he would take them all with him. It was a graphic illustration of the power he held over life and death.

Tyler took out his pistol and fired it into the air.

'Now listen to me, cops,' he roared. 'You will do exactly what I say. If you do not, these three girls will die. Understand that there is nothing you can threaten me with. I know I'm dying. I don't care about my own life.'

Gillard was rooted to the spot by the sound of Tyler's voice. He watched Sergeant Sparkes as she ran around the back of the house, expecting him to follow. Instead, he looked upwards. The side of this wing of Imperial Hanover House was virtually windowless, with just a few small casements at the third-floor level. The Edwardian builders had preserved its clean lines by clustering all the downpipes from bathrooms and gutters into a narrow vertical slot, a perfect rock climber's chimney set back into the rendered brickwork at the side of the house. With his years of experience on some of the hardest ascents in Wales and the Lake District, he knew he could climb it, even in his cumbersome flak jacket. The biggest problem was his footwear, polished work brogues with limited grip at the toe. His upper body would have to do the work. The crucial part was the first. Ten feet of sheer metal downpipe before the first branch to the network of spreading feeder pipes. He braced his feet at either side of the chimney, where a rough render coating had been applied, and gradually eased his way up. It required all his strength to keep the outward pressure on his feet while he climbed hand over hand up the pipe.

As soon as he reached the first feeder pipe, he was able to move faster and he was at the second floor before the first message to him came over the radio.

'Gillard, what the hell do you think you're playing at?'

He realised that DCS Simpson and all the others could see his bodycam live feed. He paused, balancing himself, and looked behind him down into the portico of the neighbouring house. The two sharpshooters he had seen before were giving him an encouraging thumbs up.

Gillard pressed the radio button and said: 'I'm using my initiative. You need someone on the roof to stand a chance of saving those girls.'

'All right, Gillard.' Tyler emerged from the front gable window at the far end of the other wing. 'What you can't see from your position is that he and the hostages are roped together, and the girls' arms are bound behind. They are utterly helpless.'

'So you can't take him down?'

'Precisely. Do not put yourself in view. And do try not to break your neck.'

'It wasn't my intention, sir.'

He switched the radio off and turned back to his task. He couldn't have the crackle of messages giving his position away. He manoeuvred carefully, putting his weight on some aged and slender pipes, edging upwards towards the rear of the house, trying to be as quiet as possible. Finally, he got onto a bathroom window ledge on the highest floor. Looking over the lip onto the mansard roof could see the three rear gables on each wing. He calculated Tyler was more than a hundred yards away, at the furthest end of the other wing, effectively diagonally opposite. The slate roof was forty-five degrees from gutter level for five feet to above the dormer windows, and then became quite shallow, in normal mansard fashion. The gables themselves had flat roofs of bitumen felting. The ledge between the bottom of the slates and the gutter was four inches. It was probably identical on the other side. He was not afraid of heights, but then he had the use of both his hands and feet. He could only imagine the terror of those three girls with their hands bound leaning against the slates and contemplating a fall that would certainly kill them. He began to carefully edge his way along the ledge, without any clear plan of what he would do when he reached Tyler.

Then he spotted something that inspired a plan. Crazy, but workable. He'd only have once chance and would have to do it just right.

Chapter Thirty-two

Gillard could clearly hear Tyler's voice, bellowing out into the road. 'First off, get those sharpshooters off the building opposite,' he yelled. 'And clear the street. Then I want the head of Britain's police service to come and stand down here in front of me, and beg for my forgiveness. I want a public apology for failing to track down the hit-and-run driver who killed my mother when she was here in 1982.'

There was a tannoy response, relayed in Simpson's calm tones. 'Mr Tyler, we are more than happy to consider any of your requests once the hostages are safely released…'

'No way!' he yelled. 'Do you think I'm stupid? I've got three good insurance policies here.' He pointed the pistol at each of the girls in turn. 'I'm keeping them paid up until my demands are met in full.'

Gillard had spotted a discarded coil of coaxial cable in the gutter. It was the uncut end of a TV aerial line which was pinned with cleats to a massive chimney stack, one of three that straddled the roof front to back. The aerial itself was out of reach near the apex of the stack. He leaned forward and picked up the roll, which looked to have a good twenty yards of cable in it. He just needed to cut it away from the cleated section. He had no knife, and searching the pockets of his flak jacket found nothing there either. With no alternative, he started to bite it, but quickly realised he was merely flattening the cable without tearing it. This would take too long. Then he saw how he could do it. He cursed himself for not thinking of it immediately.

He grasped at one of the loosest-looking slates, eased his fingers under the edge, and tried to break it. He tried three different slates before one broke readily, the removed portion showing a thin jagged edge. Promising. He leaned back against the roof, with the broken slate gripped between his knees, and worked the cable backwards and forwards on the edge until the plastic insulation split. He then worked through the metal sheath, which frayed readily. The central wire he tackled by bending the cable backwards and forwards in his hands until it snapped.

Now he was ready to tackle Tyler.

–

Zoe Barnes had never been more terrified. Standing on a narrow ledge, leaning against the steep roof, only a few inches of stone ledge and metal guttering between her and the paving slabs four floors below. She was helpless to move her wrists at all. Tyler had taken no chances and had used multiple cable ties on her hands. The cord around her waist he had pulled from curtains in another room. It had all been done at gunpoint.

She looked to her left, where Tyler was balanced on the window ledge of the room they had exited. Lucy, between her and Tyler, was sobbing. Azalea was on the other side, quivering. They could just see each other. Tyler had warned them to be quiet on pain of death, and they believed him. To Zoe's right, police marksmen were lying on the roof of the house next door, separated from them only by the drive. Their guns seemed to be pointing at her. However hard she thought about it, Zoe couldn't imagine how this could end except with all of their deaths.

The exchanges continued between Tyler and an apparently senior police officer with silver braid on his epaulettes who had introduced himself on the tannoy as Detective Chief Superintendent Alan Simpson. While Tyler was shouting, Zoe thought she heard a slight noise on the roof. She quickly glanced at Azalea, who shifted her eyes up and behind and then nodded. She had heard it too.

–

Gillard leaned forward on the slates and sidestepped his way right along the rear ledge, until he was level with the corresponding front window from which Tyler had emerged. He clambered stealthily up onto the flat roof of the last dormer and then onto the shallow rising slates. From there he could just see over the central ridgeline, with glimpses of the back of Tyler's head and waving gun arm on the other side. With the coil of cable in one hand he eased himself up the tiles, crawling to the apex. Tyler was still shouting and making threats, masking the small scrapes and rattle of the roof as Gillard made his way up it. Crouched behind the ridgeline, Gillard carefully tied the cable, making it into a large lasso with a sliding knot. He needed to anchor the other end, but all he could see were a couple of rusted cast-iron pegs cemented into the chimney stack, five feet to his right. They would have to do. Using his one free hand to steady himself, he moved crab-wise along the ridge, now able to see not only Tyler's shoulders and back, but the heads of Azalea and Zoe too, and beyond them into Marloes Road. Simpson was in full uniform standing with loud hailer in the middle of the street, behind him a fire tender with a long-armed aerial platform easing its way down the road.

'Do not bring that thing anywhere near,' Tyler bellowed. 'Now apologise!'

There was a pause before Simpson began. 'On behalf of all the branches of the British police, I apologise that the suspect in the hit-and-run on your mother was never identified. This was an inexcusable error, for which we are truly sorry...'

'My mother is buried in Highgate Cemetery, as was her wish,' Tyler yelled. 'You are not fit to kiss her grave. I want flowers, roses, with all your apologies, laid on it.'

Gillard had now knotted the end of the cable to a rusted peg, and tied it as tight as he could, before edging back to his original position, then advancing over the ridgeline with the lasso gripped in his right hand, the unwinding coil in his left. One stealthy foot at a time he moved down the shallow slated incline, fifteen feet from Tyler, then ten, then onto the rear of the dormer. That step dislodged a fragment of cement which skittered noisily down the sloping slates. He swept his arm from behind and tossed the loop of cable.

Just as Tyler whipped round, gun pointing right at him.

'Die, cop,' he yelled, and fired just as the looped cable landed over his head and gun arm. Gillard felt the immense blow of a bullet in the midriff, which knocked the wind out of him. As he fell backwards, a second shot ricocheted from the slates. The cable tautened as Gillard toppled, and Tyler lurched forwards. Another shot rang out as Tyler struggled, first trying to free himself, then grabbing hold of Lucy.

'They're all gonna die,' Tyler bellowed. He picked up a screaming Lucy, and as Zoe and Azalea pleaded for the young girl's life, tossed her out into mid-air.

Screaming, she fell from view in a second, and Tyler leaned out to follow her. But restrained by Gillard's cable, he could not. Gillard could hear Lucy wailing, and saw the taut rope from Tyler's waist, swinging back and forth. The cable, now with Tyler's full leaning weight on it plus Lucy's, jerked tightly in Gillard's hands. He gripped as hard as he could but was dragged three feet forward on his side almost to the lip of the dormer roof. As he scrabbled for purchase, he heard at least three high velocity shots ring out, far to his right. Tyler's head jerked, spraying blood, then slumped forward. His gun dangled and then fell from a lifeless hand.

Tyler was dead.

But still teetering, a belly flop into the void, frozen in time, his feet on the ledge and Lucy dangling help-lessly beneath him. Zoe and Azalea, either side of the dormer, were leaning back against the steep slates, terri-fied. There was still a little slack on the ropes connecting them to Tyler's corpse, and without it they would have been dragged over the edge. Even now, unless Gillard could hold the weight, they were all going over.

'Zoe, Azalea, help me,' Gillard gasped, as he was dragged on his chest across the rough gravelly flat roof. His radio fell off, the bodycam disintegrated in a hail of plastic splinters. 'Loop your ropes on something fixed.'

'There's nothing,' Zoe said, glancing around desper-ately for a hook, peg or even a protruding nail.

'I can help!' Azalea called, as she began to rotate her body, winding in the slack on the rope to Tyler.

'No, stop!' Gillard called. 'You need that free play.'

'But I'm taking some of his weight from you.'

'No!' As he feared, her movement disturbed Tyler's equilibrium, and the corpse jerked forward again. Azalea had the presence of mind to turn the other way and let the rope unwind, as Tyler tipped to 45 degrees. The sudden extra leverage dragged Gillard another six inches on his front until he was just above Zoe, his hands over the lip of the dormer roof. Further back, the tips of his shoes found a tiny fissure, barely a crease in the flat roofing material, where he buried the protruding edges of his soles, and tensed his ankles. On the far side, he could see that Tyler's movement had given Azalea a space, a delicate chance to squeeze behind him through the open window into the room.

'Should I?' she gave Gillard a wide-eyed gaze, a question.

'Yes,' Gillard gasped. 'Don't dislodge his feet, his legs are carrying half the weight.'

Gingerly, she slipped behind Tyler's leaning torso to get in front of the dormer, unable to move her arms because they were bound, but lifting her feet one at a time around the back of his obliquely angled legs. She then threw herself head-first into the open window, jerking the rope which connected her to Tyler. For a moment that took some weight off and created a few inches of slack that Gillard hauled in, hand over hand.

'Hook your rope around a radiator or something,' Gillard shouted to her. 'Zoe, can you do the same?'

'I can't get past!' she cried. It was true; with bound arms, she couldn't duck under or climb over the cable which stretched diagonally from the dormer roof down to Tyler's neck and torso. There was now no slack whatever on the cable behind Gillard back to the chimney peg. If that gave way, they were dead, no question. Wrapping the cable tightly around one forearm, he called down to Zoe.

'Can you lie on the edge and crawl underneath?' The cable was agony, cutting off the blood supply in his hands. But he must not let go. Everyone's lives depended on it.

She gasped as she looked up at him, her eyes wide. 'I don't know.'

The ledge was a foot wide where she was standing, leaning against the slates, but narrowed to six inches wide in front of the dormer window. 'Can you crouch down?'

'I think so.' She slowly sat on her haunches, the tips of her trainers peeping over the edge of the ledge, to the dizzying fall to the terrace far below.

'Now, can you feel the protruding bottom edge of the slates with your fingers?'

'Yes.' She had her hands behind her bottom, fingers curled under the edges of the steep roof.

'Use that to keep you steady, while you lie on your side.'

A sob escaped her. 'I'm going to fall.'

'No, you're not. Breathe deeply. Help is coming.'

But it wasn't there yet.

A fire service cherry-picker was in position in the street but it was too wide for the narrow driveway, its boom too short to reach across the garden. Firemen were busy trying to dismantle the garden railings to get it further in, while others were running up to the front of the house carrying what looked like a deflated orange dinghy. Gillard had seen these fall cushions before, on a training course. He recalled the newest versions inflated into ten-foot cubes in only thirty-eight seconds. A drastic improvement on previous versions, but still a lifetime up here. There were loud male voices now both inside the dormer he was lying on, and much further back, on the roof. More help, but not yet there.

'Help, I'm stuck,' Zoe yelled, her knees out in the void, the rope running between them to Tyler.

An assault helmet emerged from the window to her left and its male owner looked across towards her, three feet away. 'Hold on, miss,' he said. 'We'll have you down in a jiffy.'

'Grab my cable first, take the strain,' Gillard yelled to him. His arms were in agony, the cable biting deeply into his flesh.

'Can't reach, just let me get a bit further out.' The armoured bulk of the officer began to squeeze clumsily through the casement window.

Gillard was just beginning to feel hope when disaster struck. The anchor peg on the chimney behind him shot out like a bullet, clattering onto the slates. He was dragged another few inches, his arms now entirely stretched over the lip of the dormer roof. Tyler had lurched from 45 degrees from vertical to 60, massively increasing the weight that Gillard was trying to hold. Strong arms inside had Azalea's rope, but it was barely enough.

'Aarrgh, help,' Zoe wailed. She was literally hanging on by her fingertips to the slates behind her, her waist squeezed and strained by the now-taut rope linking her to Tyler. Lucy, dangling beneath, was spinning backwards and forwards, squealing in terror. For a full half minute, the fragile equilibrium held, with Tyler's heels still in the gutter, his body trying to dive into space, his head and one shoulder restrained by the cable, his torso held by the cord from inside the room.

'I'm going, I'm going!' screamed Zoe. Her arms were taut behind her, her feet in the gutter, as if she too was reluctantly going to dive. The emerging cop now had one arm on Gillard's cable, while another officer was reaching out for Tyler's feet.

It was a risk Gillard had to take.

He let go of the cable with his right hand and snatched at Zoe's rope. It was enough to stop her falling, and Tyler jigged on his restraints like a puppet.

'Just hang in there a few more seconds,' Gillard said.

But though dead, Tyler now had one more cruel trick to play. His corpse twisted as his legs were seized by police at the window. He folded at the knees, giving a massive jerk on the cable.

Gillard now knew he was going to fall.

There was absolutely nothing he could do about that.

His last act was to push Zoe into the arms of the nearby armoured officer, before Tyler's weight dragged him off the dormer. He tumbled head-first out into the void. In those milliseconds he registered a series of glimpses: missing Lucy by an inch, as she was being pulled in by officers at a window on the floor beneath, of seeing Tyler's body dangling face down, legs held by flak-jacketed arms from the dormer. One final question occurred as he plunged towards a soggy-looking orange blancmange: *was that thirty-eight seconds?*

He felt an impact and knew no more.

-

DCS Alan Simpson had watched the drama playing out, as he was forced by Tyler to apologise for historic failings. Words were cheap, and contrition too. What was expensive was life, and particularly the as-yet-unlived decades of innocent children, hanging by a thread. The snipers had in the end done their job. The last order he'd given before emerging with his loud hailer to confront Tyler had been to only kill the abductor when Gillard had taken the strain of his body. Even then, it was a tough judgement. Nothing was certain. No doubt there would be years of inquiry by those even better paid than he, second-guessing decisions made in milliseconds in real time by officers on the ground, judging with the luxury of hindsight.

When Gillard fell Simpson's heart almost stopped. The cushion wasn't fully inflated, and Gillard wasn't quite over it. But as he fell, he pushed out right arm and leg, steering himself leftwards by a crucial foot or two. The chest-first impact was on the cushion's edge, and caused the entire structure to shudder, puffs of dusty air blasted from under the inflated skirt.

For a second there was silence, then two firemen clambered up to Gillard. One officer turned to Simpson, as he was running with several other officers towards the cushion. And gave a thumbs-up.

Gillard was alive.

Chapter Thirty-three

Jonathan Hale awoke in hospital, with a female doctor leaning over his bed. Behind her stood a worried-looking Xolwa and Azalea. Above her face mask his daughter showed a swollen purple bruise from cheek to hairline.

'Oh Azalea, thank God you're all right,' he gasped.

'Can we hug him?' Azalea asked.

'Yes, but gently,' the doctor said.

As his daughter rested her face against his, tears welled up in his eyes, and his voice became thick with emotion.

'I thought he killed you, after some awful ordeal.' He didn't even dare give voice to what he thought Tyler had done to her.

'He never had time, because of your arrival,' Azalea said, moving back to let her mother embrace him.

'And Jon, it's you who was the miracle,' Xolwa said, caressing his face. 'The bulletproof vest saved your life. You've just had a bullet removed from your thigh. You've been unconscious for three days.'

The doctor nodded. 'It was the one that hit your scalp that knocked you out and caused all the bleeding. The scan shows you have a nice little furrow across the top of your skull.'

Hale reached a tentative hand up to the bandages around the top of his head. Even the slightest touch was really sore, and his chest and abdomen felt like he had gone ten rounds with a heavyweight boxer.

'He would have thought you were dead,' Azalea said. 'And at first so did we. The vest stopped four bullets. Four!'

'At the cost of several broken ribs,' the doctor added.

Hale sighed, and then caught his breath at the pain of it. He looked at his daughter and said: 'You have to tell me how you escaped.'

Azalea gave a quick account of the final minutes on the rooftop. 'We were all tied up together so that if Tyler fell, we would all fall. But when that detective—'

'Craig Gillard,' Xolwa interjected.

'—When he managed to get a loop of cable round Tyler's neck, I had just enough time to scramble behind him and throw myself into the room. If I hadn't got the cord wrapped around the window catch, he would have pulled me out when he started to fall. By the time the police had broken through the door, poor Zoe had been almost dragged over the edge.'

'Dear little Lucy,' Xolwa said. 'She spent five minutes upside down sixty feet in the air, dangling with Tyler's body. She must have been hysterical.'

'That unlucky policeman sitting next to me,' Hale said. 'Shot dead in the car before he could do anything.'

'He saved Oliver's life,' Xolwa said. 'If he hadn't replaced Oliver, Zoe and Lucy would no longer have a dad.'

'He was brave,' Hale said. 'Laying down his life for his public duty.'

'He was,' Xolwa said. 'But we shouldn't forget that you were willing to die to save your daughter, your family, from this monstrosity of a man. You never hesitated, and I will always love you for it.'

At that moment, there was a knock on the door and Gillard walked in, accompanied by family liaison officer Gabby Underwood.

'Ah, the hero of the hour,' Xolwa said.

Gillard smiled. 'I think your daughter, and Zoe and Lucy were the heroines.'

'We couldn't have done it without you,' Azalea said.

'Are you all right now?' Xolwa asked him. 'I hear you hit the ground pretty hard.'

'There was a bit of concussion. But the cushion did its job, despite not being fully inflated.'

Hale sighed, and grasped the hands of Xolwa and Azalea. 'Ever since I was arrested and dragged off the States, I have regretted getting involved with Richard Tyler and his friends. Every night I worried about what might happen to you, and it got worse and worse. But now I think we're waking up from the nightmare. From now on, it's the straight and narrow for me. Because I owe it to you both.'

Epilogue

The funeral of Detective Constable Gregory Marshall took place two weeks later in Hammersmith in pouring rain. A cortège of mounted officers was preceded by motorcycle outriders. Rank upon rank of helmeted uniformed officers followed the hearse. The service was attended by senior officers of both the Met and Surrey Police. On the second row in the church, the one in front of Gillard and Sam, were the Barnes family: Oliver, Jenny, Zoe and Lucy. Zoe had not met this man, who gave his life to save hers, but she was thankful people like him existed. People like Craig Gillard too. As the coffin was slid onto the dais by six white-gloved officers, Zoe slid her arm around the shoulders of her younger sister. Many people were crying.

Stella Anderson was there too, but wearing civvies. Gillard had heard that she had just resigned from Surrey Police to resume her career as a forensic auditor. The prospect of disciplinary action over her absence during operations was not one she had relished. Rainy Macintosh wasn't there, but had just passed her sergeant exams with flying colours. He looked forward to retaining her on his team.

–

It was the following Saturday when Gillard and Sam were again invited over by Oliver and Jenny Barnes. This time the autumn weather was too poor to use the garden, so they sat on opposite sides of the lounge, keeping a good social distance. Gillard had finally dispensed with the sling for his strained shoulder, and his bruises had gone down. Oliver had put on a good spread of sandwiches, cold meats, hummous and taramasalata. This time Zoe didn't need to be called down from upstairs to join her sister.

'So how are you two girls recovering from your ordeal?' Sam asked.

'Fine,' Zoe said, peering briefly at her phone, before glancing at her parents. 'I mean, very well thank you. Thank you for asking.'

Jenny nodded her approval.

'I've had nightmares,' Lucy said, with a pout.

'They've both been remarkable, really,' Oliver said to Gillard. 'Considering what they've been through.'

'I've got way more followers than anyone in my year now,' Zoe said.

'The best-looking boy in the class asked her out,' Jenny said with a smile. 'She's always the centre of attention.'

'Mu-um,' Zoe squealed. 'You're embarrassing me.'

'They and Azalea have been nominated for a bravery award,' Oliver said.

'Quite right too,' Gillard said. 'They saved their own lives and Lucy's, as well as mine.'

'I hit him in the face with a sock full of bullets!' Zoe said, miming the action.

'And I showed her how to break her the cable ties with shoelaces,' Lucy said.

'How on earth did you know how to do it?' Sam asked.

'This boy at school was showing everyone how to do it, his big brother had seen it on YouTube,' Lucy said.

'But you really saved us,' Zoe said to Gillard. The two girls looked at each other and left the room. They came back in with a large iced chocolate cake with a candle on top.

'This is to say thank you,' Lucy said, then whispered: 'I did the icing. Zoe only did the sponge.'

The cake was set down on the coffee table and Jenny dispensed generous slices to everyone around. 'It's delicious,' Gillard said. 'Thank you.'

'Your tummy's got bigger,' Lucy said to Sam. 'Plenty of room for cake!'

'Lucy!' her mother said.

'It's packed full of baby,' Sam replied, and glanced adoringly at her husband.

Socks the cat wandered into the room, glanced haughtily around, and then climbed gracefully onto Lucy's lap, where he began purring.

'Another brave survivor,' Gillard said.

Zoe was staring at her phone again. 'Azalea's family is moving away.' She looked up, frowning. 'They've just agreed a sale on the house, and she'll be starting at a new school.'

'Where are they going?' Jenny asked.

'It's supposed to be a secret,' Zoe said. She looked forlorn.

'You've got other friends now, haven't you?'

'Hangers on,' Lucy said, cuddling the cat. 'Not real friends.'

'Who are you to judge, madam?' Oliver said.

'Azalea said it. She says real friends are there for you in your disasters as well as your triumphs.'

'Wise words,' said Sam. 'Still, it's good to have fun friends as well as serious ones.'

Lucy looked at Gillard. 'Did it hurt, falling on the cushion thing?'

'Yes, at the time. I had bruises all down my front, and I strained my shoulder with the cable.'

'Are you off sick?' Zoe asked.

'No, not now. I'm far too busy for that. I've got criminals to catch.'

–

A week later the man known as Pegasus was at Sandown Park racecourse, in a crowded hospitality tent. He was sipping Dom Pérignon and nibbling crackers smeared with foie gras while he waited for his contact to take his place at the table opposite him. His own place marker was labelled the Rev Martin Greene. It could equally have been labelled plain Martin Greene, Martin van der Groen or any number of other aliases. His real name, Vincent McCann, and his real origins in rural County Down were only hinted at in his slight Irish accent.

He looked at his watch. The contact was late, perhaps unsurprising with the long journey from Calabria, and all the Covid regulations to contend with. Their scheme had almost worked. Part one, the complex set-up described by Hale on the data stick, was perfect. The structures put in place had allowed them to pump huge amounts of drug money into London property, the purchases of which were being arranged that very week. But Hale hadn't known about part two.

The money launderer, having set up an almost perfect cash washing scheme, had made himself redundant. That's a very dangerous thing to be, if you are a man who is party to secrets and a record of ratting under pressure. For McCann, being contacted by Tyler was a happy coincidence. Why kill Hale himself when the American felon was happy to do it for his own reasons? The IRA gun and ammunition McCann had supplied and left at a London car park for Tyler was all he'd had to provide. His bosses would keep their hands clean, even after the only man who could implicate them had been rubbed out.

The only trouble was that Hale was still alive.

Tyler had got greedy. Staging an abduction, trying to get Hale's daughter for himself. He should have kept the job simple.

McCann looked up as three suited guys made their way through the crowds. There was something familiar about the older guy, a rugged-looking guy of fifty, with grey hair and a firm jaw. Who was he? He looked to be heading across the room to a different table, until he suddenly turned and grabbed the chair opposite.

'Vincent McCann, I'm DCI Gillard and I'm arresting you for supplying a firearm in contravention of the—'

'You have the wrong man, detective chief inspector. My name is Martin Greene, look at the place marker. Here, let me show you my passport too—'

As he reached inside his jacket the two younger officers who were now standing behind him seized his arms and handcuffed him. Everyone in the hospitality tent was now staring at them.

'We know about your many identities,' Gillard said. 'We're not fooled. And you, I'm afraid, have breached the terms of your immunity under the Good Friday Agreement by committing a fresh crime.'

'You've nothing on me.'

'No? Ballistics matched the gun you supplied to Richard Tyler to one you had in your possession when you were held in 1987 for the murder of a British soldier.'

As McCann was being led out, he saw at the door that his contact had just arrived. A dark-haired Italian-looking man, who looked him straight in the eye. The Italian put a finger up to his lips, and raised an eyebrow for emphasis.

McCann understood omertà, the Mafia code of silence. He knew how to keep his mouth shut. He was not about to make the same mistake as Jonathan Hale.

CANELOCRIME

Do you love crime fiction and are always on the lookout for brilliant authors?

Canelo Crime is home to some of the most exciting novels around. Thousands of readers are already enjoying our compulsive stories. Are you ready to find your new favourite writer?

Find out more and sign up to our newsletter at canelocrime.com